"Believe me, Hunter, I ask myself these questions every day.

"In fact, when I was in the hospital, recuperating from the accident, I kept expecting and hoping that someone would show up—a family member, a friend, any acquaintance—but no one ever came. And I had to face the fact that, clearly, I hadn't been important to anyone."

Hunter groaned out loud. She'd been more than important to him. But something had kept him from trying to locate her. Clearly, she'd not loved him enough to stay in their marriage.

"I'm sure there were people in your past life who cared about you. But they probably didn't hear about your accident or had no idea how to start searching for you. As for a husband, he, uh, surely would have reported you missing."

"You'd think." She grimaced with a wistful sigh. "But I simply have no way of knowing. Still, I was thinking... maybe you could take a photo of me and show it to your friends back in Utah... One of them might recognize me?"

"I can't see it would hurt anything to try," Hunter said. "Unless..."

"Unless what?" She urged him to continue. "You think I'm some sort of fugitive from justice or something?"

Her question put a wan smile on his face. The only crime Willow Anderson Hollister had committed was breaking his heart.

Dear Reader,

When Hunter Hollister rolls into Red Bluff, California, with his rodeo company, the Flying H, the only thing on his mind is producing the River Bend Stampede or the next seven days. Keeping his livestock healthy and the shows running on schedule isn't an easy task, and he always tries to be prepared to deal with unexpected hurdles and snags. But no amount of preparation could brace him for the emotional storm he encounters when he literally runs into his ex-wife, a woman who'd disappeared from his life four long years ago.

Willow had left their home on Stone Creek Ranch in Utah while Hunter had been on the road with the Flying H. He'd been devastated to return to an empty house without so much as a note of explanation and even more crushed when, a month later, he'd received divorce papers in the mail. Yet in spite of her desertion, his heart has never stopped loving her.

Running into her in Red Bluff feels like an answer to Hunter's prayers, until he calls her name and she stares at him blankly. She isn't Willow! She's Anna Jones and she's never seen him before in her life! What is Hunter going to do? She doesn't remember him or anything about their life together back in Utah!

I hope you'll enjoy reading how Willow finally realizes the cowboy she'd forgotten is the man she's always loved.

God bless the trails you ride,

Stella

A COWBOY TO REMEMBER

STELLA BAGWELL

SPECIAL EDITION

Recycling programs for this product may not exist in your area.

ISBN-13: 978-1-335-40205-9

A Cowboy to Remember

Harlequin Enterprises ULC
22 Adelaide St. West, 41st Floor
Toronto, Ontario M5H 4E3, Canada
www.Harlequin.com

Printed in Lithuania

MIX
Paper | Supporting responsible forestry
FSC® C021394

After writing more than one hundred books for Harlequin, **Stella Bagwell** still finds writing about two people discovering everlasting love very rewarding. She loves all things Western and has been married to her own real cowboy for fifty-one years. Living on the south Texas coast, she also enjoys being outdoors and helping her husband care for the animals on the small ranch they call home. The couple has one son, who teaches high school mathematics and coaches football and powerlifting.

Books by Stella Bagwell

Harlequin Special Edition

Montana Mavericks: The Trail to Tenacity

The Maverick Makes the Grade

Men of the West

A Ranger for Christmas
His Texas Runaway
Home to Blue Stallion Ranch
The Rancher's Best Gift
Her Man Behind the Badge
His Forever Texas Rose
The Baby That Binds Them
Sleigh Ride with the Rancher
The Wrangler Rides Again
The Other Hollister Man
Rancher to the Rescue
The Cowboy's Road Trip
A Cowboy to Remember

Visit the Author Profile page
at Harlequin.com for more titles.

To all the readers
who continue to read my Men of the West stories.
Thank you from the bottom of my heart.

Chapter One

Hunter Hollister parked his truck in a slot not far from the portico covering the entrance to the hotel and shut off the engine. However, he didn't immediately climb out of the vehicle. Not because it had started to rain and he was reluctant to get wet. No, he was staring blindly out the rain-splattered windshield, wondering what the hell was wrong with him.

He'd quit searching the rodeo crowds for *her* face a long time ago. He'd believed he'd grown past the aching urge to catch a glimpse of her. He'd pretty much convinced himself that seeing her again would only make the ache inside him even worse. But tonight, when the performance had ended and the spectators had begun spilling out of the stadium, he'd stood to one side and hopelessly scanned the crowds for a tall, curvy brunette.

Damn it! Being back in Red Bluff, California, must be causing his mind to dredge up these old, painful memories. Especially with Christmas only a little more than a week away. Nearly four years ago to the day, he'd been right here in this same town putting on one of his first large-sized rodeo, the River Bend Christmas Stampede, while his wife had been packing up and leaving their home on Stone Creek Ranch in Beaver County, Utah.

Heaving out a weary breath, Hunter shoved away the dark thoughts and departed the truck. He'd been going since four thirty this morning and now it was well past midnight. Which was actually an early night for him. Usually, he'd be at the rodeo grounds until two or three o'clock in the morning. Thankfully, his right-hand man had insisted he could finish up and make sure the livestock was cared for and settled in for the night. Hunter was grateful to the younger man. He was dog-tired. All he wanted now was a stiff drink and a bed.

The entrance to the hotel was well lit with a row of foot lamps lining each side of the covered portico and colorful Christmas lights hanging from the protective awning. However, Hunter had his head down to shield his face from the rain and missed seeing the woman about to step down from the curb in front of him.

As soon as his shoulder collided with hers, he instinctively reached out and wrapped a steadying hand around her arm.

"Oh, I'm sorry! I didn't see you!" he swiftly apologized. "Are you okay?"

"Uh—yes. I'm fine," she said. "Sorry, I wasn't watching where I was going, either."

Lifting her head, she looked directly at him and Hunter very nearly staggered backward.

"Willow! Is that you?"

Shock had caused his voice to lower to little more than a whisper, but she must have heard him because she continued to stare at him blankly.

"Willow? Excuse me, but—do you think you know me?"

Wind was beginning to blow cold rain onto the portico and he instinctively drew her deeper beneath the awning to prevent the both of them from getting soaked.

"You're Willow. Aren't you? If you're not, you could be her twin."

Her head shook slowly back and forth as though she was struggling to absorb his words. Hunter wondered who she was trying to fool. Him or herself? In any case, he didn't appreciate the confused act she was giving him.

"I'm sorry," she said. "You must have me mixed up with someone else."

Hunter came close to blurting out the words burning on the tip of his tongue. He knew exactly who she was—the wife who'd walked out on him four years ago! But the dark, frantic look in her eyes held him back. Maybe he was being delusional, but some sixth sense was telling him that she honestly didn't recognize him. How could that be?

His heart was beating in his throat and he tried to swallow away the rapid throb before he attempted to speak again. "Oh. My mistake. If you don't mind me asking, what is your name?"

"Anna Jones."

Really? Where had that come from? Why wasn't she Willow Hollister or using her maiden name of Anderson? If she'd remarried a man with the surname of Jones, he could understand the change in the last name. But *Anna* made no sense at all. Still, a little voice in his head was yelling at him to be cautious and go along with this woman. Otherwise, she might run hard and fast and he wouldn't have a clue as to where to find her.

"Nice to meet you, Anna Jones." He extended his hand to her. "I'm Hunter Hollister. I own the Flying H

Rodeo Company and I'm here in town producing the River Bend Christmas Stampede."

There wasn't one iota of recognition on her face as she slipped her hand into his, but as for Hunter, the contact of her soft fingers was assaulting him with endless memories. Four years was a long time, he thought. But not nearly long enough to forget.

"Yes, I've heard about the rodeo. The town is in full celebration for the event, plus all the added holiday festivities," she said. "How do you do, Mr. Hollister? I hope you enjoy your stay here in Red Bluff this week. Now, it's getting very late. I need to be on my way."

Until this moment, there'd been too many other questions hurtling through his mind for him to wonder why she'd been leaving this plush hotel at this time of night. And the questions were still striking him from all the directions. She couldn't just walk away, he thought desperately. Not without learning how he might contact her again.

Deliberately retaining his hold on her hand, he asked, "Do you work here at the hotel?"

Her expression turned wary. "I do. I'm secretary to the hotel manager. I was working extra late tonight. Our computer system is being upgraded. Are you a guest of the hotel?"

His mind was whirling at such a high rate of speed, Hunter could barely think, much less talk. Yet somehow he managed to make his voice sound normal when he finally answered, "As a matter of fact, I'm booked here for the whole week. Maybe we'll bump into each other again."

She eased her hand from his and adjusted the strap

of her purse onto her shoulder. "Perhaps. Good night, Mr. Hollister."

Mr. Hollister. She'd called him plenty of things during their marriage, but never Mr. Hollister. Oh God, did she really not recognize him? As far as he could tell, there wasn't one sign of recollection on her face, or a light of dawning familiarity in her eyes. He couldn't believe it! Nothing about this, or her, made sense.

"Good night."

Feeling as though someone had just sucker punched him, he watched her step from beneath the awning and jog off through the falling rain.

He didn't wait around to see her climb into a vehicle and drive away. What was the point? She was gone. At least, for the night. Tomorrow, he might be able to come up with a reasonable excuse to look her up here at the hotel. But should he? Wouldn't that just be asking for trouble?

His senses were too scattered to answer that question. At the moment, his heart was pounding and his hands were shaking. After four years, he'd given up on ever seeing Willow again. She'd disappeared and he'd decided there wasn't any point in trying to find a woman who'd wanted to end their marriage. To practically stumble across her path on a dark, rainy night felt like a dream. Or a nightmare. He couldn't decide which.

Inside the hotel, he strode past the large lobby furnished with several plush couches and armchairs, along with two large fireplaces with fake burning logs situated on opposite walls. A giant Christmas tree ablaze with lights and colorful adornments took up a lot of space, while nearby a long table draped with a red garland held a large bouquet of red poinsettias. Normally, he appreciated the holiday decorations. And considering the cold, rainy night, the cheery sight of the fireplaces would have warmed him. But Hunter wasn't feeling cheered or warmed. Seeing Anna or Willow, or whoever the hell she was, had left him chilled to the bone.

At the entrance to the elevator, he dug the pass card from his wallet and was about to slide it into the entry slot when the rapid sound of approaching footsteps sounded behind him and a female voice called out.

"Mr. Hollister! May I speak to you for a moment?"

Pausing, he glanced over his shoulder and stared in stunned fascination as *she* hurried toward him. What was this about? Had she decided to come clean and confess that she'd been faking not remembering him—and having some new name he'd never heard before? This was getting more surreal by the minute.

Quickly, he jammed the pass card back into his wallet, then turned to face her. With the two of them now standing in a pool of overhead lighting, he could see the details of her soft features and a faint spark of fire in her dark hair. Her eyes were the same warm brown and so was the bow shape of her full lips. Were those the lips he'd kissed hundreds of times? The same lips that had drove him crazy with desire as they slid against his skin, whispered loving words in his ears? They had to be. He couldn't mistake them. But what if it was just nostalgia playing tricks on him, making him see a resemblance that wasn't real? How could this be Willow when she looked at him with no recognition at all?

"Sure, I have a moment," he told her, then, deciding

to get straight to the point, asked, "What did you want to speak to me about?"

She looked a little distressed and he braced himself for the truth to come spilling out any second.

"Uh—well, first of all, I apologize for taking up your time. But out in the parking lot, I decided I couldn't drive away. I kept thinking there might be a tiny chance you could possibly help me find the truth."

The truth? He'd definitely appreciate hearing the truth of why she ran away and ended their marriage so callously. But he'd look pretty damn stupid if he spewed those bitter words at her and it turned out that she wasn't actually Willow.

"I don't understand," he said. "Perhaps we could go to the bar and talk over a drink?"

She glanced over her shoulder to where an arched open doorway led into a spacious bar before turning her attention back to him.

"Yes. That would be nice," she said with a grateful little smile. "And I promise not to keep you long."

After four years of searching, wondering and trying to forget, a few more minutes was nothing, he thought. "Don't worry about it," he said. "I was planning on having a drink before I went to bed anyway."

Instinctively, he cupped a hand beneath her elbow and urged her in the direction of the bar. She glanced up and gave him a tentative smile.

"I'm glad," she said. "I realize the night is getting late and I shouldn't be detaining you. But I was afraid I might not have the chance to see you again. And then I'd be—well, I'll explain once we get our drinks."

That voice, Hunter thought. It had the same husky

quality he remembered. And he couldn't help but notice how the top of her head was level with his shoulder, just as hers had been. But those details didn't prove this was his ex-wife, he tried to tell himself.

Are you blind, Hunter? Everything about her screams Willow. Are you afraid to admit to yourself that this is actually her?

Ignoring the questions sounding off in his head, he escorted her into the dimly lit bar furnished with small round tables and chairs, plus a long bar that ran the length of one wall. They chose to sit at a table situated near the entrance. Other than the two of them, there was only a handful of customers scattered around the room. A loop of standard holiday music filtered over the sound system, while behind the bar, a basketball game with the sound muted was playing on a flat-screen TV.

As soon as they'd taken their seats, a waitress appeared and took their orders. Hunter lifted his black cowboy hat from his head and placed it on the floor next to his chair.

He was raking his fingers through his hair when he noticed she was watching him closely. A tiny frown marred the space between her brows and he wondered if she was worried that he might press her to come clean about her identity.

"This is—"

"I don't—"

They both spoke at once and she laughed. The sound was a bit awkward, he thought, but he appreciated her attempt to lighten the moment.

"You go first, Mr. Hollister," she said.

"Just call me Hunter," he told her. "And ladies first, so you go ahead."

One hand reached up and clutched the throat of her coat together as though she was chilled. Hunter could see the shoulders of the olive green fabric were soaked from the rain. He started to suggest she'd be more comfortable if she slipped off the wet garment, but it was hardly his place to advise her about her clothing.

"I—uh, really don't know where to start. I'm sure you're thinking I'm a weird woman or something. But believe me, I don't normally go chasing after men."

He gave her an easy smile in hopes it would ease the tension on her face. Even if this truly was Willow and she was trying to fool him, he didn't want to see her suffer. He didn't have time for revenge, hate or spite. Those sorts of feelings crippled a person.

"Especially on a rainy night, huh?"

A wan smile touched her lips as she nodded. "Right. When we collided out there on the portico, I wasn't thinking too clearly. I heard what you said, but it didn't really have a chance to sink in. Then by the time I reached my car, it dawned on me that you—well, that perhaps you did actually recognize me."

"Is that important?" He supposed his question sounded inane, but how was he supposed to respond to this woman who might—or might not—be the woman who'd been his wife for two short years?

"Probably not to you," she answered. "But it's very important to me."

At that moment, the waitress arrived with their drinks and Hunter didn't hesitate to reach for the squat tumbler filled with bourbon and soda and take a sip. When he put the glass back down again, he carefully weighed his words before he spoke. "I'm not sure I understand why my recognizing you would be important. You said you didn't know me."

She reached for the glass of wine and Hunter noticed her hand was trembling. The sight of her distress bothered him far more than he wanted to admit.

"I don't know you. But as far as I'm concerned that doesn't mean a whole lot. You see, as far as I can remember, I didn't exist until about four years ago. Before then—well, it's all a blank slate."

This was Willow! His Willow!

Hunter swallowed a hefty drink of the bourbon and soda and hoped it would slow the whirling in his head. Questions were hurtling at him from all directions. The main one being what would happen if he blurted out her true identity? Would it throw her into some sort of mental shock? Damage the bit of memory she had now?

Oh God, he needed help.

Swallowing another drink of the bourbon, he asked, "What happened? You suffered some sort of medical issue?"

"Sort of. I was involved in a serious car crash. When I woke up in the hospital, the doctors told me I'd been in a coma for three weeks. They explained I had brain swelling and bleeding."

Hunter couldn't absorb what he was hearing. All these years he'd never thought of Willow being ill or injured. He'd always pictured her living happily with a family of her own. To think of her being that close to death left him dazed and even a little sick.

"Must have been a horrific crash." He sounded like a robot, but he couldn't help it. He'd never been so stunned.

"I was unconscious when the first responders rescued me. But I remember nothing about the wreck. They tell me my car skidded off a rain-slick mountain road and crashed down to a creek below."

"Somewhere near here?" he asked, while wondering if she'd been in this area ever since she'd left Stone Creek Ranch.

"North of here. Toward Redding. That's where I remained in the hospital for a month before I was well enough to leave. The doctors told me that I had amnesia, but at the time, they believed it would probably go away on its own. It hasn't." She leaned slightly toward him. "So you see, when you called me by that name—what was it?"

His throat was so tight it was a struggle to swallow. "Willow," he said.

"Oh, yes. Willow. Well, I thought you'd mistaken me for someone—or, forgive me, but that you were just using that as an excuse to talk to me. And then, after you'd entered the hotel, I realized I had to find out if maybe I was someone you knew in the past. Am I?"

From the moment he'd bumped into her and she'd stared at him with blank brown eyes, something had made him pick and choose his words. Something had made him hesitant to say anything that would tie her to him, or the past. *Slow. Careful. Cautious.* The words had been revolving around in his head, warning him not to make a hasty step. Now he was glad he'd not blurted out the truth. Springing something like that on her might do more damage than good. He needed to talk to a medical professional for advice before he said anything.

"Well, I—to be honest it was dark out there on the portico and I thought you looked exactly like someone I used to know. But now that we're inside under the light I can't say for sure. You see, I haven't seen the woman in years. She's probably changed, and you've probably changed, too."

"What was her surname? Was she around my age?"

He hated to lie outright, but maybe he could work around her questions without actually lying. It was for her own good, he told himself. At least, until he could talk to a professional who could advise him on such matters as amnesia.

"I'm not sure. How old are you?"

She shrugged one shoulder, then took a sip from the wine goblet. "You can't imagine how it feels not to know your age or your birth date. It's maddening. Not to mention lonely."

He looked across the table at her and their gazes clashed. The contact caused Hunter's heart to lurch, then jump into a slow, anxious thump. How could she look into his eyes and not remember the times they'd made love? The nights they'd slept with their bodies wrapped closely together?

"Lonely?" He turned the one word into a question.

"That probably doesn't make sense to you," she said wanly. "But I feel as though I'm the only one in the world like this and no one understands how isolated it makes my life."

Her forefinger was absently tracing the base of the wine goblet, and Hunter noticed her nails were perfectly manicured and painted a pale pink. While they'd been married, she'd never worn nail enamel. Nor had she worn anything like the sexy black sweater dress she was wearing tonight. Showcasing her perfect curves had never been Willow's style. She'd been a quiet, modest woman who'd never wanted to draw attention to herself. Apparently, she'd changed since their divorce—or maybe just since her accident.

"No. Unless a person has experienced such a thing, it would be impossible to understand," he replied. "But maybe you should look at it this way. You survived and you're healthy now. You have a lot to be thankful for."

Nodding, she picked up the wine goblet. "True. I'm blessed to be alive and healthy." She took a sip of the wine, then glanced over at him. "You asked about my age. Well, the doctors gauged me to be around thirty at the time of my accident. That makes me around thirty-four or thirty-five."

The doctors had gauged right, he thought. She was thirty-five now. He wanted to tell her the exact date of her birth and so many other things, but he didn't feel he could—not yet.

Feeling more helpless than he'd ever felt in his life, he said, "Well, that's a good age."

"I suppose. How old are you, Hunter?"

She remembered his name, he thought. Clearly there was nothing wrong with her short-term memory.

"Forty-one." By most accounts, he was still a young man. But tonight, as he faced his ex-wife, he felt as though he'd already lived the life of a ninety-year-old.

"Oh. I thought—uh, you look younger. Do you have a family?"

The question chilled him and he swallowed the last of the bourbon in an effort to chase the coldness away. "No. I'm single. What about you?"

Her soft laugh had nothing to do with humor. It was more like self-mockery.

"No. I'm afraid to let myself think about marriage."

Her answer caught him off guard and he frowned as his gaze slid over her beautiful face. She'd never have a problem finding herself another husband. The fact that she was still single amazed him. "Why?"

"Why?" She shook her head. "It seems simple to you because you can remember your past. You know whether you have a family, a wife or a girlfriend. I don't. For all I know, I could already be married with children."

Yes, he could see how the blank spaces in her mind would be preventing her from taking steps forward. How tragic, he thought, that she'd been living in limbo these past years. No matter how much it had hurt to lose Willow, he wanted her to be happy.

You could change her situation this very minute, Hunter. All you have to do is open your mouth and tell her all about her life back in Utah.

Yeah, but would that make her happy, he silently argued with the voice in his head. Would that fix her loss of memory? Or would it just make it worse? He had no way of knowing for sure, and he wasn't ready to take that chance. At least, not until he talked to a physician.

"If you had a husband or children, don't you think they would've been searching for you? That they would have located you long before now?" he asked.

"Believe me, Hunter, I ask myself those same questions every day. In fact, when I was in the hospital, recuperating from the accident, I kept expecting and hoping that someone would show up—a family member, a friend or even an acquaintance, but no one ever came. And I had to face the fact that I hadn't been important to anyone."

Hunter struggled not to groan out loud. She'd been more than important to him. But pride had kept him from trying to locate her after she'd proven that she'd not loved him enough to stay in their marriage. The only reason he might've elected to track her down would've been to simply ask why she'd divorced him in such a backhanded way. Now, after all this time, and in light of her current situation, her method of divorce hardly seemed to matter.

"I'm sure there were people in your past life who cared about you. But they probably never heard about your accident or knew where to start searching for you. As for a husband, he—uh—surely would've reported you missing."

"You'd think." She grimaced, then, with a wistful sigh, reached for her wine goblet. "Unless he was relieved to be rid of me. I simply have no way of knowing."

She'd not only been living in limbo, Hunter thought, but she believed the person she used to be had been unwanted. Dear God, this whole situation was unimaginable. But what could he do? How could he fix anything for her? And if she did learn her true identity, she'd probably resent him. She'd most likely tell him to get out of her life and stay out. On the other hand, if he kept the truth to himself, at least for a while, it might give him a chance to make her fall in love with him again. Wasn't that really what he wanted?

The questions were buzzing around in his head, sending him into such deep thoughts he didn't realize she was speaking until the last of her words caught his attention.

"...a photo. Someone might recognize me."

Mentally shaking himself, he said, "I'm sorry. What were you saying?"

Sighing, she said, "You look very tired and uncomfortable. And I've kept you far too long. I really should be leaving."

She started to rise, but he quickly reached over and placed his hand over her forearm. "Don't worry about me. You were saying something about a photo?"

Nodding, she said, "I was thinking if you took a photo of me and showed it to some of your friends back in your hometown one of them might recognize me. Do you think it's possible?"

Yeah. About three-fourths of the population in Beaver County would recognize Willow. She'd lived there her entire life. Until the need to get away had sent her packing, he thought ruefully. So how was he going to handle this innocent suggestion of hers?

Unable to hold her gaze, he glanced down at the empty tumbler. At the moment, he could use a double bourbon or even a triple. Anything to calm the chaos going on inside of him.

"I can't see it would hurt anything to try," he said. "Unless—"

"Unless what?" she urged him to continue. "You think I'm some sort of fugitive from justice or something?"

Her question put a wan smile on his face. The only crime Willow Anderson Hollister had ever committed was breaking his heart.

Lifting his gaze back to hers, he said, "No. I was only thinking that all my friends in Utah *will* think you're Willow. But resembling her doesn't prove you are actually her. You understand what I'm trying to say?"

The hand she had resting on the table top turned palm up in a helpless gesture. "Of course. But I can't just give up on trying to find my past identity. Even if it's an inkling of a chance, I'm willing to grab it. And you're the first person I've run into who's come close to recognizing me."

He could see desperation in her brown eyes. The same sort of desperation he'd seen when she'd argued and begged for him to give up his career as a rodeo producer. He'd refused and she'd walked out. On the surface, the problem between them had been as simple as that. Yet beneath the surface, there'd been so much more dividing their wants and wishes.

"Well, I don't suppose it would hurt to try." He pulled the phone from the pocket of his western shirt and snapped a close-up of her face. "I'd better take another one. Be sure to smile this time. Folks might remember you as a happy young woman."

"Okay."

She flipped her long hair back over her shoulders, then spread her lips into a wide smile. The expression transformed her lovely features and all he could think about were the days back when he'd made her happy enough to smile like that. He thought back on endless kisses they'd shared, the way she'd tasted, the soft little breaths that had brushed his skin.

Clearing his throat, he said, "That should do it."

He started to put away his phone, but she quickly

stopped him. "Wait. I'll give you my cell number so you'll know how to contact me. Just in case you get a response about the pics," she added.

Once she was confident he had the number safely stored in his contacts, she stood and tugged the strap of her handbag onto her shoulder. Hunter politely rose to his feet.

"Will I see you tomorrow?" she asked.

Feeling slightly dazed, Hunter stared at her. Because she wanted to see him, or because she hoped he might give her answers about the photos?

What the hell does it matter, Hunter? This is Willow. You want to be with her for any reason!

Shoving the mocking voice aside, he explained to her, "I probably won't get away from the rodeo grounds until very late. But if you think you might be here at the hotel, I'll look you up."

She extended her hand to him. "Thank you, Hunter. I'll try to be around. Good night."

"Good night, Anna."

He gave her hand a squeeze, then she turned and quickly walked away.

As soon as she was out of sight, Hunter motioned to the waitress, who was passing nearby his table.

Balancing a tray of beer mugs against her hip, the petite blonde maneuvered her way over to him.

"Want something else, cowboy?"

The blue-eyed woman was giving him all kinds of flirtatious signals, but he wasn't interested. All he could see was Willow's brown eyes. Willow's face. Why was this happening to him? He'd been growing closer to being over her, or so he'd thought. At least over her enough to go through a whole day without thinking of her more than twenty times. Hell, he couldn't have been more wrong.

"Yeah. Another bourbon and soda and make it a double this time."

The young woman's brows lifted perceptively. "Trouble with your woman?"

He grimaced. "I don't have a woman," he said bluntly.

"Maybe that's your problem," she suggested. "You need one."

He needed one, all right. But he also needed one particular woman to remember him and how very much he'd loved her.

"Not tonight," he said curtly.

Disappointment flashed across the waitress's face. "I'll go get your drink."

The waitress walked away and Hunter immediately pulled out his phone. At this late hour of the night, his sister Grace would already be in bed and he wasn't about to disturb her with a call. Being a doctor in a small town like Beaver County kept her going at full speed from early in the morning until late at night. She needed all the rest she could get. So instead of calling, he tapped out a text message with hopes she'd read it early in the morning and call him.

Need to talk with you. It's kinda urgent. Call whenever you can.

Chapter Two

Hunter was about to return the phone back to his pocket when it suddenly vibrated with Grace's call. Eagerly, he punched the accept button and jammed it to his ear.

Not bothering with a greeting, he asked, "Grace, did I wake you?"

"No. I'm sitting at my desk at home, going over some patient test results. What's wrong?"

"What makes you think anything is wrong?" he asked.

She groaned. "You normally don't call in the middle of the night. And your text said urgent. Or was that an exaggeration?"

"I'm sorry if I scared you. I'm fine. Everyone with the Flying H is fine—even the livestock. But something has happened and you're the only person who might be able to advise me about what to do."

She laughed softly. "Since when has my big brother ever needed my advice? Unless it was medical."

Despite all the time Hunter spent away from Beaver County and Stone Creek Ranch, he was still very close to his parents and all seven of his siblings, especially Grace. Even now, just hearing her strong, steady voice calmed him somewhat.

"This is medical," he said. "No. It's more than medical—it's incredible."

"Hmm. Now you've piqued my curiosity. By the way, where are you? I hear Christmas music in the background."

"I'm in a hotel bar in Red Bluff, California. The rodeo wound up about three hours ago."

"Okay, I'll give you some medical advice right now," she said. "You should've gone straight to bed. Not to a bar."

"I had my reasons."

"And those reasons were?" she asked.

He drew in a deep, bracing breath. "You're not going to believe this, Grace, but I ran into Willow tonight."

His sister was silent for a long moment and Hunter realized the news had stunned her.

"Willow?" she finally asked. "Is this some sort of joke, Hunter? I mean, yes, I always expected you'd see her again sooner or later, but in Red Bluff? No. I believed she'd eventually show up in Beaver County again."

He very nearly groaned, but managed to stifle the helpless sound before it slipped out. "Well, believe me, she's here in Red Bluff. She lives here and she works as a secretary at this hotel."

There was another long pause and then Grace said, "Oh. What did she have to say? I'm sure she was just as shocked to see you as you were to see her."

"No. She wasn't shocked at all. She didn't recognize me."

Grace let out a grunt of disbelief. "Are you trying to tell me that you saw her from a distance, but she didn't spot you? But no, that doesn't make sense. You must've talked to her. Otherwise, you wouldn't have known where she works."

"Oh, I talked with her," he said wryly. "We had drinks together here in the bar. When she left a few minutes ago, she still didn't recognize me. She—uh—" Seeing the waitress approaching with his drink, he said, "Just a moment, Grace."

By the time she'd served him the drink and turned to leave, Grace had grown impatient. "She what, Hunter? Please explain, because I'm not understanding any of this."

He swallowed a big gulp of the drink and grimaced as it slowly burned its way to his gut. "I apologize, sis. This is—hard. Really hard. Willow has no idea she was once my wife. She doesn't even know her real name. She's going by Anna Jones."

The doctor in Grace must have kicked in as she said, "Something has happened to her. Some sort of brain trauma."

Hunter swiped a hand over his face, while wishing he could wipe the away the desperation he'd spotted in Willow's eyes when she'd asked him for help.

"A car accident four years ago. She was in a coma for three weeks. From the way she described her injuries she's lucky to be alive. However, her only health issue now appears to be a case of amnesia."

"Amnesia," Grace repeated in a stricken voice. "Oh my. How awful!"

"Yes. And, Grace, from what I can gather, the accident happened not long after she left Stone Creek."

He could hear his sister's sharp intake of breath.

"You're saying she's had amnesia for four years?

That's a long time, Hunter. I'm not really trained in that sort of medical issue, but I'd think her memory should've returned before now if it was going to come back. Unless there's some underlying health reason like permanent damage to that part of her brain. Or, I suppose, the problem could be something psychosomatic. And by that, I mean there might be something in her subconscious that's making her afraid to remember. I confess I know very little on the subject, Hunter, but it's a complicated problem."

He swallowed another mouthful of the drink. "I was afraid you might say something like this. So, what am I supposed to do, Grace? Just let her go on being Anna Jones?"

"You didn't tell her anything about her past?"

"No. I was afraid to say anything. I didn't want to send her into shock. Could hearing the truth do that to her?"

"Like I say, I'm not that qualified on the subject, so I'm not able to answer your question. But I do know a doctor in Salt Lake City who works on such cases. I'll call him in the morning. Until you hear from me, I'd say avoid giving her any concrete information."

He gripped the tumbler as torn emotions threatened to overtake him. "The not knowing is hurting her, Grace," he said in a low, gruff voice. "She doesn't know if she had a family. I think she's almost hoping she didn't, because at least that would explain why they didn't care enough to search for her. She has no birth date. No hometown or old acquaintances. No—nothing."

"And you want to help her," Grace said matter-of-factly.

"Is that so strange? I haven't forgotten how she walked away from our marriage. But that doesn't mean I can turn my back on her. I'm not made that way, Grace. And neither are you. When Mack came back to Beaver County after all those years—you still loved him."

She sighed. "You don't have to explain yourself, Hunter. I understand. I only hope—she hurt you so badly. I can't see how reconnecting with her can result in anything good for you. But that's your business. And I'll help any way I can."

"Thanks, sis. Now I'd better let you go. I'll talk to you tomorrow."

"Before you hang up, Hunter, I should ask whether you want me to mention this to the family or keep it quiet?"

Of course their parents, Claire and Hadley, would be surprised at the news and probably concerned to learn of Willow's loss of memory. Most likely, his brothers— Jack, Cordell, Flint and Quint—would contact him to advise him to steer clear of his ex. But Hunter was accustomed to their negative attitude toward Willow. He knew it was because his brothers loved him and wanted to protect him. They'd never understood that his heart had always been bound up with Willow. As for his twin sisters, Beatrice and Bonnie, their mindset was more like Grace's. They simply wanted their brother to be happy.

Raking a hand through his hair, Hunter momentarily closed his eyes and thought how he'd searched for Willow among the rodeo crowd earlier. Something must have been telling him she was nearby. It was an unsettling thought.

"No need to keep anything quiet," he told her. "Willow was a Hollister once. The family has a right to know what's happened to her. And I'd rather them hear it now than spring it on them when I come home for Christmas. The news would ruin the holiday."

"Okay, Hunter. I'll call tomorrow."

"Thanks, sis. Good night. And—in case I haven't told you in a while—I love you."

"I never doubted that, dear brother. Good night."

With the call ended, Hunter finished his bourbon, then paid for the drinks and left the bar. As he walked through the lobby toward the elevators, his head was still spinning with thoughts of Willow, and he seriously doubted he'd get more than an hour of sleep tonight.

And tomorrow night? Well, one way or the other, he was going to make damned sure he found her again.

The next morning, Anna was studying the monitor on her desk, trying to acquaint herself with the new computer program the hotel had implemented, when her boss walked by her desk, then turned on his heel and returned to her side.

"Anna, I hear you worked past midnight last night. I hope you know I didn't expect you to stay so late."

She looked up at the tall man. He was in his midthirties, with dark blond hair and an affable smile. Ian Brennan had been her boss for three years now and during that time, he often urged Anna to call him Ian like the rest of the hotel staff did. But she'd never felt comfortable using his first name. Probably because she, and everyone else who worked in the hotel, knew he had a crush on her. If she started calling him Ian, he'd immediately get the idea he had one foot in the door to her apartment. And even though her boss was a nice guy, that sort of thing wasn't going to happen.

"I know you don't expect me to work overtime." She tacked a reassuring smile onto her words. "It was something I wanted to do. Getting familiar with the new system will make my job easier down the line."

As it turned out, Anna was glad she had stayed late at the hotel. Otherwise, she might have never run into Hunter Hollister. After four long years, the man had given her hope for discovering her true identity. True, it might be only a sliver of hope, but even a sliver was better than nothing.

"Well, if you'd like to take off early this afternoon, I'm sure I can manage," he said.

Normally, she'd jump at the idea of having an afternoon to herself, but not tonight—not when she was planning to stay at the hotel long enough to run into the rodeo producer again. She shook her head. "Thank you, Mr. Brennan, but I'm fine. In fact, I'm eager to get all the quarterly expenditures entered into our new system."

He gave her a long, thoughtful look, then said, "There are times we need to ease up on ourselves, Anna."

"Don't worry about me, Mr. Brennan, I'll let you know if I need time off."

He frowned and as she watched him shove his hands into the pockets of his slacks, she couldn't help thinking how different her boss was from Hunter Hollister. The rodeo man was not quite as tall as Ian, but he was thick with muscle and looked as strong as a bull. As for her boss, he was slender with hardly enough flesh on his shoulders to fill out his shirt. Ian was always perfectly groomed from his head to his feet and smelled of expensive cologne. Hunter Hollister had been a little rough around the edges with his dirty cowboy boots and unruly waves of hair brushing the collar of a denim jacket that had seen better days. He'd smelled like sage and juniper and a dark windy night, while the hand holding the glass of bourbon had been big with tanned, leathery skin. Something about him had made her heart beat a little faster.

"Alright. I'll be in my office for most of the morning. I have that luncheon meeting with a food distributor today, so I probably won't be back until one or later. If anything urgent pops up, you can text me. Okay?"

"Okay. Of course."

He went on to his office and Anna got back to work—until a clerk from the bookkeeping department stuck her head around the door and scanned the small office space. Celia, a petite blonde with a giggly personality, was the exact opposite of herself, but somehow they'd become friends over the course of the past couple of years.

"Good morning, Celia. Looking for someone?"

"No. Just making sure you were alone."

"Mr. Brennan is in his office and I don't have time for chitchat."

Undeterred, Celia slipped into the room and propped one hip on the corner of Anna's desk. Today, the young woman was dressed in a sparkly green sweater and a white pencil skirt. A rhinestone reindeer pin was pinned to one shoulder of the sweater. She looked festive and pretty and made Anna feel bland and boring in comparison, especially with Christmas just days away.

"I can only stay a minute," she said. "I heard some gossip and wanted you to verify if it was true or not."

Frowning, Anna looked away from the monitor and over to her friend. "Me? I haven't heard any hotel gossip."

Celia rolled her blue eyes. "No, silly. You *are* the gossip. I heard you were seen in the bar last night having a drink with a hunky cowboy. Anna! I didn't even know you went to the hotel bar, much less knew a hot-looking cowboy."

Anna couldn't stop a blush from rushing to her cheeks. "Who told you this?"

Celia plucked a pencil from a can on the desk and tapped it thoughtfully against her palm. "Well, I'm not a tattler."

"No. You're just a gossiper," Anna said curtly, then smiled to soften her words.

"Okay, fine. One of the other bookkeepers knows the waitress who waited on you two in the bar. Apparently, she thought the cowboy was Mr. Dreamy." Celia leaned closer to Anna. "So I've got to know! Where did you meet him?"

Anna pressed her lips tightly together. Celia was a friend, but there were times that Anna wanted to tell her she talked far too much. Especially about things that were none of her business.

"We accidently bumped into each other out on the portico and we ended up having a drink together. That's all."

Celia's eyes widened with disbelief. "That's all? Anna, since we became friends more than two years ago, you've probably been on four or five dates, and that's probably stretching the number. This guy must have been awfully persuasive to get you into the bar."

"You make me sound like a stuffed shirt or something. I do like men. I just haven't run across one who interested me enough to go on more than one date."

Rolling her eyes again, Celia leaned even closer and whispered, "Your boss wants you to be interested in him. Why not give him a chance?" Then she laughed. "Silly question, right? Why would you give Ian a chance if you've become acquainted with a sexy cowboy?"

"Listen, Celia, I'm not that acquainted with the man. We met, had a drink and a little talk. That's all. He'll be leaving town as soon as the River Bend Christmas Stampede is finished."

Celia was clearly disappointed by this news. "Really? How do you know he'll be leaving?"

"He's the rodeo's producer. I think the event goes for a week, but once it's over he'll be moving on to the next town."

Strange, how the thought of him leaving left her feeling a little lost. Especially when she'd already been the definition of *lost* for the last four years. Hunter Hollister couldn't change her life. Not unless he could somehow connect her to the woman she used to be.

Slipping off the edge of the desk, Celia headed toward the door. "Darn. I was hoping I was going to finally see you with a guy."

Anna sighed. "Celia, you know my situation. I can't get *that* involved with any man. Not until I find out whether I had a fiancé or husband in my prior life."

Celia marched back over to the desk and hammered her forefinger on an empty section of the wood top. "You've put your life on pause for four years while waiting for your memory to return. What are you going to do?

Waste another four years? And then another? At some point you're going to have to let go and start over. You're Anna Jones now. A name you chose for yourself. Whoever you were in the past is gone. And who knows, maybe you're better off not knowing. Did you ever think of that?"

"Only a million times, Celia." She let out a weary sigh and for one split second she considered telling her friend about Hunter thinking he recognized her. But no, it was too soon to talk to anyone about Hunter Hollister and a woman named Willow. "Anyway, you need to tell your gossiping friends that there's nothing to gossip about. Now you'd better get to work and so should I."

"Right. I need to get back to my desk before Amelia gets back from her coffee break. The old woman has forgotten how to say a kind word. I'll bet while she's at home her husband wears earplugs." She hurried over to the door, then paused. "Did you bring your lunch today?"

"No. I slept late and didn't have time to make one." Thanks to Hunter Hollister keeping her awake last night, she thought, feeling a bit foolish.

"Great. Let's go to Loretta's. I want one of those sinful Reuben sandwiches. You know, piled high with meat and cheese. They're so yummy. And she's been offering Italian cream cake in honor of the Christmas holiday. A slice of it is to die for."

"From an overload of calories," Anna replied.

"Bah, humbug," Celia said with a laugh, then headed out the door.

Once she was out of sight, Anna slumped back in her chair. So someone had spotted her in the bar with Hunter Hollister. No doubt the news had spread like wildfire through the hotel staff. Most everyone thought of her as a quiet mystery. The woman with a fake name and no memory. A woman who mostly kept to herself and never discussed her personal life. Just like Celia, they were probably all wondering what had come over her to be sharing a drink with a man. Thank goodness she wasn't going to be eating lunch in the staff break room today. She wasn't in the mood to deal with any covert looks or sly remarks. Not when her mind was consumed with every word the rodeo man had spoken—and with thoughts about what he might say when they met again.

Chapter Three

"Hunter, I'm thinking I should drive out to Red Bluff and find out for myself what's really going on."

Of the five Hollister brothers, Jack was second to the eldest. He was also the manager of Stone Creek Ranch, the family-owned and -operated ranch in Utah, which meant he had a workload that would crush a regular man. Not to mention, Jack had a wife and a baby son. All of which added up to him being the last person who should consider taking a trip to California on a whim. Just to prove how shocked his brother was to hear about his run-in with Willow.

Holding the cell phone to his ear, Hunter shifted around on the metal bleacher and gazed out at the freshly plowed arena. For the past hour, he and his main assistant, Malachai, had been checking the pens of stock to make sure each animal was healthy and sound, but already he'd been interrupted with phone calls from two of his brothers. First Cordell and now Jack. No doubt the pic he'd texted his family of Willow had knocked them all for a loop. He sympathized with their surprise, but he sure hoped that Jack would be the last one to call. He couldn't deal with talking to all seven of his siblings today.

"Don't talk nonsense, Jack! You don't have the time to waste on me," Hunter told his brother. "Besides, there's nothing wrong."

"Nothing wrong! Are you kidding? After all this time you've finally found Willow and the woman turns out to be a walking blank slate! Or so she says. Frankly, I wouldn't believe a word she told me."

The morning sun suddenly burst through a bank of clouds and Hunter instinctively tugged the brim of his cowboy hat lower on his forehead to shade his eyes from the glare. Thank goodness the rain had moved out and slightly warmer weather was forecasted. Snow on an outside rodeo would spell disaster and he already had more than enough on his mind.

"Jack, I know you never cared much for Willow. You or anyone else in the family. But—"

"I never really *knew* Willow," Jack interrupted. "None of the family did. Because she didn't want to be close to any of us. You can't deny that."

Hunter grimaced and wearily pinched the bridge of his nose. This wasn't the first time he'd heard that accusation, and he doubted it would be the last. "I'm not trying to deny it. Yes, I remember how Willow was with all of you. She was—it wasn't that she wanted to keep her distance. She just never felt comfortable trying to be a part of the Hollister clan. And yes, her discomfort showed. I won't deny that, either. But the problem she had was with herself. Not any of you."

"Hell, Hunter. All Willow ever wanted was you. She didn't care about much of anything except being with you. That kind of obsession isn't healthy. Nothing was ever going to be enough for her. Frankly, it shouldn't have come as a surprise to any of us when she ran off like she did. She was probably hoping to force your hand—make you chase after her and give her your full attention. There was something missing in the woman's psyche all along. And from what you're telling me, even more is missing now."

"Thanks for being helpful and understanding, Jack," Hunter retorted, not bothering to spare the sarcasm from his voice. "Is that why you called me this morning? To remind me what a fool I am?"

"Sorry if it sounds that way, Hunter. That's not my intention. I called because I'm worried about you. When Grace gave us the news about you finding Willow, I found myself praying to God that you wouldn't be hurt again."

Again? The hurting had never stopped, Hunter thought. "I'm sure you're thinking that now that I've found her, I'm going to jump right back into the fire."

"Well, aren't you? From what Grace said, you want to help her regain her memory. That's not only a tricky situation, it's dangerous."

"For me? Or her?" Hunter asked bitterly.

There was a long pause and Hunter supposed his question had caused Jack to stop and consider the situation.

"For both of you, I suppose." Then, with a rueful groan, he said, "Look, Hunter, I don't wish Willow any ill will. I hope she does get her memory back. Maybe then she'll be able to find happiness with someone—just not you."

"If this was Vanessa, you'd view this differently," Hunter said.

"And why wouldn't I? Van is my wife. I love her. I'd want to do everything possible to help her."

Unexpected sorrow welled in the middle of Hunter's chest, making it difficult to draw in a decent breath. "Willow was my wife," he said flatly. "And I loved her."

This time, there was a very long pause before Jack finally replied.

"Yeah, I know. So I—need to quit with the lectures and warnings, don't I?" He let out a long sigh, and when he spoke again, his voice was softer. "Is there anything I can do to help? Maybe you have some old pictures of the two of you stored away in your house that might jog her memory? Or some of her grandparents? I could express the photos out to you or take pics of them and text them to you."

Hunter felt a rush of gratitude. While he might get annoyed at his family for sticking their noses in his feelings, it was good to know that they had his back, no matter what. "Thanks, Jack. But at this point I can't see that as an option. Explaining how I came by the photos would mean I'd have to tell her everything and I'm not sure she's capable of handling that yet. Besides, for the info to mean anything to her, she'd have to remember it on her own."

"Hmm. Yes, I understand what you're saying," he said. "How much longer will you be in Red Bluff? You'll be here for Christmas, won't you? Mom and Dad are counting on you."

"No worries, I'll be home for the holidays. I'm only here in Red Bluff for seven more days."

"Must be a big rodeo."

"It is. Ten performances. It's the River Bend Christmas Stampede. With the rodeo and the holiday coming, the whole town is in festival mode. There's not a vacant room to be had. Last night's crowd at the rodeo was close to a sellout and that's on a Monday night. As the week goes on I expect it will be standing room only. We're being televised, you know. So you might tune in one night for a performance."

"I'll try my best to watch," he said. Then he added, "You've really made it to the big time, Hunter. I'm proud of you. We're all proud of you."

A cowboy at the far end of the arena pushed a gate wide open and allowed a herd of mares and colts to run into the huge pen. Seeing the babies buck and frolic at their mothers' sides would normally put a huge smile on Hunter's face. As would Jack's compliment. But this morning he couldn't manage to muster a smile. All he could think about was Willow and how he could possibly help her.

"Thanks, Jack. And you and the rest of the family shouldn't be worrying about me. Things happen for a reason. It was meant for me to run into Willow again. I figure by the time I leave Red Bluff I'll know the reason."

The connection went quiet and then Jack asked, "What will you do if Willow doesn't remember anything in these next seven days? What then? Are you just going to walk away and let her go on living in the present?"

Hunter momentarily closed his eyes. "She isn't just living in the present, Jack. She's living in limbo. I'm not sure I could leave her that way. But I—just don't know. Not yet."

He could hear Jack heave out a heavy breath.

"Okay, brother. Talk to you later."

"Yeah. Later."

Hunter Hollister had warned her he would be late getting back to the hotel and he was right. For the past hour, Anna had been sitting in the lobby, attempting to read a book while keeping an eye on the doors of the front entrance. Now the hands of her watch were getting closer to one o'clock in the morning. How much longer should she wait for the cowboy to appear?

She was trying to come up with an answer to that question when she heard the doors swish open and she looked up to see him striding through the glass-enclosed foyer. He was dressed much the same as he'd been the previous night, in a pair of jeans and a short denim jacket, only this time he wasn't half-wet from rain.

Her heart pounding at a ridiculous rate, she rose from the couch and walked over to intercept his path.

"Good evening, Mr. Hollister."

A look of surprise crossed his face before a crooked smile slanted his lips. "I think it might be morning now. Working late again?"

Not seeing any point in lying, she said, "No. I've been waiting for you."

The crook to his lips deepened and she wondered what he might be thinking. Did he think she was too brazen, too pushy?

"I'd like to feel flattered," he said, "but I'm sure your reasons are centered around finding out what happened when I sent your photo to my family."

She nodded. "You can probably guess how anxious

I am to hear their reactions. But I was looking forward to your company, too."

"Really?"

She gave him a timid smile. "Yes. Really."

He studied her for a moment and Anna got the feeling he wasn't sure what to say or do next. Which surprised her. Hunter Hollister didn't strike her as an indecisive man.

"Have you eaten?" he finally asked.

"Yes. Hours ago."

"Guess that was a silly question. You're not living on my weird schedule." He glanced down the lobby to the entrance to the hotel restaurant. "Is the restaurant already closed for the night? I've not eaten since this morning."

He must be an extremely busy man, she thought. Probably far too busy to deal with her. Out of consideration, she should let him off the hook and tell him to be on his way so he could eat and retire for what bit of night there was left before the next day started for him. But she was desperate for whatever help he might give her. And yes, she was selfish, too. Because she did want the handsome cowboy's company.

"I'm sorry. The restaurant closed more than two hours ago," she told him. "But there is a twenty-four-hour diner across the street. It's not fancy, but the food is generally good."

"Would you care to join me?" he asked. "If you're not hungry, you might have a cup of coffee or something while I eat."

"I'd like that. Just let me get my things."

She collected her jacket and handbag from the couch where she'd been sitting and he was quick to step closer and help her ease the black twill jacket onto her shoulders. The faint scent of alfalfa hay and horse wafted up to her nostrils, while the touch of his hands slightly brushing against her rattled her senses.

"It's cool out tonight, but at least it's not raining," he told her.

They started toward the door and she was surprised when he wrapped a hand beneath her elbow. She'd not expected him to be that familiar with her. Nor had she expected his hold on her arm to feel so natural.

Trying to ignore the strange thoughts going through her head, she said, "I'm sure the better weather helped draw out the rodeo crowd. Although, I think I recall the grandstands having a cover."

"Yes. It's a very nice facility. The rodeo committee has made some huge improvements in the past few years," he told her. "So far it's been a joy working with the group. Which makes my job a whole lot easier."

Outside, the area around the building was quiet and traffic nearly nonexistent. As they crossed the street, a cold wind slapped her cheeks and ruffled her hair, but the sky was clear and lit with stars. Normally at this hour, she'd be in asleep, or reading a book and drinking a cup of hot chocolate, she thought. Not meeting up with a man she'd met barely twenty-four hours ago. She had no idea if she'd been an impulsive person in her past life, but for the past four years, she'd been much more likely to lean heavily on common sense. It helped her feel in control. But nothing about this situation was controlled. She certainly wasn't exercising her usual caution with Hunter Hollister.

"Do you always keep a graveyard schedule?" she asked.

He grunted with amusement. "It's a part of the job. I'm used to it."

She suddenly realized she wanted to ask him a thousand questions. And none of them had a thing to do about her or whether his family back home had recognized her. No, she wanted to know all about him and his life.

Careful, Anna. Much more of that sort of thinking is going to have you treading on dangerous ground. This man is forty-one and still single. That's enough to show you that he's not interested in being a family man.

The voice darting through her head caused her lips to press into a thin line of self-reproach. She wasn't looking for a family man or any kind of man. Not with her blank background.

The building that housed the diner had a red brick front with a wide, lime-green door sporting a wreath of evergreens bound with a wide, red ribbon. Several paned windows bracketed both sides of the entrance, while above the door a neon sign glowed the name Happy Hen. To the left of the diner was a women's boutique, displaying a Christmas tree in its plate-glass window along with an assortment of holiday fashions, shoes and jewelry. To the right, a real estate agency advertised ranch property for sale. Both businesses were presently dark, but the diner was always busy.

Inside the long room, the faint scent of frying bacon, coffee and apple pie permeated the air. Most of the stools at the bar were occupied, but several of the booths that lined one wall were vacant. Hunter ushered her to the one in the very back. After Anna had slid into one of the bench seats, he eased into the seat on the opposite side of the table, then removed his hat and placed it beside him.

"Do you eat in here often?" he asked.

"At least a couple of times a week," she answered. "There's a restaurant called Loretta's about three blocks from the hotel where a friend and I often eat, too. It serves mostly grilled food and salads—that type of thing. But it closes around nine."

"Too early for night owls like me, huh?"

Smiling, she glanced at her watch. "I'd say about three and a half hours too early."

A waitress with a messy blond bun and a red bib apron over jeans and a white blouse approached their table carrying two small glasses of ice water and two menus.

"Hello. My name is Becky. How are you two tonight?"

They both gave her an agreeable reply as she placed the items on the table. "So what can I get you tonight? Dinner or breakfast?"

Hunter looked at the waitress as though he didn't quite catch her question. "I have a choice?"

"Sure. The cook stays ready for whatever."

"Great," he said. "Then I'll have breakfast. A tall stack of pancakes, bacon, sausage, fried eggs sunny-side up and a side of hash browns. And plenty of coffee."

She finished writing his order on a pad, then glanced at Anna. "Is he always this hungry?"

The waitress clearly assumed they were a couple. Anna expected Hunter to quickly speak up and set the situation straight, but he simply cast her a teasing smile.

"Uh—he hasn't eaten all day," Anna explained. "But I have. So I'll just have a cup of coffee."

The waitress groaned her objection. "Oh, come on. You've got to eat something with the man. How about a cinnamon roll? Or a piece of pumpkin pie?"

Anna conceded. "All right. A piece of the pie."

With a pleased smile, she jotted Anna's order on the same pad. "You won't be sorry. It's delicious," she told her. "I'll be right back with the coffee."

Once the waitress walked away, Hunter said, "You didn't have to give in to her, you know."

"Don't worry. If I decide I don't want the pie, you appear to be hungry enough to eat it."

He chuckled. "I have four brothers and I can outeat all of them." He pulled off his jacket and after placing it next to his hat, he leveled a pointed look at her. "You're wondering about your pic and how my family and friends responded, so I'll just tell you straight-out. They all thought you resembled Willow, but none of them could swear you're the same woman."

Her spirits sank like a rock in a shallow pool of water. "In other words, they don't believe I'm her," she said, trying not to sound as glum as she felt. "Well, it was worth a try."

His brows drew together in a faint frown. "I wouldn't jump to conclusions yet. Time has a way of blurring images in a person's mind, Anna. And seeing a picture of someone they've not seen in years can hardly be regarded as concrete proof one way or the other."

"Do you have any other suggestions? Maybe this Willow you knew had some detail about her that would settle the question? Like a scar or birthmark."

"I don't recall any. But I…"

When his words awkwardly trailed away, the direction of his thoughts dawned on her. "I'm sorry, Hunter. I wasn't thinking. Only a man who'd been intimate with Willow would know what was underneath her clothing. That was a bad suggestion on my part."

He looked away from her and across the room to where Becky was skirting around the end of the bar with a tray loaded with coffee cups and a thermos carafe.

"Your suggestion wasn't bad. It's just that I can't give you the answers you need. Not right now."

Not right now. What did that mean? That later on he might have answers? She wanted to question him and yet she didn't. Reckless not, the idea of spending more time with this man had suddenly become just as important as finding her identity. And she'd already gotten the impression that questioning him about Willow made him uncomfortable. Was that because he'd had some sort of relationship with her? More than just friendship?

She'd only met Hunter last night. It would be crass of her to ask him such a personal question. Instead, she needed to bide her time and wait for him to talk about the woman. But there was one huge problem with that plan—she only had a few days before he'd be leaving Red Bluff. Once he moved on, her chance to learn about him, and possibly herself, would be over.

"I understand," she murmured, then gave him a rueful smile. "Don't feel bad about not having better news for me. I've been disappointed many times before and will probably be again. It's not your fault."

Becky reached their table and Anna was relieved for the interruption. She wanted to quit thinking about a woman named Willow and the idea of Hunter saying goodbye.

It's not your fault. Her words continued to swirl around in Hunter's head like the cream he was absently stirring into his coffee. If she looked across the table and suddenly recognized him, she'd be saying the exact opposite. She'd be telling him, most likely in a bitter voice, that everything had been his fault. He'd been the reason for her unhappiness, the reason she'd left without a word, the reason she'd obtained a divorce directly through a lawyer.

Oh Lord, how much more of this subterfuge could he take? How much longer could he go on pretending he didn't know her? Go on telling himself that he didn't want to sweep her into his arms and swear how much he loved her? How much he'd always loved her?

If he had any sense, he'd tell her flat out that she wasn't the woman he used to know. She'd be better off not knowing about their past. After all, she'd been so unhappy that she'd run away from him and everything about her life back in Utah. Why inject those dark memories back into her memory bank?

Happy or sad, she has a right to know her roots, Hunter. You can't play God with her life.

Giving himself a hard mental shake, he tried to tiptoe around the truth. He still needed to find out more from Grace's doctor-friend before he threw any major bombshells her way. "Well, I wouldn't give up on this just yet, Anna. There are plenty of old acquaintances back in Beaver who might be able to positively identify your photo. Trouble is, I don't have their phone numbers. Once I go home, I can show the pic around town. Someone might recognize you."

A flicker of hope returned to her eyes and Hunter decided he had to be the biggest fraud to walk the earth.

"Or they might have an idea of where Willow went once she left Beaver," she said brightly. "That might help track her whereabouts. If she ended up in this area of the country it might mean we're one and the same."

Hunter thoughtfully continued to stir his coffee. "Possibly. The authorities didn't recover any kind of information from the vehicle you were driving?"

"No. Except for the metal frame, everything had burned to ash. And unfortunately, the VIN was destroyed."

From what she'd told him about the accident, it seemed as though fate had stepped in to carefully wipe away her identity. Ironically, his rodeo trail—the very thing that had parted them—had caused their paths to collide.

"Oh. I thought you said the vehicle had ended up in the bottom of a ravine in a creek. If it was in the water, how did it burn?"

She shook her head. "I'm sorry. I guess I didn't explain the crash very well. From what the authorities told me, I was thrown from the vehicle before it rolled to a stop on a ledge just above the creek. Even though it had been raining that night, it wasn't enough to douse a fire ignited by gasoline."

"No. Gasoline doesn't just burn, it explodes."

She fidgeted as if the topic made her uncomfortable, fiddling absentmindedly with the necklace she was wearing. It was odd to see her in a necklace—matching earrings, too. They were far from showy, but the Willow he'd known would've never worn the set. Which could only mean the conservative woman, who'd wanted to remain unnoticed, had been squashed along with her memory. "Sounds like you haven't had any sort of break since the accident. I mean, regarding clues to your identity."

"Not until you. You've been my one and only break."

Now her well-being seemed to hang in his hands and the responsibility was lying heavy on his mind. He couldn't do this alone. He needed Grace's guidance. But the only word he'd heard from her had been disappointing. Her neurologist acquaintance in Salt Lake City was out of town on vacation and wouldn't return for two more weeks. By then Hunter had to have his staff and stock moved four hundred miles or more away from here.

"Well, I do want to help you, Anna. But I can't see your problem being solved quickly."

Shrugging, she lifted the coffee cup to her lips. After she'd taken a sip, she said, "Like I said, I've already waited four years. I can wait a little longer."

Becky's arrival with the food saved him from making any sort of reply. After the waitress placed the food on the table and made sure they had everything they needed, she left to tend to the next customer. While Hunter got busy seasoning his eggs and drenching the pancakes with maple syrup, Anna pushed the pie in his direction.

"The pie looks delicious," she said, "but I'm not the least bit hungry."

His Willow had always had a healthy appetite. She'd loved to cook and eat and as a result she'd been fleshier than she was now. Last night, as she'd sat across from him in the hotel bar, one of the first things he'd noticed was how slender and frail she'd looked. Gaunt hollows shadowed the area beneath her cheekbones, while her arms and shoulders were close to being bony. He supposed nearly dying from a head injury would cause major setbacks in her health. But that had been four years ago. Could she have developed some other medical issue? Maybe her turmoil over her identity was making her too anxious to eat as heartily as she used to?

"You should eat the pie, Anna." He used his fork to motion toward the platter of breakfast food. "I have more than enough here to fill me up. And it would make my meal nicer if you'd eat along with me."

His last remark caused her dark brows to lift ever so slightly and then she relented. "Okay. If it will please you that much, then I'll eat."

She positioned the plate in front of her and sliced a fork into the pumpkin pie topped with mounds of whipped cream.

"So tell me," he said between bites of food, "what do you do around here in your spare time? I imagine you have friends who keep you busy."

"A few," she said. "But I don't go out all that much with them. I have a good friend at work, who's constantly trying to get me to go to the movies and that sort of thing, but I—well, my job keeps me very busy and usually it's nice just to have quiet and rest."

He looked up at her. "Is this good friend a male?"

Her short laugh was a brittle sound. "No. Like I said, I don't want to…to begin something that can't develop. It's rather—meaningless. I'm thinking about getting a pair of cats. Everyone tells me they're very good company."

Hunter didn't know whether to feel sad or relieved that she avoided having a relationship with a man. True, he still thought of himself as her husband, her lover. He didn't like the image of some other man taking his place. But it was foolish of him to think in those terms. Sending him divorce papers in the mail was a clear statement that she'd ended his role as her husband and lover and anything else he'd ever been to her.

"My mother has cats. She lets them stay inside or outside, whatever they choose. They're her babies. And my father has a number of cats roaming around the ranch yard. He says it's much safer to have cats around than rat poison."

"Definitely," she said with a wan smile. Then she asked, "Have you always lived in the Beaver County, Utah, area?"

He nodded. "Yes. My grandfather, Lionel Hollister, purchased property in the northern part of Beaver County way back in the 1960s and built Stone Creek Ranch. My dad and his three brothers were born there. Then later, my parents married and had eight children. Five boys and three girls."

She seemed genuinely interested in what he was saying, but if anything was ringing a bell with her, she didn't show it.

"Stone Creek Ranch," she repeated. "That's a pretty name. Do you actually have a creek on the property?"

He nodded as he chewed a bite of pancake. "One fairly large one and two smaller ones. All of them originate in the mountains on the north side of the property."

"I see. I'm assuming you raise cattle on the ranch," she said.

Her hands were dainty and slender, even more so than he remembered. His eyes followed their movements as she continued to eat small bites of pie. She wore no rings and he thought about the plain gold wedding band she'd worn while they were married. A few days after she'd left Stone Creek Ranch, he found the ring among some of her things she'd not bothered to take with her. And like a hopeful fool, he'd put the ring away in a safe place thinking one day she might return and want it back. It was still in that same drawer in his bedroom. Waiting.

"Cattle and sheep. Jack helps my father manage the ranch. Cordell is foreman over the cattle division and Quint is responsible for the sheep. Flint is a deputy sheriff for Beaver County, so he only works on the ranch when his schedule allows."

"And you?"

"I'm only home a few weeks out of the year," he told her. "I have a degree in agribusiness and for a short while, when I was much younger, I helped Dad manage the ranch. But I'd always had the dream of owning my own rodeo company. So when I was financially able to put one together, I hit the road and Jack stepped into my place."

She continued to study his face with an unreadable expression. He wondered what would happen if hearing some of his family history began to trigger her memory. Would it throw her into shock? Send her into a rage at him? Or would she simply feel relieved to finally know who she really was? Oh Lord, if he only knew the answers.

"I see. And what did your family think about you leaving?" she asked.

"In the beginning, I think they were all doubtful I'd be able to make a go of producing rodeos for a living. The business is costly and competitive."

"So in other words, they didn't encourage you to go chase your dream."

Chase your dream. He couldn't count the times Willow had said that same phrase to him. She'd accused him of always chasing his own dream and never their dreams together. He supposed in some ways, she'd been right. But in his eyes, a man wasn't much of a man if he didn't try to succeed in what was important to him. Besides, each time she'd accused him of ignoring her so that he could chase his dream, he'd practically begged her to join him on the road so the two of them would have more time together. And always, she'd refused. They'd been like two stubborn mules butting their heads together.

He said, "No. We've always been a close-knit bunch. They didn't like seeing me go for any reason. But in the end they wanted me to be happy. And now I think I can safely say they're proud of my accomplishments—even though the rodeo does keep me away from the ranch."

She ate a few more bites of the pie before she tossed another question at him. "Is Stone Creek Ranch the place you call home now? And the headquarters for your business?"

"Yes. I have a place of my own away from the main ranch house. In recent years, I've built more stock pens and barns to house all my rodeo stock during downtimes. It's actually a good location for me because most of the rodeos I produce are here in the west and northwest."

"You must live a busy and exciting life." Her smile was wan as she glanced over at him. "Makes mine sound as boring as watching paint dry."

Willow had never wanted excitement in her life. She'd never been particularly outgoing, either. Hell, like Jack had said, she'd never even wanted to be around the Hollisters. Even during holiday celebrations, he'd had to practically force her into joining the family at the big house. But a part of him had understood why she'd wanted to linger in the background. Neither one of her parents had been fit enough to rear a child. Ultimately, she'd been passed on to poor grandparents. They'd raised her with love, but little more than the bare necessities of life. And in spite of her being beautiful and extremely smart, she'd held a low opinion of herself. He felt like she'd never considered herself worthy to be a Hollister. And he could only blame himself for never managing to convince her.

"Busy, yes. And I do love what I do. But I admit it's sometimes a lonely life. That's why having you for company tonight is a pleasure."

The faint smile on her face deepened into a real one. "I'm glad you said so because I feel very guilty monopolizing your time like this. I'm sure you always have plenty to do. And at this time of night you should be sleeping and getting your rest."

"That's not the same as talking with you," he said. "And I've been doing most of that about myself. Tell me about your job and how you ended up here in Red Bluff."

"A nurse who cared for me while I was in the hospital has a friend in the hotel's management. She knew about the job opening and suggested I try for it. So that's how I ended up in Red Bluff."

"I see. Well, I imagine dealing with hotel business is interesting."

She nodded. "For the most part. Some of it gets mundane. But I have a nice boss and a nice salary to go with it, so I can't complain. Actually, I felt very fortunate when I was promoted to Mr. Brennan's secretary. Without a past or knowing what sort of education I had, the hotel owners had no idea what sort of job I was capable of doing. Frankly, neither did I. But at that time they needed another clerk in bookkeeping, so they put me in that department sort of as a learn-as-I-go type thing."

"Obviously that must have gone well." It should have, he thought. During their marriage she'd worked as a bookkeeper for a bank in Beaver County and she'd been so good at the job, she'd eventually been promoted to office manager. A position she'd not wanted, but had finally accepted after Hunter's urging.

She said, "It was strange really. Once I started the job it was like I'd done it all my life. Everything about working with a computer and dealing with numbers felt as natural as breathing. Actually, it was a relief to find out I had a work skill that I'd not forgotten."

The more Hunter talked to her, the more he realized her amnesia meant more than not remembering her name or birth date, or where she'd lived. It touched every aspect of her life. He couldn't imagine trying to live under such frustrating limitations.

"So you don't have any idea what kind of job you had before the accident?"

"No. Just an intuition that it involved numbers." Shaking her head, she leveled a helpless look at him. "Sometimes I wonder if I might've been a criminal. Maybe I embezzled money or cooked the books for someone, and that's why my brain refuses to remember the bad things I've done."

"No! You're wrong!"

The words blurted out of him so forcefully that she stared at him in wonder.

"How could you sound so emphatic? You have no idea what kind of life I used to lead."

Oh yes, he knew. Other than committing the crime of breaking his heart, she'd be the last person on earth to ever do anything criminal.

"My job exposes me to all kinds of people, and I like to think I can spot a shady one," he said reasonably. "Anyway, I'm sure the lawmen who dealt with your accident must have searched their database to see if you had warrants or anything of that nature, didn't they?"

She nodded. "Yes. They ran my fingerprints and found no match in the system. But what does that really prove? I could've committed a crime and was never caught."

He scowled at her. "Why would you think such a sordid thing about yourself?"

She peered into her coffee cup as though the swirling brown liquid could give her answers. "Like I said, something is blocking my memory. Even the neurologist who examined me a few months ago believes my memory loss is due to subconscious fear."

"Perhaps. But you told me you suffered a brain bleed and three weeks of being in a coma. I'd say that has everything to do with you not being able to remember."

"He believes the damage to my head was the initial cause of my amnesia. But everything about the injury healed a long time ago. That's why I feel like—well, like there's something about my past that I don't want to face."

Like marrying a Hollister, he thought dully. Just getting Willow to agree to go on a date with him had been a major challenge. She'd viewed him and his family as

Beaver County royalty and she'd believed she would never fit in with his family or friends. But he'd persisted and once she'd given in, the rapport between them had been instant and hot. Yet in spite of the intensity of their feelings, she'd refused to discuss marriage for a long while. At that time she'd been twenty-nine and even though most of her old school friends were married and starting families, she'd remained steadfastly single. Her grandmother, Marcella, had passed on some years before and her grandfather, Angus, was in poor health. Willow had devoted herself to taking care of him and she'd not wanted to leave him alone without anyone to see to his needs.

His brothers had all advised him to let Willow go and find a woman who'd be glad to be his wife. And perhaps he should've listened to them. But Hunter hadn't wanted another woman. He still didn't want another woman.

"Hunter? You've been quiet for a long while. Are you thinking I've lost more than my memory? Like part of my senses?"

Her voice interrupted his thoughts and he looked across the table at her, regret clamping his heart.

"No. For what it's worth, I don't think you've slipped a cog or two. And I don't believe you ever committed a crime."

Suddenly, a wide smile spread across her face. The sight of it warmed him far more than the hot coffee.

"Your opinion is worth lots to me. Thanks for not thinking I'm a shady character."

He chuckled and then decided to try another angle to prick her memory. "Do the names Angus or Marcella mean anything to you?"

She carefully considered his question for a moment, then gave her head a slight shake. "No. Why?"

He swallowed the last bite of pancake and pushed the empty plate aside. "They were some of Willow's relatives in Beaver County."

"Then they might recognize my picture!" Her eyes widened and then just as quickly her features drooped. "But they probably weren't *my* relatives."

Averting his gaze from hers, he asked, "Why would you say that?"

"Because if they had a missing relative, they would have been searching. And no one was searching for me."

He felt sick to his stomach and the feeling had nothing to do with the large meal he'd just consumed. "Well, in this case, you're wrong. See, Angus and Marcella passed away some years back. Even before you had your accident."

"Oh. I see. Well, that's another roadblock," she said glumly. "Unless you can think of any other relatives Willow had who lived in the Beaver County area."

Only the big Hollister family, he thought. To her, he said, "No. No one else. I just thought I'd toss those names at you to see if they sparked your memory. Obviously they didn't. I'm not being much help, am I?"

"More help than you know. You're the first person who's given me even a glimmer of hope. That means a lot," she said. "And honestly, none of the friends I've made here in Red Bluff really get what I'm going through. In their opinion, I'm healthy with a good job and a decent apartment. I should be satisfied. They can't understand why I'd want to rock the boat and risk uncovering something unpleasant. They don't realize I'm living my life in limbo. I'm a woman without a past and no path to a future. I mean, not the kind of future I want."

As he looked at the helpless expression on her face, all sorts of thoughts rushed through his head. The main one being that somehow, someway he had to help her be Willow Hollister once again. And maybe then they could start over. Together.

Chapter Four

"What kind of future do you want, Anna?"

Did he really care? Anna wondered. Or was he simply being nice to her because of her situation? She wanted to believe he cared. But why would it matter to her either way? She hardly knew him. And yet something about him felt so familiar. Was it his husky voice or the way he phrased his words? Was it something about his rugged features that made her feel as if she'd gazed at them for years instead of a few hours?

"I suppose I want the same things that most women want. A loving husband. Children to nurture and support as they grow to be adults. I don't want a fancy house or lots of pointless things. I don't want lavish vacations or a closet full of designer clothes and shoes. None of that interests me. I just want family around me—to share and love and laugh with."

He drank the last of his coffee and set the cup aside. "I hope you find those things, Anna. And I believe you will. Even if you don't get over the amnesia."

She frowned. "You think I could be happy just moving on with another man, while not knowing whether I already have a husband somewhere?"

"After this length of time, he's probably moved on. That is, if you had a husband."

She acknowledged grimly to herself that she couldn't argue his point. "You're right. A husband who wanted a future with me would've reported me as a missing person. And no one did. Which meant I had no husband or he was glad to see me go."

He shook his head. "Anna, you could suppose all day and night and still not be anywhere near the truth of the matter."

Nodding, she said, "I'm afraid I spend half of my waking hours going over different scenarios in my mind. What ifs. Whys. Suppose this and suppose that. It all gets so very wearisome. That's why—after I ran into you last night, I prayed you were the answer."

He picked up his hat and levered it onto his head. "I don't know if I can be the answer you need. But I'll try."

Glancing over at him, she said, "Hunter, it's wrong of me to drag you into this. You're in town on a job and I'm creating a headache for you. So please don't feel as if you need to take time to text my pic to anyone else. If later on, after you go home to Stone Creek Ranch, someone happens to recognize me, you can always get in touch with me here at the hotel."

She reached for her jacket and handbag, then scooted across the vinyl to the edge of the seat. He got to his feet and reached down to give her a helping hand from the booth. As she placed her hand in his, little shock waves spread through her palm and shot all the way up to her shoulder.

Had she ever experienced this sort of reaction from having a man hold her hand? Not in the past four years.

But if it had ever happened before her accident, she had no way of knowing. Yet, she had a strong feeling this had to be a first. A woman couldn't forget something like that, could she?

"So you're letting me off the hook," he said with a twisted grin. "Or you're trying to tell me that our new-found friendship has reached its end."

Once she was standing, she found herself looking straight into his dark blue eyes. For a moment, she wondered if she was going to drown in the blue depths. But before that happened, the heat flowing from his hand into hers was probably going to cause her to combust.

"Uh—yes. You're off the hook. As for the two of us—I didn't realize you considered us friends."

His smile widened, and she decided the expression of pleasure made him look like an entirely different man. One that was more approachable and even endearing.

He released his hold on her hand, then slid his hand up her forearm and cupped her elbow. "I do consider us friends. And as long as I'm here in Red Bluff, I hope we can remain friends. I'm just sorry I'm keeping you up so late."

"I don't have to be at work until nine. I'm not worried about losing sleep," she told him.

He urged her away from the booth. "Come on. I'll pay my ticket and we'll get out of here."

Once they left the diner, they crossed the quiet street and walked toward the hotel. His hand remained on her elbow and she realized this was the first time since she'd left the hospital four years ago that she'd felt protected by a man.

Watch it, Anna. Much more of this and you're going to

start thinking of Hunter as your knight in shining armor. How will you feel when he gallops out of your life? You'll feel empty, that's how. Emptier than your memory bank.

Shutting her mind to the warning voice going off in her head, she glanced up at his rugged profile. "Do you ride a white horse?"

He looked at her and chuckled. "I have a couple of mares in my saddle bronc pen that are mostly white. Do they count?"

She laughed. "If they're yours, then they count."

"Am I supposed to understand your question?"

"No. I was just thinking that you're kind of like a knight on a white horse, slaying my fears of the past. Thank you, Hunter."

His fingers faintly squeezed her arm. "I've not really slayed your dragon, Anna. But you're welcome all the same."

"I'll bet you're one of those people who goes around helping others even if they're strangers to you."

He said, "You're putting me on too high a pedestal, Anna. I do lend a hand to others, if I'm able. But I mostly tend to my own business."

What was he trying to say? That he was making her his business? No. Just because he was being friendly and offered to help, didn't mean he wanted to be more than a Good Samaritan to her.

Gesturing toward a dark blue hatchback at the end of the sidewalk, she said, "My car is parked right over there. Next to the row of hedges."

"I'll walk with you."

When they reached the driver's side of her car, he released his hold on her, but he didn't step back. Anna had the strangest feeling that he wanted to kiss her. Or was it actually her who wanted to kiss him? Either way, her heart was pounding at the mere thought of touching her lips to his.

"Thank you for the pie, Hunter. And the company."

He reached for her hand and her heart thumped even harder as he stroked his fingers over the back of her palm.

"My pleasure, Anna." He glanced toward the hotel entrance, then back to her face. "I was wondering if you might consider coming out to the rodeo tomorrow night. I'll be tied up with work during the performance, but as soon as it ends my assistant, Malachai, will take over for me and I can show you around. That is, if you'd care to see the horses and bulls and some of the other stock. If the outing sounds a bit too dirty for you, I'll understand."

She laughed softly as pleasure rippled through her. "This almost sounds like you're asking me on a date."

A grin lifted one corner of his lips. "I guess I am."

She smiled back at him. "Then, yes. I'd like to go. What time does the performance start?"

"Seven thirty. It will end around ten or so. The arena director and I try to keep things moving, but sometimes unforeseen things happen to bog down the schedule," he said. "I'll leave a ticket for you at the front gate. Just give them your name. And I'll make sure the seating is in a good spot."

"Okay. I'll be there," she promised.

His gaze continued to make a slow survey of her face. Anna got the impression that she'd surprised him by accepting his invitation. She couldn't imagine why. She figured he had women chasing him. Probably had a different woman in every town he visited.

"Have you ever eaten a rodeo hot dog?" he asked.

Chuckling, she said, "Not that I know of. The closest I've been to a rodeo is seeing one on the TV screen."

"Then you're in for a treat. There's nothing like a good rodeo hot dog from the concession stand. We'll have one after the performance."

"I'll look forward to it," she said, while thinking if he didn't let go of her hand soon, it was going to melt away.

He didn't make any sort of reply and suddenly Anna was very aware of their quiet surroundings and how the glow from the nearest streetlamp shed only enough light for her to see his chiseled features, leaving his eyes in shadows. She couldn't begin to guess what he was thinking. But the thoughts going through her head were loud and clear. If she didn't step away from him soon, she was going to end up doing something rash.

She was trying to summon up the strength to tell him good-night, when his hands came up to rest on her shoulders. Something quivered deep inside her and she was struck with the wild urge to fling herself against his chest, to hold on to him with all her might. How could she feel such deep longing for a man she'd only met yesterday? It made no sense.

"Anna. You're very beautiful. And warm. And I— I've been wanting to kiss you ever since we sat down in the bar together last night."

Beneath her breast, her heart was fluttering like a happy butterfly. "I know," she whispered. "Because I've been wanting to kiss you."

"You have?"

"This isn't like me at all," she murmured. "I've never

felt so drawn to a man I've just met. But meeting you has knocked me a little off-kilter."

"It's kind of knocked me a little crazy, too."

His head descended toward hers and she automatically closed her eyes and angled her mouth up to his. She felt his warm breath brush against her skin and then finally his lips were covering hers in an all-consuming kiss. The contact jolted her all the way down to the soles of her feet. It felt like there was a mini earthquake going on inside her, causing her body to sway into his. At the same time, she felt his arms slip around her. After that, the only thing her brain was able to register was the dark, rich taste of his mouth moving against hers and the warm bands of his arms holding her tight against him.

His kiss was like magic and she didn't want it to end. Didn't want to leave his arms. But the moment her hands clutched at the front of his jacket, he lifted his head and stepped back.

"I think—uh, it's time I went up to my room and you went home," he said gently. "I'll see you tomorrow night. Okay?"

She drew in a ragged breath and wondered how he could form a coherent sentence when her senses were spinning in a drunken circle.

"I—yes. Tomorrow night." She turned and opened the driver's door on her car, then twisted around to where he remained standing. The look on his face said he was stunned or worried, or both. "What's wrong? Are you sorry you kissed me?"

His groan was a sound of disbelief. "No. Why? Are you sorry?"

"No. Should I be?"

His lips took on a wry slant. "I'll let you decide about that—later on. Good night, Anna."

With a hand firmly around hers, he helped her into the car, then stepped back.

"Good night, Hunter."

Her voice sounded small and shaky and she wondered if he had any idea of the upheaval he was creating inside her. She hoped not. She didn't want him leaving Red Bluff in a few days thinking he'd gotten another notch on his belt.

With a faint nod of his head, he shut the door, then stepped away to allow her to back out of the parking spot.

Without a glance in his direction, she started the engine, then quickly put the vehicle in Reverse. She'd driven out of the parking lot and started down the street toward her apartment before she realized she was holding her breath and the back of her eyes were stinging with inexplicable tears.

Damn it, she didn't know what was wrong with her. But she *was* certain about one thing. She couldn't let herself fall for Hunter Hollister. She couldn't deal with a blank memory and a broken heart at the same time.

Standing outside the fence midway down the arena, Hunter watched the auburn-haired woman jump her white horse through a ring of fire, then over three burning hurdles. Neither the horse nor the rider made a bobble, but Carlotta Dalhart and her two sisters, Chastity and Cheyenne, rarely made mistakes in their trick riding acts. Their skill, showcased through daredevil stunts, had made them widely known across rodeo arenas in the western half of the United States. Hunter considered himself fortunate to include them in his Flying H productions.

Lotta, as her friends and family called her, pulled the horse to a stop where he was standing. "Okay, Hunter, what do you think? It's been a while since we've done the fire act and because the crowds have been so large these past couple of nights, we wanted to give them a few more thrills. We thought we might jazz the whole thing up with some of our Christmas costumes."

"I've always liked this part of your act, Lotta. My only concern is time. The roster of contestants is longer tonight. How much time will it take you to set up the fire rings?"

"Three minutes. Tops. Some of the guys have already offered to help. And Malachi is always somewhere in the arena, so he's going to light everything up for us."

Hunter chuckled. "Yeah, he would like to get the blaze going. He's always trying to talk me into pyrotechnics. But as far as I'm concerned, those will always be off the table. Too many risks involved. Your horses are good with fire and smoke and explosions, but most aren't. I don't want any animal or person getting injured."

As he finished speaking, Carlotta's sister Chastity walked up to the fence where Hunter was standing. At thirty, the tall, copper-haired woman was the middle sister of the Dalhart trio. Last spring, when Hunter had attended his sister Beatrice's wedding up in Idaho, Chasta, as most called her, had gone with him as a faux date just so he wouldn't have to attend the function alone. When his family had spotted the pretty redhead at his side, they'd all jumped to the conclusion that he'd finally gotten over losing Willow. If the situation hadn't been so pitiful, their thrilled reaction would've been laughable. But Hunter would never get over Willow—and Chastity had been safe as a date because he knew she had no interest in him. At the time of Beatrice's wedding, Chastity had been going through a bad breakup with her fiancé.

"What do you say, Hunter? Are you giving a thumbs-up on the fire tonight?" Chastity asked.

His gaze vacillated between the two women as he weighed the pros and cons of extending the riding act. The added excitement would definitely be a boost to the midweek performance. "Okay," he said. "Thumbs-up. We'll see how things go tonight. If you can get the ring and hurdles out of the arena quickly, then I'll be all for it."

Chastity clapped with glee while her older sister smiled with pleasure. "They'll be out by the time you blink your eyes twice."

"Two blinks," he repeated with wry humor. "Would those be slow blinks or rapid ones?"

The sisters laughed, then Carlotta said, "Thanks, Hunter. You know you can trust us to keep things rolling." She looked over at Chastity. "Go get Chey and saddle the other horses. We need to take them through the routine to get them and us tuned up."

As Chastity hurried away and Carlotta rode off, Hunter left his spot by the fence. At the far end of the arena, he found his assistant, Malachi Yellow Hawk, helping two other hired helpers move bulls from one pen to another. The animals looked fresh and lively, a testament to the meticulous care Hunter and his employees gave them. And not only the bulls, but every single head of stock belonging to the Flying H.

Grinning from ear to ear, Malachi raised an arm to

acknowledge Hunter. "Hey, Hunter, how do the bulls look to you this morning?"

"Couldn't look better," Hunter called to him.

A little more than two years ago, Hunter had been producing a rodeo on the Wind River Reservation in Wyoming when Malachi had approached him to ask for a job. At that time, the young man had been twenty-five, living on the reservation with his elderly father, and doing daywork on a local ranch. Hunter hadn't necessarily wanted to take on an extra salary, but something about Malachi had gotten to him and he'd hired him as a general helper. It had only taken a few weeks for Hunter to see that Malachi was not only dependable and reliable, he was also well educated about the care and health of everything from the horses to the steers and from the calves to the bulls. In two months' time, he'd become Hunter's right-hand man. These days, he often wondered how he'd managed to run the Flying H without him.

The tall Shoshone climbed over the pipe fence and joined Hunter where he stood at the edge of the holding pen.

"The weather is going to be chilly tonight so all the stock should be feeling frisky," Malachi commented.

"Should make for a good show," Hunter replied. "And as you already know, the sisters are going to do their fire stunts. Lotta tells me you're going to light everything up for them."

Malachi chuckled. "You know me. I love playing with fire."

Hunter grunted. "From some of the girls you've dated, I believe it."

"When you're on the road all the time, it's not easy

finding a decent woman to date. A little fire makes things fun," he added with another naughty chuckle.

Even though Malachi was half joking, he had a point. It wasn't easy finding a woman willing to hook up for any length of time with a man who lived on the road. Hunter had tried it with Willow and the result had been tragic in more ways than one.

So what are you doing now, Hunter? Why did you invite Willow to the rodeo tonight? Moreover, why did you pull her into your arms and kiss her like there was no tomorrow? You're playing with something far worse than fire. You're playing with her heart all over again. And she doesn't even know it.

Trying to shut off the critical voice going round in his head, he looked over at his friend and assistant. "Speaking of women, I'm going to have a guest here at the rodeo tonight. I'll be meeting up with her after the performance. So if you can handle things for me, I'll make it up to you later with money or time off, or both. Whatever you want."

A playful grin split Malachi's face. "Well, well. A woman. Finally. Or is this business? I recall you're supposed to meet the woman with the Alturus rodeo committee pretty soon. Must be her."

Clearing his throat, Hunter turned his gaze on the pen of bulls. Minutes ago, the hired hands had spread alfalfa in several mangers and now the animals were munching contentedly on the green, pungent hay.

"No. It's not Ms. Welch. She wanted to make the trip down here to Red Bluff before we ended on Sunday, but family issues came up and changed her plans. We agreed to do a FaceTime call next week." He glanced over at

Malachi. "My guest tonight is just someone I—want to spend time with."

Malachi folded his arms against his chest as he studied Hunter's face. "The only other times I've seen red in your face is when you're mad as a hornet and that doesn't happen very often. This woman must be special."

Hunter opened his mouth to give Malachi some sort of excuse for the blush on his face, but just as quickly he decided there wasn't any point in trying to hide the truth from his friend. The guy was trustworthy. When it came to important issues, he could always count on Malachi to be tight-lipped.

Motioning toward a long bench located at the side of a small storage shed, he said, "Let's sit down for a minute. I think I should tell you something."

"I'm not getting fired, am I?" Malachi joked as they crossed the barren slope of ground to the bench.

Hunter snorted. "As far as I'm concerned, you'll have a job with the Flying H for the rest of your life. It's nothing like that. I want to explain about this woman."

The two men took a seat on the bench. Malachi spoke first. "Look," he said. "You don't need to explain anything about who you're seeing or why. That's your business."

"I'd expected you to say something like that. And I appreciate you, Malachi. But I want to tell you because I—frankly, I need to talk to someone about this. Someone other than my family. They don't understand. And you probably won't either. All I want from you is—well, to tell me whether I'm being a fool or not."

Malachi laughed. His sense of humor was one of the very things that had first drawn him to the man. He could find humor in even the worst situations, unlike Hunter.

"I wish my dad could hear that. He thinks I'm the one who lives with my head in the clouds. But I'll do my best to be honest."

"Yeah. Brutally, I imagine. But anyway, it's a long story, but the short version is…well, you remember me telling you I was married for a while?"

Malachi nodded. "Yes. You said she left and got a divorce. But that's all you ever said about the situation."

"Basically, she got tired of me being on the road with the rodeo company. She wanted me to stay home and be a husband and have children. At that time the Flying H was just starting to make good money and I told her I needed more time. I wanted to save as much as I could in order to better support her and our future children. In the meantime, I wanted her to travel with me, so we could experience the rodeo life together. She refused. Eventually, she left while I was away working—ironically, here in Red Bluff."

Shaking his head, Malachi murmured, "That's rough, Hunter. I mean, I can see her perspective up to a point. But she knew what you did for a living when you married her, didn't she?"

Hunter nodded. "Yes. But she thought she could persuade me to give up the rodeo business and work on the family ranch."

"Hah! That would be like asking it not to get hot in Tucson, Arizona, in July. Rodeo is your life. You'd be lost without it."

"True," Hunter muttered. "But I was lost without her. I've been lost for four long years. I never tried to find her, but I've continued to wonder where she was and what she was doing. And then a couple of nights ago I practically ran into her on my way into the hotel."

Malachi stared at him. "You're pulling my leg."

"No. But that's not the wildest part of this thing, Malachi. She didn't recognize me, or my name, or anything about me. She doesn't even know who she really is. She was in a bad car accident four years ago. From the sound of it, she was lucky to survive. She was in a coma for three weeks with a head injury and ever since she's had amnesia."

"Oh, heck. That's like something you hear about in books or movies," Malachi said with a snort. "That stuff isn't real, is it?"

"Trust me, in Willow's case it's real."

The other man lifted the gray cowboy hat from his head and swiped a hand over his black hair. "Wow! A real case of amnesia! So what did you say to her? Did you tell her everything?"

"When I first bumped into her I naturally called her Willow. And then when I realized she didn't recognize me, I tried to smooth it over by saying she looked like someone I used to know. Now she believes I can help her find out her real name and past life. It's—all so crazy."

Malachi's head swung back and forth. "Why not just tell her? Wouldn't that solve everything?"

"I'm afraid it might send her into shock or something. I talked to Grace about it. You remember my sister who's a doctor?"

"Sure. I remember meeting her when I went with you to Stone Creek Ranch a few months ago. What did she tell you to do?"

"Be careful and wait until she consults with a neurologist before I tell Willow anything about her past. But now—Willow's been single all this time, Malachi, and I can feel she's warming up to me. Not to mention, I'm—"

"Still in love with her," Malachi finished for him. "Oh man, you're in a fix. A real heck of a fix."

"You got that right. I want Willow back in my life. But then I ask myself, how smart would that be? She's already divorced me once. And if her memory returned, she'd only start hounding me to give up the Flying H again. If it didn't work between us before, why would it now? But I hate the thought of giving her up when it feels like we've gotten a second chance. No matter which way I turn, I'm going to lose."

Malachi frowned. "So your date tonight is actually your ex-wife who doesn't know she's your ex. That's a hell of a situation, my friend."

"You don't have to tell me what a mess this is. I've been living it for the past three days," he muttered. "But just remember, when I introduce you two, don't let anything slip. And if she asks if you knew Willow, just tell her you never met the woman in your life. Which would be true enough. You won't have met her until tonight."

Malachi rolled his brown eyes. "Even that sounds screwy. Maybe it would be better if I purposely avoided running in to you two. That way there won't be any chance of me slipping up."

Hunter shook his head. "You won't slip up. And I want the two of you to meet. You're a big part of the Flying H and before we leave town, I want her to become acquainted with the company."

Malachi's brows pulled together in a puzzled frown.

"Why? What good will that do? Especially if she hated your rodeo life."

With a heavy sigh, he looked over to where the bucking horses were penned in several adjoining corrals. The new foals, along with the older yearlings, couldn't be separated from their mothers, so they always had to come along on each trip. But the extra work and expense to haul the babies had actually turned out to be a boon. The audience loved it when the mares and little ones were turned into the arena long enough to strut their stuff with enthusiastic bucks and gallops. The horses had always been Hunter's favorite animal of all the stock in the Flying H repertoire. Because Willow enjoyed horses, he'd hoped they would be enough to get her interested in his work. He'd been delusional in thinking he could warm her up to the idea of traveling the rodeo circuit with him. And perhaps he was being more delusional now to think that four years and a bout of amnesia could make any difference. But he had to try.

"I honestly can't answer that, Malachi. Except—well, I suppose I'm curious as to how she'll react to the rodeo and everything that goes into putting on a show. I guess I need to hear her tell me straight-out that it's not her cup of tea, even now. Then maybe I'll be able to put her out of my mind once and for all."

Shaking his head, Malachi said, "If you haven't forgotten her after four years, I wouldn't bet on that happening."

"Well, I can hope," Hunter muttered. Rising from the bench, he gestured to the far end of the arena where the steers were corralled. "That's enough about Willow. Let's go check on the steers. There's a couple of them I'm thinking about cutting from tonight's lineup."

Malachi stood and as the two men began walking through a maze of parked cattle haulers, he cast a look of concern over at Hunter.

"You're probably not going to appreciate my asking," Malachi told him, "but is there any chance you'd ever give up the Flying H?"

Stopping in his tracks, Hunter stared at his assistant. "What would make you ask such a question? I've scraped and worked really hard for years to get to this point, Malachi. The Flying H is making good money now. And this—" he made a sweeping gesture with his arm to their surroundings "—is what I dreamed about since I was a teenager. No. There's not one iota of a chance I'd ever give it up or sell it. So quit worrying. Okay?"

"Yeah. Okay. I just thought—well, the way you talk about this Willow, you sound pretty crazy about her. And a man in love doesn't always think clearly."

A man in love. For years now, Hunter had been telling himself he didn't love Willow anymore. He'd tried to tell himself he was fortunate to be rid of her. But he'd never managed to convince himself of either of those ideas. And last night when he'd kissed her, the same emotions he'd always felt for her swelled inside him like an ocean wave pushed by a stormy wind. Kissing her again had given him the same intense pleasure it had given him years ago. Only this time there'd been an extra sweetness to her lips and a sweeter appreciation on his part that he'd been allowed to find her and hold her close once more.

"I've already gone through the brain fog of being in love, Malachi. I can see things clearly now. And no matter what happens with Willow, the Flying H is my life. Giving it up wouldn't solve anything. It would only make me miserable."

With a wan smile, Malachi gave Hunter's shoulder a friendly slap. "Okay. I'm not worried. Now let's go look at those steers."

Since Anna had never been to a rodeo, at least during her short, four-year memory, she was uncertain as to what to wear. She wanted to look appropriate for the occasion, but more importantly, she wanted to appear attractive in Hunter's eyes.

Silly girl. You're letting one breathtaking kiss put you under some sort of hypnotic spell. You need to think of Hunter Hollister as a lifeline to your true identity. Not as a love interest. He's a rambling man. Just the kind you don't need.

Anna silently snorted at the mocking voice in her head. It didn't even matter if Hunter was a rambling man—not really. That wasn't the main reason why she couldn't allow herself to fall for him, or any man. No, the real problem was that she couldn't commit without knowing if there'd been someone special in her past, someone who still might be wondering what happened to her, or even thinking she might return to him. Maybe that kind of thinking was a bit ridiculous after all this time, but she couldn't help it. Each time she thought about getting married and having children, some nagging voice in the back of her mind kept warning her to forget the notion, that a man was out there somewhere whom she'd once loved very deeply.

Shaking her head against that hopeless thought, she reached for the mustard-colored button-down shirt she'd laid out on the bed. She didn't want all the jumbled thoughts of her amnesia to ruin the night. Hunter had invited her on a date, and it was the first time she'd gone out with a man in months. She wanted to simply enjoy the moment and not dwell on the loss of her past, or the worry over her future.

She was pulling on a pair of black knee-high boots when the cell phone lying on her dresser rang. When she plucked up the phone and saw the caller was Celia, she groaned out loud. She didn't have time for a frivolous conversation with her coworker, but she decided to answer the call anyway. Otherwise, Celia would just keep calling.

"Hello, Celia. What are you up to?"

"Nothing. Just double-checking to see if you're still planning on going to the rodeo tonight."

"I'm getting ready right now. In fact, I don't have time to do much chatting."

"I won't keep you long," Celia promised. "I'm only going to ask you again if you think meeting up with Mr. Hollister is the right thing to do."

Ever since Anna made the mistake of telling Celia about her date, the other woman had been hounding her. Which was rather strange because Celia was often encouraging her to start dating more. Now that Anna was actually going to spend some time with a man, Celia was acting like she was headed out on some sort of dangerous mission.

"What do you mean, 'the right thing'? I'm simply going to watch a rodeo and have a hot dog with a good-looking cowboy. There's no right or wrong about it."

Celia groaned. "Okay. I confess, I'm being a pest and sticking my nose where it doesn't belong. But I'm a little worried about this sudden connection you've made with this stranger. Up until a few days ago, you'd never met him. I'm afraid you're going to end up getting your heart broken."

Even though Celia couldn't see her, Anna rolled her eyes. "Celia, you sound like some Victorian spinster with the vapors. Hunter is leaving town at the end of this week. He won't have time to break my heart."

"Hmm. True. So why am I worried?"

Anna said, "Probably because you've been stopping and visiting your grandmother after work these past few days. Is she feeling better?"

"Yes, she's feeling much better. She's already planning a day for the two of us to go Christmas shopping. Thanks for asking about her," Celia said, then sighed. "Okay. I'll let you finish getting ready for your date. Have a good time."

"After all those warnings, I wasn't sure you wanted me to enjoy myself tonight," Anna said with a bit of dry sarcasm.

Celia laughed. "I did kind of sound like Gran, didn't I?"

Anna chuckled. "I've met your grandmother. You sounded much worse."

"Sorry, Anna. I honestly do want you to enjoy yourself. And be prepared to tell me all about it in the morning."

Anna would inform Celia about the rodeo and the cowboys who participated in the competitions. But she'd already decided that she wouldn't relate anything about the private time she spent with Hunter, no matter what happened. That was something she'd hold close to her heart.

"Bye, Celia."

Not giving her friend a chance to say more, she ended the call and exchanged the phone in her hand for a hairbrush. As she thoughtfully pulled the brush through her long hair, her thoughts drifted back to when she'd first emerged from the coma and was able to view her image in the mirror. A stranger with dark, wavy hair to her shoulders had stared back at her and since then, she'd made it a point to keep her hair the same, just in case she happened to cross paths with someone who'd known her in the past. Her thinking had been if she looked the same, she'd be more easily recognized. But nowadays, she simply wore her hair the same because it suited her. Or perhaps she wanted to hold on to that part of herself from before the accident.

Had Willow, the woman Hunter used to know, had long, dark mahogany hair? The question had her leaning closer to the mirror and studying her big brown eyes and full lips, which tilted upward at the corners. There had been times when, as she'd gazed at her image, a name had pushed at the outer fringes of her mind. But always the name would slip away and she'd be left frustrated and filled with even more questions.

Who had she been in the past? What had she done with her life that meant no one cared to come looking for her once she was gone? Part of her still wondered if she'd been a criminal. Hunter had been quick to dismiss that idea, but he didn't know her well enough to make that judgement. He couldn't know she often held the notion that when her car had skidded off the highway, she'd been running from something or someone. But a new idea had occurred to her since she'd met Hunter. Now she was wondering if she might've been running to something or someone, rather than away.

Whatever the case might've been, Anna had to find the truth of the matter. Otherwise, she'd be living the rest of her life in limbo.

Chapter Five

During the last two events of the rodeo, a strong wind blew in. Hunter kept one eye on the sky and hoped rain or snow would hold off until the show was over and the spectators had left the rodeo grounds. As for Anna, he didn't have to worry that she might get wet. The seat he'd picked for her was in the covered area of the stadium.

Before the performance had started, he'd sent her a text, telling her that once the show was over, he'd join her at her seat. He'd not wanted her to have to elbow her way through the crowds, or dodge mounds of horse manure behind the bucking chutes in an effort to find him. Now, when the show had concluded and the rush to the exits was well underway, Hunter made his way up the steps to where she was waiting. He was thinking that this was the way he'd always wanted things to be. Willow joining him after a night's work.

But this isn't real, Hunter. You're pretending and Willow thinks she's Anna Jones. A woman who, until three nights ago, had never met you.

Pushing the dire voice out of his mind, he looked up to see Anna was standing and waving to get his attention. Hunter lifted a hand in acknowledgement and though he tried to tell himself not to let himself get too excited about being with her again, his spirits were suddenly soaring.

"Hi, Hunter!"

She quickly maneuvered her way to the end of the bench seating and met him on the stairway.

"Hello, Anna." Without thinking, he rested a hand on her shoulder and, leaning in, placed a kiss on her cheek. "Thank you for coming."

When he eased his head away from hers, he was thrilled to see a wide smile on her face. "Thank you for asking me," she told him. "The rodeo was so exciting! I enjoyed every minute of the performance."

He had to remind himself that this was Anna Jones he was talking to, not Willow Hollister. Willow hated rodeos. Because in her eyes she'd seen the profession as something that stood like a wall between them.

"Really?" he asked.

Her brows arched upward. "Why, yes. Does that surprise you?"

It surprised the hell out of him, but to her, he only said, "A bit. I wasn't sure you'd enjoy such a rough, outdoor sport. Especially with the weather turning colder tonight."

The smile remained on her lips and Hunter had to fight not to pull her into his arms and kiss her with all the pent-up longing he was feeling.

"It's not terribly cold!" she exclaimed. "And I wore my sock cap and sherpa-lined coat, so I've been comfortable."

His gaze swept over her oval face, then down the length of her slender curves. "You look very pretty tonight."

"Thank you. I don't own any rodeo-style clothing, so I hoped this would do," she told him.

"It does just fine," he said, then, with a hand on her arm, he urged her down the steep concrete steps. "Come on. I'll show you around. And if you don't mind, I'll introduce you to my assistant."

"I'd love to meet your assistant," she said. "And tell me, do you contract the sisters' trick riding act? They were fantastic! Jumping a horse through a ring of fire! They must be loaded with courage!"

Her enthusiasm caught him off guard. For one split second, a part of him wished she'd never get her memory back. This was the woman he needed in his life. Yet deep down, he realized that wouldn't work, either. He wanted Willow, with all the love that they'd shared. Not just a woman who looked like her who didn't remember being his wife.

"Yes, I do contract the Dalhart sisters. They perform at all my rodeos, exclusively. And yes, all three of them are fearless. I'd be terrified to do the things they do on horseback."

"Are any of them married or have children?" she asked curiously.

"No. They're all single. Carlotta, the eldest, was married once, but she ended it years ago. Chastity, who's next to Lotta in age, was engaged for a year, but it didn't work out for her. Cheyenne is the baby of the bunch and she's not that keen to find a steady boyfriend."

"They're all very beautiful. I'm betting they don't lack suitors."

"The sisters have plenty of those," he said, while thinking the women were somewhat smarter than Hunter.

They'd figured out beforehand that crisscrossing the western states with a rodeo company wasn't conducive to making and keeping a family.

She slanted him a clever glance. "Are you one of them?"

He laughed and tightened his hand on her arm. "No. Technically, I'm their boss. But beyond that, we're all just friends. Nothing more."

By now, they'd reached the bottom step and Hunter waited to make sure she had her footing before they took off in the direction of the holding pens.

"I can't imagine having enough trucks and trailers to haul all these animals," she said, as they approached a pen of bucking horses.

"It takes several big rigs to move the stock from point A to point B. And from California, it's a long haul to take them back to Stone Creek, but during a bit of downtime, I like for them to be home and turned out in the pasture. It's a stress reliever for them. Like a person taking a vacation from work."

She looked at him with interest and as Hunter studied her brown eyes, he wondered if the mention of the Hollister family ranch had sparked anything in her sleeping memory this time.

"Stone Creek Ranch must be huge," she commented.

"Several thousand acres. I don't know the exact size of our ranch now. Recently my dad made some purchases to the north and west of our boundary."

She smiled at him. "In other words, the ranch is massive. With enough space to home your rodeo stock."

"Right. And you know, as much as we travel, the animals always know Stone Creek is their home and that coming back there means they're away from work. They kick up their heels and lounge beneath the aspen and cottonwood trees."

Her expression turned curious as they moved on to the adjoining pen. "And what do you do when you're home? Away from work?"

"I help my dad and family on the ranch. There's always loads of work to be done and I like being out with them and the hired hands. The three regular hands that work on the ranch every day have been there for several years. So those guys are like family, too."

"Sounds like a lovely place to be," she murmured, then turned her gaze on the pen of mares with foals at their sides.

You thought so once, Willow. But then you ran away from Stone Creek and me. If you could remember now, what would you think? That the ranch and our marriage hadn't been so lovely, after all?

Stop it! he silently yelled at himself. He shouldn't be focusing on the past. He had to plan for the future. With or without this woman.

He glanced over to see her features had softened as she watched the mothers interacting with their offspring. It was clear that whatever changes had occurred in her since the accident, she still held a deep maternal instinct. She'd wanted him to give her babies and he'd failed her on that count. Hell, he'd not only failed her, but also himself.

"Hey, Hunter. Want to introduce me to your friend?"

Malachi's voice sounded behind him, and he looked over his shoulder to see the tall Shoshone striding up to them.

"I sure do," he told him. "Come meet Anna. This is her first rodeo. And believe it or not, she enjoyed it."

Laughing lightly, Anna turned away from the fence to face the two men. "I think Hunter was a little shocked that I loved the rodeo," she told Malachi in an impish voice. "I think he had the idea that because I work as a secretary in a big hotel, I don't ever walk on bare ground."

She extended her hand to Malachi. "Hello. I'm Anna Jones. And I'm betting you're Hunter's assistant. Right?"

"Nice to meet you, Anna. I'm Malachi Yellow Hawk," he said with a friendly grin. "How did you guess I was Hunter's assistant? Do I look like I'm worked to the bone?"

With another chuckle, she said, "No. Why? Is he a taskmaster?"

Malachi slapped a hand on Hunter's shoulder. "Hunter is the best. I don't think he's ever given me an order since I started to work for him."

Hunter explained to Anna, "That's because I don't have to tell Malachi what to do. He always knows what needs to be done and does it."

Anna slanted Hunter a coquettish smile, then asked Malachi, "Are you from Beaver County, Utah, also?"

Hunter could see Malachi was looking at her and, no doubt, thinking about the whole eerie situation. Yet Hunter had no worries that Malachi would inadvertently let anything slip. The Shoshone liked to joke around, but he also respected Hunter's privacy.

"No. I'm from the Wind River Reservation over in Wyoming," Malachi told her. "That's where I met Hunter. He was there putting on a rodeo."

"Yeah, that was a fortunate time for me," Hunter spoke up.

"And me," Malachi responded. After a thoughtful glance at the both of them, he asked, "So have you two eaten yet? I think they're getting ready to shut the concessions down for the night. Or maybe you're going to drive into town and have a sit-down meal?"

"We're going to have a sit-down meal in my trailer," Hunter told him. "And if you're right about the concessions, we'd better get moving."

"I need to go, too. I don't think the horns have been unwrapped on the roping steers yet." He lifted a hand in farewell as he started backing away. "Nice to have met you, Anna. Make sure Hunter treats you to anything you want at the concession stand."

Smiling, she gave the other man a little wave. "I will. And I hope I get to see you again before you leave town."

Malachi gave her a thumbs-up, then trotted off toward another set of corrals.

"What a nice young man," she said to Hunter.

"I'm glad you like him. He's like a little brother to me."

"I can tell he looks up to you," she replied. "It's good that you have a respectful employee—one who you can trust."

He cocked a brow at her. "I'm sure you respect your employer."

She glanced away from him. "I do. But it's—at times, working for him is difficult."

"Why?"

"I—uh, I'll explain later," she told him.

He wrapped an arm around her waist and urged her

away from the pen of mares. "All right. We need to get over to the concession stand before it closes, anyway."

Throughout the two-minute walk to the concession stand, Anna was extremely aware of Hunter's arm locked around her waist and the side of his body brushing lightly against hers. In spite of him calling this outing tonight a genuine date, she had not been sure if he'd treat this time he spent with her in that way. Even the hot kiss they'd shared in the hotel parking lot had not totally convinced her that he was interested in her romantically. But when they'd met on the grandstand and he'd kissed her cheek, she'd sensed that he'd allowed a bit of his guard to drop. And she definitely liked the change.

"Good show tonight, Hunter! The bulls were great!"

Anna glanced around to see a young cowboy walking a few feet away and giving Hunter a big thumbs-up sign.

"Thanks, Cody! That was a nice ride you made," Hunter called out to him.

As they moved on, he said to Anna, "You probably didn't keep score, but I think he came in third tonight in the bull riding."

"Is tonight the only time he'll be performing here at the River Bend Christmas Stampede?" Anna asked.

"No. Each contestant performs on three consecutive nights. The top twelve contenders from each event will compete Sunday for the championship round. That's the most exciting day. I realize Christmas is getting closer and you probably have shopping and things to do to get ready for the holiday, but I hope you're free Sunday afternoon. I'd like for you to see the final go-around. That is, if you'd like to."

He was inviting her out again? Sunday would be the last performance, she knew. The next day he and his company would be leaving town. He'd probably be heading home to be with his family for the holidays, or moving on to the next rodeo on their schedule.

In spite of telling herself not to read too much into his invitation, her heart was suddenly beating fast. "Well, I—as far as I know, I'll be free that day. The rodeo will take place in the afternoon?"

"Yes. From two o'clock to whenever all the events are wrapped up."

Her mind was whirling. No matter if he was only viewing her as a short-term girlfriend, she couldn't resist the idea of spending more time with him. Especially since it would be the last time she'd see him.

"Honestly, Hunter, I'd love to come to the last performance."

Smiling, he tightened his hold on her waist. "I'm glad."

They strolled on toward the concession stand, only to be stopped twice more by cowboys who wanted to shake Hunter's hand and praise his rodeo stock. He humbly thanked each one before they moved on.

"At this rate, we'll never get a hot dog," he joked as they crossed the last few yards to the white cinder block building.

Anna smiled at him. "I don't know anything about rodeo stock or producing a show, but it appears that you're doing it right."

"Thanks. It's taken years of trial and error to get to this point. And even when you know what you're doing, unexpected glitches and snags always happen."

"But I can see that you like the challenge," she replied.

Beneath the brim of his gray Stetson, she could see his brows arch.

"You surprise me, Anna."

"Why? Because you don't expect me to see such things in you?"

"Yes. Sort of." Shrugging one shoulder, he glanced away from her. "You just surprise me, that's all."

By now they'd reached the wide window where the food and drink orders were taken. Hunter ordered four chili dogs, a bucket of fries, sodas and three candy bars.

Once the attendant handed him a box filled with their meal, they walked to the far end of the grounds where a long enclosed horse trailer was parked next to a pair of large juniper trees.

"There are small living quarters located at the front of the trailer. Normally that's where I stay when working a rodeo. But there are times I like to indulge myself and stay in a hotel. This was one of those times," he told her.

"I'm glad you did. Otherwise, I would've never met you," she told him.

He glanced at her as he reached to open the door. "If you hadn't been working late that night, I would have missed running into you in the rain."

"And if you hadn't called me by someone else's name, I would have gone on home without giving you another thought. Funny how things happen sometimes."

"My dad always says things happen for a reason," he said. "I guess the reason for our meeting is to give me a pretty dinner partner while I'm here in Red Bluff."

"And friend," she added. "I hope you'll still put me in that category, too."

He opened the door wide, then motioned for her to precede him up the two narrow metal steps.

"There's a switch just to the right," he said. "If you flip it on we should have lights."

Anna found the switch. Once the interior of trailer was flooded with light, she stepped inside and looked curiously around her.

"Oh, this is roomy!" she exclaimed. "I thought it was going to be tiny!"

He followed her inside and carefully shut the door behind him.

"My living room." He gestured toward the couch running along one wall, then to the opposite wall where a tiny booth-type table and chairs were located next to a refrigerator, sink and cookstove. "And this is the dining room–kitchen."

"Nice. All the comforts of home away from home." She glanced around, admiring the fancy wood trim around the windows and doors and the varnished cabinets over the sink and cookstove. There was also a small built-in TV set hanging from the ceiling at the end of the couch, though something told her that Hunter wasn't the type to use his time watching the small screen.

"Where do you sleep when you're not staying in a hotel room?" she asked curiously. "Here on the couch?"

He placed the box of food on the table, then walked past her and over to a drawn drape. When he drew it aside, she was surprised to see a full-size mattress positioned on a wide shelf.

"It sleeps great. Just as long as you don't forget and try to sit straight up. I've knocked my head on the ceiling too many times to count."

She eyed the bed while wondering if he'd ever had a woman sleep there with him. She'd be naïve to think he hadn't. A hunk of a man who looked like him would never lack for female company...if he wanted it. She supposed that was the question she wondered about the most. Did Hunter want a woman to be that close to him? Did he ever want one on a permanent basis?

Why are you asking yourself those questions, Anna? Even if Hunter wanted you on a permanent basis, you couldn't pledge yourself to him. Not without knowing who you are!

"If you need the restroom, just open that little door right behind you," he said. "It's small, but it offers all the necessities."

"Thanks. I didn't take time to visit the restroom during the rodeo. I didn't want to miss any of the performance."

He stared at her. "Wow! When you said you enjoyed the rodeo, you must've really meant it."

Frowning, she wondered why he would have doubted her. "Did you think I was just pretending to be nice?"

His expression turned a bit sheepish. "Sort of. Anyway, you've made me happy."

That one word was enough to exchange her frown for a smile. "It doesn't take much for a woman to make you happy, does it?"

He cleared his throat. "In your case, no. Your company is enough to do that," he said, then gestured toward the door to the bathroom. "Go ahead. I'll have this ready when you come out."

Moments later, after she'd used the facilities, she emerged from the tiny bathroom to see he had all the food and drinks laid out on the table, along with a bottle of ketchup and salt and pepper shakers.

"Have a seat and we'll eat before it gets cold," he told her. "I have plates and utensils if you'd like them. I usually just eat my hot dogs out of the wrapper and the fries with my fingers."

"I'll eat mine the same way. Then we won't have any dirty dishes to deal with."

He chuckled. "That's my way of thinking."

She slipped into the bench seat on one side of the table and he seated himself opposite her.

As they both began to eat, Anna asked, "If I wasn't here tonight, what would you be doing? Helping Malachi?"

He nodded. "Tending to the stock takes a while. And there's usually a few rodeo contestants who need to find empty pens for their horses. Sometimes the sisters want me to check out their horses. Not that they're uncertain about caring for them. They know horses like the backs of their hands. But when it comes to their horses' health, all three of them fret and worry over insignificant things. Like a fly bite or a teeny-weeny chip on the edge of a hoof. I guess you'd say it's my job to reassure the girls that all is well."

Nodding that she understood, she said, "We all need reassurance about what's important to us. And, in my opinion, I'd much rather have the sisters overly protective of their animals than to be indifferent to their health."

"So had I. And just in case you might've misunderstood me, I never mind helping them. All of them are like sisters to me."

"How did you come to hire them exclusively for your rodeos? Did they seek you out?"

"Actually, they did. Lotta approached me one night at a rodeo down in Arizona. At that time, I'd heard about the sister act, but had never seen them. She told me they were tired of freelancing. Especially for rodeo companies that treated them as an afterthought and dragged their heels about paying the money owed to them. To be honest, I wasn't sure I wanted to incorporate a permanent act into my productions. But Lotta was persuasive and talked me into watching them work. Once I did, I was sold."

When Anna had first seen the sisters ride into the arena, she'd been struck by their beauty and glamorous showmanship. And she'd instinctively wondered if Hunter was attracted to any of them, or if one or more of the sisters had ever had an eye on him. But the more he talked about the women, the more she realized they were nothing more than friends and employees.

She asked, "Are you glad you made the choice to hire them?"

"More than glad. Adding them to the roster has turned out to be very beneficial for the Flying H." He reached for a fry while leveling his gaze on her face. "Now that we're sitting here in the quiet, why don't you tell me about your employer. You said working for him was hard at times. What did you mean?"

She didn't have to see herself in the mirror to know her cheeks were turning pink. She quickly fastened her gaze on the food in her hand rather than his dark blue eyes. "I shouldn't have said that. It's not exactly hard. Awkward is more like it."

"Why? Does he sexually harass you?"

Her gaze flew back to his face. "Oh, no! Ian is very much a gentleman. It's just that he has a crush on me, and I have no interest in him—romantically, that is. Everyone in the office thinks he wants to propose marriage to me. Even though I've never dated the man. So you see, whenever he's around I feel like I have to stay on guard—watch what I say or how I act. It gets tiresome."

He grimaced. "Because you're afraid he'll take certain remarks the wrong way and get the idea that you're interested in him."

She released a lungful of air. "Exactly. How did you know?"

His lips twisted to a wry slant. "I'm a man. I know how their brains work. And you're a beautiful woman. It's not hard to see why he developed a crush on you."

He'd called her *beautiful*. Did that mean Willow had been beautiful? She wanted to ask him so many things about her, but each time she mentioned the woman she could sense him drawing a curtain between them. It made her wonder if this Willow person had been some kind of troublemaker while living in Hunter's hometown.

He asked, "Have you ever considered getting a different job?"

Nodding, she said, "Yes. But as far as my work goes, I love what I do. And I like my coworkers. Plus, the hotel took a chance hiring me in the first place. I had no past references. No way of even knowing where I had worked, or the type of job I could do. I'm very grateful to them for looking beyond my amnesia. Especially since they quickly promoted me to Ian's office."

He ate a few more fries before he replied, "I can see

how you'd be grateful to the hotel's management for hiring you. Frankly, if I'd been in your shoes, I don't know if I would've had the courage to look for a job. Not without references or even your own true name or birth date."

She shrugged one shoulder. "I was determined not to be a charity case. The good people of Redding raised funds to help me get on my feet, but I wanted to take care of myself. No matter how employers perceived my lack of background, I had to try."

He reached across the small table and enfolded her hand within his. The sudden contact of his calloused skin against hers made Anna want to shiver and sigh at the same time.

"You know what I think?" he asked softly.

She breathed deeply before she finally managed to answer, "No. What do you think?"

His gaze delved deep into hers and as she searched the blue depths of his eyes, something flashed briefly in her mind. Another set of blue eyes? A kiss that stole her breath? Frowning, she tried to hold on to the foggy pictures in her head, but they were gone as quickly as they'd appeared.

"I think that you're a very brave woman," he said, then quickly asked, "Is something wrong? You're frowning."

Shaking her head, she gave him a wobbly smile. There was no way she could admit that another man's kiss had flashed through her mind. "Nothing is wrong. I—just for a second I thought I remembered something. But whatever it was has already left."

His hold on her hand tightened slightly. "Does this happen often? Or is this something new?"

"This past year I've had a few images flash through my mind that feel like fragments of memories. Sometimes they give me hope that the gates of my memory bank will burst open and everything will be clear again. Obviously, that kind of miracle hasn't happened." Her gaze dropped to their entwined hands. "And this will probably sound absurd to you, but at times it terrifies me to think I might remember or find out who I really am."

"Oh, Anna, why would you be afraid?" he asked gently. "You're still not holding on to to the idea that you might've been a bad person, are you?"

She lifted her gaze back to his face. "Not exactly. But maybe my life had been filled with turmoil. I could've been terribly unhappy. Or I could've made some huge mistakes with loved ones or been in dire financial straits. If my memory returned, then I'd have all those troubles facing me again. And right now—well, I'm basically settled and happy."

"Are you—happy? When we first bumped into each other the other night, you seemed desperate to find your past." His gaze continued to search her face. "Now you act as though you almost don't want to know what was behind you."

She released another long breath. "I told you that my feelings would sound strange. I guess what I'm trying to say is I want to know who the real Anna is, but I'm a little afraid of who she might have been."

"I can tell you who the real Anna is," he said softly. "You're a gentle and lovely woman, who's also courageous and hardworking. A woman who anyone would be proud to have for a friend, or a part of their family."

By the time he finished speaking, tears had formed in her eyes and were beginning to roll down her cheeks.

Mortified that she'd become so emotional in front of him, she quickly stood and turned her back to him. As she attempted to wipe the moisture from her face, she said in a choked voice, "Forgive me, Hunter. I didn't mean to get all weepy on you. I just need a minute. Okay?"

He didn't answer. Instead, she heard the scrape of his jeans sliding against the seat and then he was standing behind her and his hands were clasped firmly around both shoulders.

"Anna, don't apologize for your tears. I think you've probably held too many of them inside you for far too long."

He was right. From the time she'd learned she had amnesia, she'd been determined to be strong and never allow herself to dissolve into a puddle of helpless tears. A voice deep inside her had continued to push her to plod on and not allow anyone to see how utterly terrified she'd been. But now this strong cowboy's comforting presence had caused something inside her to go all soft and needy.

"Tears don't fix anything." She turned to face him, and rested her palms against the middle of his broad chest. "But thank you for understanding."

Lifting his hand, he lightly brushed the hair at her temple with his fingers. "I don't think you realize how happy it makes me to have you here with me tonight. With or without the tears."

Being this close to him felt so good and right. She didn't understand it. If Ian, or any other man she knew, attempted to touch her in such a way, she would be running backward. But with Hunter, she wanted to get closer and closer.

"We've not known each other for very long, Hunter," she murmured, "and it's impossible for me to explain— but I feel like I've known you all my life. What do you think that means?"

His hands slipped to the back of her shoulders and gently urged her forward until the front of her body was pressed to his. "That we have chemistry. And we shouldn't waste it."

Her gaze met his and the glint she saw in the blue depths made her heart race. There was no doubt that this sexy cowboy wanted her, and with everything inside her, she wanted him. Maybe she was being impulsive and reckless. Maybe she was opening herself up to a big heartache. But she couldn't turn away from Hunter and the special feelings he had created inside of her.

"No," she whispered. "We shouldn't waste a moment."

His head lowered and as his lips settled over hers, she thought she heard him groan, but she couldn't be sure. Not with the loud roar rushing through her ears. But she didn't need to hear or to think. All she needed was the hungry search of his mouth upon her lips and the tight circle of his arms holding her close to his hard body.

He tasted like a dark, sexy dream. One that she'd experienced over and over. His hard, muscled body felt like a familiar piece of clothing wrapped around her, cocooning her with hot desire.

She didn't know when his tongue slipped between her teeth, or when her arms circled tightly around his neck. The only thing she knew was that she couldn't get enough of the taste of his lips, the scent of his skin or the warmth of his hard muscles pressing against her. She'd never felt anything so good. Or had she? Had she experienced this same sort of magic in another man's arms? How could she know? Would she ever know?

The questions popping through her head were like cold water thrown in her face and with a groan of frustration, she pulled her mouth from his and turned her head aside.

"Anna? What's wrong? I thought you wanted that kiss," he said huskily.

Groaning again, she forced herself to meet his gaze. "I did. I do. But I started thinking—too much, I guess."

His fingertips gently traced a circle upon her cheek. "What were you thinking? That we might end up going to bed together? Are you not ready for that?"

"No. I was thinking about *him*."

His drowsy eyes narrowed to suspicious slits. "Him? I thought you didn't have a man in your life?"

Feeling beyond foolish, she glanced away from him. "I don't. I mean not that I know of. But I keep thinking there's a man out there somewhere who loved me, who's waiting on me to come home. I don't want to cheat on him."

His thumb and forefinger slipped around her chin and as she looked up at him, she didn't miss the odd expression on his face. She could hardly guess what it meant. Probably that he was losing his patience with her, she thought ruefully. If so, she couldn't blame him.

"You are thinking too much, Anna. If there was a man out there, he's had four years to find you and he hasn't."

"True. No one has found me."

His lips formed a faint smile. "I've found you. And I think the present is more important for you and for me than the past. Don't you?"

Doubt pulled her brows together. "You and me together. Is that how you see the two of us?"

"That's why I asked you on a date tonight. To be with you. For the two of us to be together. I don't know what might happen when it's time for me to leave Red Bluff, but we have a few more days before the rodeo ends. By then, I believe we'll both know whether we want to pursue whatever this is between us."

His arms were still around her and the heat of his flesh was warming her, reminding her that she wanted him and the pleasure he could give her. What she didn't need was to let her blank memory take over her thoughts and ruin this precious time she had with him.

"Yes. We'll know," she murmured. Then, placing her lips against his, whispered, "But for now, let's not think about you leaving. Let's just think about this."

"It'll be my pleasure."

Anna wrapped her arms around him and as he initiated another full-blown kiss, she let her mind go blank to everything except the magic of his embrace.

Chapter Six

When a knock sounded on the door of Hunter's trailer, he had no idea how long he and Willow had been kissing, or if the passion between them would have led them to his bed. He was totally caught up in the pleasure of kissing the woman he'd never stopped loving. Because of that, it took several long seconds before the noise of knuckles rapping on the outside of the metal door penetrated his foggy brain.

Easing his head back, he sucked in a deep breath. "I better see who that is," he said in a low, frustrated voice. "Something might've happened."

"Yes. You might be needed," she said thickly, then dropped her arms from around his neck.

He raked a hand through his hair as he stepped over to the door. "Who is it?" he called out.

"It's Chasta," a female voice answered. "Are you decent in there?"

He glanced over at Willow and she gave him a single nod as she straightened the front of her blouse.

"Uh—yeah." He opened the door and invited the middle Dalhart sister into the trailer. "Come on in, Chasta. There's someone here I'd like you to meet."

The tall redhead stepped into the trailer and glanced

around Hunter's shoulder to where Willow was standing. She was clearly surprised to see he had female company.

"Oh," she said. "I'm sorry, Hunter. I didn't realize you had a guest."

"No problem, Chasta. Come over here and meet— Anna."

God help him, he'd almost said *Willow*. He wondered if she would have noticed. Probably. And that would've caused her to ply him with questions he wouldn't be able to answer yet. Before he revealed anything to Willow, he needed reassurance from a qualified doctor as to whether hearing the truth would send her into irreversible shock.

Willow gave Chastity a friendly smile as she stepped forward. "Hello. You're one of the trick riders, aren't you?"

Chuckling, Chastity extended her hand to Willow. "My sisters would say that's debatable, since they say I'm the least talented of the Dalharts," she joked. "I'm Chastity. But everyone calls me Chasta."

"I'm Anna Jones. Happy to meet you, Chasta. Actually, I was going to ask Hunter if he'd introduce me to you and your sisters. I was totally amazed with your act. All three of you and your horses were just incredible."

Chastity gave Hunter a huge grin. "I really like this beautiful woman. She knows talent when she sees it," the redhead joked.

"Why do you think she's here with me?" Hunter joked, then slanted a sly grin at Willow, who appeared to be taking their banter in stride. "So what's brought you over to see me? Anything wrong?"

Chastity's curious glance vacillated between Hunter and Willow. "Everything is great. Lotta sent me over to invite you over to our trailer to eat barbecue. Some people who work with the rodeo committee brought us a big spread of food. Beef and chicken. Beans and potato salad. Yeast rolls and peach cobbler for dessert."

Both Hunter and Willow looked at their half-eaten hot dogs and fries. Chastity laughed as she followed their gazes over to the table.

"Nothing wrong with hot dogs," she told them. "I've eaten a ton of them in my lifetime. But you two might enjoy the barbecue."

"Thanks, Chasta. We'll talk it over. You might see us in a few minutes."

"Fine." She opened the door to leave, then turned and gave Willow a little wave. "Nice to meet you, Anna."

"Yes, very nice for me, too," Willow told her.

Chastity shut the door behind her. After securing the lock, Hunter walked over to Anna.

"Sorry about that, Anna. When I stay here on the rodeo grounds, I usually don't have a lot of privacy."

Smiling, she said, "You're a wanted man."

With a naughty little grin, he moved close enough to wrap a hand over the ridge of her shoulder. "Before Chasta interrupted us I was beginning to think I was wanted."

Her gaze dropped from his as the tip of her tongue came out to moisten her top lip. "I was beginning to feel like I was wanted, too."

She couldn't begin to know that for the past four years, he'd continued to want her. By this point, all that wanting was so bottled up inside him, he could hardly contain it.

"And you'd be right." Bending his head, he kissed her

lips, but this time he didn't allow the sweet contact to get out of hand. "I think—we'd better finish eating or we might not get to eat at all. Do you want cold hot dogs, or would you like to go sample the Dalharts' barbecue?"

She hesitated, then asked, "What would you like to do?"

His lips twisted to a wry slant. "I'd better not say. And we—uh—need to spend some of our time getting to know each other better. Don't you agree?"

Smiling, she reached for his hand and gave it a gentle squeeze. "As much as I liked those kisses, it would be nice to know you better," she said, then released a wry little laugh. "As for you getting to know me, that won't take long. Four years of history isn't much."

Oh, how he wanted to wrap his arms tightly around her and confess that he knew all about her history. At two years old she'd been left behind by her parents who were both too worthless to care for a child. Her paternal grandparents, Angus and Marcella Anderson, had taken Willow in and raised her as their own child. She'd made her home with them on the Anderson farm until she'd married Hunter. By that time, Marcella had passed away and Angus's health was beginning to fail. He'd died about a year before Willow had disappeared from Stone Creek Ranch, and his death had been especially crushing for her. Angus had been the only father she'd known. As far as Hunter knew, he'd been the last close relative left on the Anderson side of the family. As for Marcella, she'd been raised in foster homes and had never really known any of her relatives. No. Willow's grandparents had been her only relatives.

Hunter had thought marrying her and bringing her

into the big Hollister family would help make up for her lack of one. But, in spite of the efforts made by his parents and siblings, she'd never felt she was truly a part of the family.

Now, as he looked at her warm smile and the gentle light in her eyes, he couldn't help but think she'd feel differently about his family now than she had in the past. That she'd actually want to be close to them. Or was he simply reading something in her that wasn't truly there?

Pulling his thoughts back to the present, he said, "I'm sure you'll have plenty of things to tell me about the four years you've been in Red Bluff. But for the moment, let's go barge in on the Dalharts. You wanted to meet them, so this is a good opportunity for me to introduce you and give you a better meal than a hot dog and fries."

She chuckled. "Honestly, the hot dogs are delicious. Let's wrap them up and save them. We might want to eat them later."

"Sounds good," he said.

After they put all the food in the refrigerator, they pulled on their jackets and left Hunter's home away from home. With his arm around her waist, he guided her across a wide expanse of ground toward the Dalharts' trailer. To one side of the trailer, a few small corrals built of portable fence had been erected, but presently they were empty. A fact that Willow hadn't missed.

"Where do the sisters keep their horses?" she asked.

"If the weather is dry and mild, they stay in those pens you see. But because it's turned so cool and damp tonight, they have them housed in the big livestock barn over there." He pointed to the far end of the property. "I have two of my own horses stalled in the barn, along with the Dalharts'. And the horses used by the pick-up men are kept with them. A Flying H employee stays in the barn at night for security purposes."

"So do you have to haul enough feed and grain with you to feed all the livestock or do you purchase it after you get in town?"

"We haul the feed and grain with us. See, you can't just abruptly change what the animals routinely eat every day. Giving them feed they aren't accustomed to can cause all sorts of digestive issues," he explained. "But there are oftentimes we have to buy local hay once we reach the town where we'll be putting on the rodeo. Some states won't allow you to transport hay across state lines because it might be carrying invasive insects or weeds."

She continued to look around her as if she'd never seen working rodeo grounds before. It dawned on Hunter that in her mind, this was all new to her. The fact stunned him and so did the interest she was displaying. Throughout their two-year marriage, she'd not wanted to share in his business or learn how it operated. Yes, she appreciated the fact that the Flying H provided him with a good income, but she'd also viewed the business as a barrier between them.

"I had no idea so much went into this business," she said. "Who takes care of all your paperwork? There must be tons of it."

Shaking away his uncertain thoughts, he focused on her question. "You're right. There is tons of bookkeeping that goes with this business. I do as much as I can with what little time I have. The remainder I send to Bonnie— my sister back on Stone Creek Ranch. But she's getting overloaded with work so eventually I'm going to have to get someone else to do the job."

"What sort of work does Bonnie do?" she asked.

"She does all the bookkeeping for the ranch and acts as Dad's secretary. And lately, she's taken on another task…but that's a whole other story," he said as the two of them reached the door of the Dalharts' living quarters. "I'll tell you about that later."

He knocked on the door of the trailer and it swung wide open. Cheyenne greeted them with a cheery smile. Not quite as tall as her two older siblings, she was, at twenty-eight, the youngest of the three sisters. Presently, her long, chestnut hair was wrapped into a thick bun at the back of her head and her face still carried the makeup she'd worn for their earlier act.

"Hi, Hunter. Come on in! We're just now getting ready to eat."

"Hi, Chey. Thanks for inviting us." He placed a supportive hand beneath Willow's elbow and helped her up the short steps and into the trailer.

They were immediately greeted by the other two women and Hunter quickly made introductions.

"Hunter is being too proper," Carlotta said as she shook Willow's hand. "Just call us Lotta, Chasta and Chey."

"Okay, I will," Willow replied. "And I hope we're not intruding."

"Not at all. We have more food than we can eat." With a hand still wrapped around Willow's, Carlotta urged her over to a long, booth-style table that ran parallel to the wall. "Have a seat and grab yourself a plate, Anna. Hunter, you join her."

"I'll just stand," Hunter told her. "So all you girls can sit."

"Nonsense," Carlotta told him. "We've made room for more than two extras in here before."

Relenting, Hunter gestured for Willow to slide into the bench seat. "We'd better not argue with the woman. Lotta can get loud."

"Boy, you got that right, Hunter," Cheyenne joked. "Lotta doesn't need a megaphone when she's hollering at me and Chasta. Her voice carries from one end of the arena to the other."

"We have to keep cotton in the horses' ears so Lotta doesn't damage their hearing," Chastity added impishly.

Carlotta rolled her eyes at her playful sisters, then looked to Hunter and Willow. "Actually, we do put cotton in the horses' ears," she told Anna. "To protect them from the crowd noise, not my big mouth. This is turning into be-mean-to-Lotta night."

Laughing, Chastity and Cheyenne both hugged their older sister.

"We're only teasing," Cheyenne said. "You're our leader and the smart one out of us."

"I don't care which one of you is the boss. You all three put on a humdinger of a show tonight," Hunter said to the women. "The audience roared when you rode your horses through the ring of fire. I'm glad you wanted to add it to tonight's performance."

Willow nodded with enthusiasm. "I'm not sure how well you could hear the crowd, but Hunter is right, it was roaring. And I was doing plenty of gasping and clapping," she told them. "You ladies are fearless."

Cheyenne slipped into the bench seat next to Willow,

while Chastity and Carlotta pulled up small stools to the opposite side of the table.

Chastity chuckled, "Our horses make us look good. And our dad says we do this job because we don't have much sense. We try to make him understand that his daughters crave excitement."

"And danger," Cheyenne said.

"And money," Carlotta tacked on.

Everyone chuckled as the eldest sister picked up a small stack of paper plates and passed them around the group.

"So what do you do, Anna?" Chastity asked. "Or are you a lady of leisure?"

Carlotta let out a dry laugh. "Do ladies of leisure still exist?"

Willow smiled. "Don't look at me. I'm a secretary for a hotel manager here in Red Bluff."

"The hotel where I'm staying," Hunter added.

"Oh, is that how you two met?" Cheyenne's expression was curious as she looked at Hunter and Willow.

"Sort of," Willow answered, then cast a faint smile at Hunter. "We ran into each other. Literally. Right?"

Hunter nodded. "It was dark and raining and I was going in the hotel while she was coming out. I very nearly knocked her down."

"She must've forgiven you," Chastity said coyly.

Hunter grinned. "After I apologized and bought her a drink."

"You sly fox," Carlotta teased, then winked at Willow.

Hunter smiled sheepishly. "It was the least I could do."

Carlotta gestured for everyone to dig into the food.

As they all filled their plates, Willow said, "Actually, that night when Hunter and I crashed into each other, he thought he recognized me."

Cheyenne let out a loud groan of disbelief. "Hunter! Don't tell me you used that ancient pickup line! Couldn't you have come up with something better than that?"

"No," Willow interrupted with a shake of her head. "Hunter actually *did* think I was someone he used to know back in his hometown. Her name was Willow."

As the sisters exchanged surprised looks, a part of Hunter stiffened with dread. He wasn't keen to discuss her amnesia while knowing he held the key to her identity. But at least none of the Dalharts could connect him to Willow. Yes, they were aware that he'd been married once, but thankfully he'd never told them his ex-wife's name, or the circumstances of his divorce.

"Is this for real?" Chastity voiced the question.

"Yes, it's true," Hunter answered, as he casually spooned a small mountain of potato salad onto his plate. "In the dark, Anna looked very much like the woman I once knew."

"If that's the case, then I forgive you for using such a stale pickup line," Cheyenne told him. "Strange things do happen like that. Back in June when we were doing the rodeo down in Camp Verde, Arizona, I swore I saw Mom sitting in the grandstand. After we finished our act, I even climbed the bleachers and looked for her. But she was gone."

None of the Dalhart sisters had ever talked to Hunter about what had happened to their mother, Marylou, except to say that about five years ago their father, Seldon, had received word that his wife had died. Supposedly,

Marylou and Seldon had been separated since Cheyenne had been small. Whatever the case, the woman
was a sore subject for the sisters and one that Hunter
was careful to avoid.

Carlotta let out a weary sigh. "She was gone, Chey,
because she was never there in the first place. She's dead.
She's been dead for more than five years."

Chastity shot a hopeless look at both her sisters.
"Let's not talk about Mom. Especially in front of Anna
and Hunter. Besides, I want to hear more about Hunter
thinking he recognized Anna. Red Bluff, California, is
a long distance from Beaver County, Utah."

Hunter cleared his throat and tried to sound convinc-
ing. "Well, to be honest, I'd not seen Willow in several
years. So I wasn't exactly sure it was her."

Cheyenne grinned at Willow. "Bet you set him straight
right off, didn't you?"

Willow looked hopelessly at Hunter, then at the three
women. "No. I couldn't exactly set him straight because
I—"

She broke off awkwardly and Hunter felt compelled
to finish for her.

"You see," he said. "Anna doesn't know who she is—
not exactly."

Chastity's jaw dropped while Cheyenne and Chastity
stared wide-eyed at their guests.

"Is this one of your jokes, Hunter?" Carlotta asked.

Frowning with confusion, Cheyenne looked to Hunter
for an explanation. "I don't understand. How can she not
know who she is?"

Hunter released a heavy breath. The Dalhart sisters
had no way of knowing he was trying to maneuver his

way through a tangled web—that he was hiding the truth from Willow, but that he was doing so to keep from hurting her. Because, no matter what happened with her memory, he wanted everything to be better for the both of them.

He glanced at her. "Would you like for me to tell them?"

She nodded. "Please."

Drawing a deep breath, Hunter turned his attention to the three women sitting around the table. "Anna was in a serious car crash four years ago. The accident nearly killed her and left her in a coma for three weeks. When she eventually regained consciousness, her memory was a total blank."

"Amnesia?" Carlotta asked with amazement.

Willow answered her question. "Unfortunately, yes. I couldn't remember anything. Not even my own name. I'm still blank about who I am and where I came from. So when Hunter acted as though he knew me, I was shaken. I thought *finally*. Someone has come along who can help identify me. But—"

All three sisters were anxiously waiting for Willow to continue, but Hunter could see she was struggling to control her emotions. He was going to have to speak for her.

He said, "It's not so simple. Quite a bit of time had passed since I'd seen Willow Anderson. She left town a few years ago and never returned. The family she had there is dead and no one else seems to know where she went." Which was true enough, Hunter thought. "I've already sent pics of Anna to my family back in Beaver

County, but they couldn't identify her with a hundred percent certainty."

Damn it, he had to be the biggest fraud to ever walk the earth. He was sitting next to his ex-wife. He had one arm around her waist. He knew exactly who she was, and yet he had to lie his way through this. No. He wasn't lying. He was pretending. He had to make believe Willow was a woman he'd met days ago, instead of the wife who'd shared his bed, his home and his life. The whole situation was tearing at him.

Carlotta shook her head. "Was there anything in your wrecked vehicle to identify you?" she asked Willow.

"It burned," Willow told her. "Only a portion of the frame was left. Even the VIN was destroyed."

"Didn't anyone come searching for you while you were in the hospital, or since then?" Cheyenne asked in an incredulous voice.

"No. I must not have had any family or friends. Or if I did, we weren't on good terms. I have no way of knowing."

"Oh, that's awful. Just awful," Chastity declared. "How have you survived without any ID? How did you get the name you're using now?"

"Getting ID was a nightmare. It took a long time and help from people working in a lot of different agencies to finally get a social security card just so I could try to get a driver's license. As for my name, a nurse who cared for me in the hospital helped me choose it." She slanted a wry smile at the sisters. "Can you imagine a grown woman picking out her own name? As you can probably imagine, I've been faced with some bizarre situations."

Cheyenne suddenly grinned. "Well, plenty of actors

and actresses pick out a different name to use other than their own. Just think of yourself as being cool, Anna, like a movie star."

The younger woman's remark lightened the moment and as laughter sounded around the table, everyone began to relax and eat.

"So, Hunter, do you have any plans to look for this Willow?" Carlotta asked. "Or do you think that's a dead end?"

"To be honest, I'm still trying to decide if Anna might actually be Willow." He glanced over at Willow to see she was gazing at him with a beseeching look in her eyes. As though he was her lifeline, and she was counting on him. The idea turned his voice husky as he spoke again. "And whether she would even want to be her."

"Hmm. Does any person have a right to choose who they want to be?" Chastity asked as she lifted a bite of barbecued chicken to her mouth.

"Of course they do, sissy," Cheyenne quickly replied. "No matter what name we go by, we can still be the person we choose to be."

Hunter was surprised to see Willow reach over and place a grateful hand on Cheyenne's forearm. She'd never been one to show her feelings with a touch or a hug. Even around his family, she'd shied away from their physical affection. Either the amnesia had changed her, he thought, or four long years of being lonely did.

She said, "Thank you, Cheyenne. Hearing you say that—it makes me feel good about myself even if a part of my brain is a blank."

Cheyenne gave her a wide smile. "I'm glad that for once I said something right. And I'll go ahead and say something else, Anna. You're a lovely lady and no matter what name you go by, I'm sure you're going to be happy and successful."

"Hear, hear. Let's all toast to that," Carlotta said.

"Well, that's a great idea, sis, but we don't have anything to drink!" Cheyenne exclaimed.

Everyone looked around the table and once it became obvious there were no glasses or drinks of any sort, they all started laughing.

"We can fix that," Chastity said. "Come on, Lotta. Let's get some glasses and soda."

When the two women returned to the table with the drinks for everyone, Carlotta lifted her glass high. "Here's to Anna," she stated cheerily. "With or without her memory, may her life be blessed with happiness."

Glasses clinked and as Hunter sipped the soda, he glanced over to Willow and saw a mist of tears had formed in her brown eyes.

Sooner rather than later, this impossible farce would reach its end, Hunter thought. But how? And once the truth was revealed, would Willow still want to be at his side?

Chapter Seven

Nearly an hour later, Anna and Hunter said good-night to the Dalharts and left their trailer. By then, she was stuffed with food and smiling with a kind of contentment she couldn't ever remember feeling. At least, not in her short memory.

"I feel like I've made new friends with the sisters," she told Hunter as they strolled alongside a corral filled with calves. "All three are so enjoyable to be around. Are they always so upbeat?"

"Usually they're a cheerful trio. Which is a testament to their character because they've not always had it easy. They've never come right out and discussed their growing up years, but from comments they make from time to time, it sounds like it was rough."

"They're obviously strong women. It didn't take me very long to pick up on that fact. But now that I've met them and see how pretty and sociable they are, I'm surprised they're not married or engaged or in long-term relationships of some sort."

He glanced down at her and Anna thought how extra sexy he looked tonight in a white shirt and a chocolate-brown western-cut jacket. His Stetson was almost the same color as his jacket and she decided the warm color suited his rusty hair and tanned complexion. And like the Dalharts, she wondered why he wasn't married with children. No doubt, with his looks, he probably had plenty of women chasing after him, hoping to snare him with a wedding ring.

"They don't discuss much about their romantic lives. Carlotta did tell me that she was married once when she was in her early twenties, but for reasons she didn't explain, the marriage ended. And last year Chastity was engaged to a guy she knew back in her hometown in Wyoming, but she broke up with him a couple of months before the ceremony was to take place. Chey told me that Chasta found out he was cheating on her. And as you might expect, Chasta doesn't want to talk about it. As for Chey, she enjoys playing the field. I can't see her wanting to get married for a long time. But that might change if she meets the right man."

The right man. Most of Anna's coworkers had been telling her over and over that Ian was the perfect man for her. He had decent looks, a good job and a home in the ritzy part of town. The two of them worked well together, the women liked to point out, and he was wealthy enough to give her a comfortable lifestyle. What more could she want?

Plenty, Anna thought. She wanted passion. The kind that made her heart pound and her head swim. Even more, she wanted love. The deep down kind of love that never faded, even during bad times. But she could never reach for any of those things unless her heart was free. And for now it didn't feel that way. She couldn't explain or understand her feelings. All she knew was that from the time she'd regained consciousness, she suspected

she'd already given her heart to a man out there somewhere. Until she found him, she couldn't expect to find
the deep love she desperately wanted.

Trying to shake away the hopeless thought, she said,
"Hmm. I guess for now the sisters are content to focus
on their rodeo careers."

"I expect they think trick riding is safer than getting
tangled up in a bad romance," he said dryly.

She glanced up at him. "Is running your rodeo company the reason you're not married?" she dared to ask.

Even though they were walking through a shadowy
stretch of ground, she could've sworn his face turned
white. She wondered if she had asked a touchy question. That first night they'd shared a drink in the hotel
bar, he'd told her he was single. But he'd not elaborated
on the subject. Now she had to wonder if a woman had
hurt him at one time in his life. If so, had it been over
his nomadic lifestyle? It was hard to imagine, but cou-
ples often split for lesser reasons.

"I guess you could say I'm single because of the
Flying H," he said in a low, cautious voice. "The job
keeps me on the road and takes up an enormous amount
of my time."

"Yes, I can see how this business would consume
your time." She smiled up at him in an effort to lighten
the moment. "But you have lots of good friends around
you and I'm sure they feel like family."

"I have a huge family back in Beaver County and a
sister and brother-in-law up in Idaho. I've never been
without a family."

So he couldn't understand how it was for her, Anna
thought. He couldn't begin to know how alone she felt

and how much she longed to be free of her amnesia, free to love and marry and have a family of her own.

"I'm sorry, Hunter, for sticking my nose in your private life. It's just that I look at you and wonder."

He darted a dubious glance at her. "You wonder what?"

She smiled at him. "Why you're not a husband and father. You seem perfect for the roles."

The taut expression on his face suddenly transformed into a smile and the sight of it filled her with relief.

"You know, Anna, I look at you and wonder the same thing—why you're not a wife and mother. 'Cause you seem perfect for the roles."

She laughed and so did he. Then, with a hand on hers, he drew her into the circle of his arms.

"It's been a long time since I felt like this," he whispered against her cheek. "Like I'm young again with a golden future stretching out in front of me."

Surprised by his words, she leaned her head back just enough to study his face. "You *are* young, Hunter. And your future looks awfully sunny to me."

"You must've forgotten I'm forty-one years old."

Smiling, she rested her palms against his chest. "That's hardly decrepit."

Because she knew they were deep in the shadows and no one else was around, she wasn't surprised when he lowered his head and kissed her. But she was surprised at the hunger she tasted on his lips. It tasted exactly like the desperate need she felt for him.

He lifted his head and sucked in a ragged breath, but then immediately dove in to kiss her again. This time, as his lips made a hot search of hers, desire flamed deep within her and urged her to press the front of her body even closer to his.

Eventually, she managed to free her hands from the tight space between their chests and slide them around to his back. The movement prompted her hips to shift and press directly against his, which caused a deep groan to rumble in his throat. Mindlessly, she thrust her tongue past his teeth and tasted the dark pleasure of his mouth.

She didn't know why it felt so right to kiss him. She couldn't understand why their bodies fit together so perfectly, or why the idea of making love to him seemed so natural. But everything about this and the two of them together was meant to be, she thought. Just like bumping into him on a dark, rainy night.

Their kisses finally came to an end when the loud nicker of a horse sounded behind them and Hunter lifted his head to glance over his shoulder.

"Malachi is seeing after the pick-up horses. He'll be coming this way soon," he murmured. "We—uh—should be getting back to the trailer."

She let out a lungful of pent-up air. "Yes. We probably should," she replied. "Because I—I'm getting a little scared."

His brows arched as he looked down at her. "Scared? Surely not of me?"

"No. Of myself. And how much I want you."

An odd look crossed his face, almost as if he was in anguish, and then he quickly bent his head long enough to press a quick kiss on her forehead.

"Oh, Anna, I want you just as much." With a hand on her arm, he said in a gruff voice, "Let's go."

By the time they walked the last fifty yards to Hunter's

trailer, a bit of cool sanity had returned to Anna's foggy brain. Before they climbed the steps to enter his living quarters, she turned to him.

"I think I'd better collect my handbag from your trailer and say good-night, Hunter. It's—uh, getting late and I have to be up early for work in the morning."

Expecting him to argue the point, she was surprised when he nodded. "Yes. I have to be up early, too. So I guess we should call it a night."

He opened the door of the trailer and she preceded him into the living quarters.

"Do you want to take your hot dog and fries home with you?" he suggested as he came in behind her. "I have plenty of plastic containers to haul it in."

"Might as well," she said, while her thoughts were already leaping to tomorrow night. She wondered whether he would suggest they meet again. And if he did, what was she going to tell him? She'd already admitted she wanted him physically. She'd look hypocritical if she turned him down.

He fetched a pair of plastic storage dishes from a cabinet and pulled the wrapped-up food back out of the refrigerator. "Use these."

While she packaged the remainder of her meal, he stood to one side and watched. The fact that his gaze was following her every movement made her extremely conscious of herself and the overpowering attraction she felt for him. Did he have any idea just how much she wanted to forget everything and throw herself into his arms? No. In spite of the eager kisses she'd planted on his lips, she doubted he'd guessed the depth of desire thrumming through her veins and pounding in her head like a drumbeat.

She had to get a grip, she thought. Otherwise, she was going to end up making a fool of herself.

"The barbecue we ate with the Dalhart sisters was yummy, but so were these hot dogs," she said, while hoping the simple act of speaking would get her mind off the wayward thoughts dancing through her mind. "I might have this for my lunch tomorrow at work."

He handed her a plastic sack to carry the containers and after she'd safely tucked them inside the tote, she reached for her purse.

"So you eat lunch at the hotel, too?" he asked. "I thought I recalled you saying you often went to Loretta's."

Surprised that he'd paid that much attention, she looked at him. "I do both. Of course, eating at the hotel saves money."

"And I'm sure that's something you need to do," he said.

His comment caused her brows to arch. "Yes. Most folks do need to be frugal. But I'm not destitute, if that's what you're thinking."

He grimaced. "Sorry, Anna. That came out all wrong. I wasn't implying you were poor. I was only thinking— well, when you said *saves money* it suddenly struck me that after your accident you probably didn't have any sort of funds. If everything in your vehicle burned and you had no memory of anything you might have saved up…"

His words trailed away on a sheepish note and Anna smiled to show she wasn't offended. "You're right. If I had any amount of money in a bank somewhere or tucked away in a drawer wherever I lived, I didn't know about it. I had to start from scratch."

Shaking his head with disbelief, he said, "I can't imagine having everything suddenly wiped away. Especially without family or friends to give me some sort of support. You have more gumption than I'd ever have."

"No. If you were in my shoes, you'd find a way to survive, just like I did." Shrugging, she went on. "But I wasn't completely alone. Initially, the hospital staff started a fund for me and eventually some of the towns-folk chipped in. By the time I was well enough to leave the hospital, there was enough for me to rent an apartment and buy food and other essentials. Then once I got the job at the hotel, it was easy to start saving from my salary. I'm not a big spender."

A wry smile twisted his lips. "No. I don't imagine you are."

There was tenderness in his blue eyes, along with a spark of admiration. To have him believe she was a strong woman filled her with pride and drew her to him even more.

A lump of emotion filled her throat and she swallowed hard as she slipped the strap of her purse onto her shoulder. "Well, I'd better be on my way."

She turned around, and was almost to the door when someone knocked. Anna stepped to one side and waited for Hunter to deal with the caller.

"Who is it?" he asked.

"Malachi."

Two strides had Hunter opening the door and motioning for his assistant to enter.

"I don't want to interrupt," Malachi said. "I only stopped by to tell you everything has been taken care of. No need for you to check on anything."

Hunter jerked his thumb toward the inside of the

trailer. "Don't be bashful, Malachi. Anna is getting ready to leave. You can tell her good-night."

The Shoshone cowboy entered the living room and, upon facing Anna, politely removed his Stetson.

"Hey again, Anna. Has Hunter been showing you some of his prize livestock?" he asked.

"He has. I especially loved seeing the mares and colts up close," she told him. "We didn't get around to the bulls, but Hunter tells me most all of them are lovable."

Malachi chuckled. "They are lovable. As long as you don't try to ride them. Did you notice the sheep we use for the children's mutton bustin' event?" he asked. "Hunter brought them from the Hollister family ranch, but he had to twist his little brother's arm to get them."

"That's an understatement," Hunter said with wry fondness. "I had to promise not to let any kid older than seven ride any of them."

"Quint's crazy about his flocks," Malachi further explained.

"Uh—we didn't make it around to the sheep either," Anna told the cowboy. They'd become a little sidetracked, and the memory of their hot kisses warmed her cheeks. She cleared her throat and glanced over at Hunter. "I recall you saying your brother oversees the sheep on your family ranch. When I watched the mutton bustin', I wondered if the animals had come from Stone Creek Ranch."

"Yes. I have a dozen of them," Hunter said. "Quint wouldn't allow me any more than that. He and his wife, Clementine, consider each ram and ewe and lamb as their babies. It's a good thing the ranch only raises sheep for wool purposes. It would break Quint's heart to have to end any of their lives early so they could be harvested as meat."

"Trust me, Anna. Hunter thinks all of the livestock are his babies, too. He treats them all with extra loving care." Malachi cast an amused glance at Hunter. "Did you tell her about Clementine being a sheepherder? That's how Quint and she got together. He hired her to watch his flock. And Quint ended up watching her."

Hunter rolled his eyes in a good-natured way. "No. I didn't tell her about Clementine. And now I don't have to. You already have."

"Well, Anna is a woman," Malachi stated as though Hunter hadn't noticed the obvious. "I thought she might appreciate hearing that little tidbit about Clementine."

Anna said, "I've never heard of a woman sheepherder before. She sounds interesting."

"She is. Beautiful and nice, too," Malachi told her. "All of Hunter's sisters-in-law are beautiful and nice. It's too bad he can't follow his brothers' footsteps."

Hunter glared at him. "Malachi, you're talking far too much. Did someone give you an energy drink?"

Malachi frowned at him, then chuckled. "Hunter, you know I don't drink those things. All I've had is a regular cup of coffee." He turned his attention to Anna. "So are you planning on coming back to the rodeo tomorrow night? The performances should be even better. Lots of top-notch cowboys are entered in most of the events. And two champion barrel racers will be running."

Anna glanced uncertainly at Hunter. So far, he'd not mentioned seeing her again until the Sunday performance and she had no intentions of inviting herself back to the rodeo tomorrow night. After those kisses she'd plastered on his lips, it would look like she was pushing herself on him. Besides, the more she thought about it the more uncertain she was about spending extra time with the man. Even if there was the slightest chance he was a link to her past, he was dangerous to her peace of mind.

"I—uh, I hadn't really thought that much about it, Malachi," she answered, while thinking she'd turned into a liar as well as a fool.

Malachi turned a look of surprise on Hunter. "Haven't you invited Anna back for tomorrow night?"

"Not yet. I was about to do that when you knocked."

Malachi grinned at him. "Well, maybe you ought to start talking before Anna leaves with the idea that you don't like her."

"Maybe I would if you'd shut up long enough," Hunter told him.

Anna smiled at the banter between the two men. It was clear they were as close as brothers.

"It's okay," she told Malachi. "Hunter has lots of work to do after the rodeo. I'm pretty sure he doesn't want to dump it all on your shoulders for a second night in a row."

Malachi batted a dismissive hand through the air. "Don't you worry about that, Anna. I can work circles around Hunter any day. Besides, he needs a break."

Hunter chuckled. "I'd like to see how many circles you can make around me, buddy," he joked. "But you're right about one thing. I could use a break." He looked away from Malachi and leveled his blue gaze at her. "If you'd like to come back to the rodeo tomorrow night, Anna, I'd enjoy having your company."

Her heart thumped as her gaze met his. If she had any sense at all, she'd make up an excuse not to accept his invitation. Nothing serious could ever develop between them and she wasn't the brief-affair type. Since her accident, she'd not had intimate relations with any man. She'd never really wanted to—until now. Until she'd met Hunter. But something was pulling her toward him; something that was too strong to deny.

She drew in a deep breath and hurriedly blew it out. "If that's the case, then I'd like to come again."

"Good. I'll leave a ticket for you at the entrance," Hunter told her.

His smile smug, Malachi made a thumbs-up sign. "Great. Now that I have that settled with you two, I'll say good-night."

"I will, too," Anna quickly added. "Would you mind, Malachi, if I walked along with you?"

"Be a pleasure, Anna."

She lifted a hand in farewell to Hunter. "I'll see you tomorrow night."

He nodded. "Yes. Tomorrow night."

Outside the trailer, Anna gestured toward a large parking area behind the stadium. "My car is parked way over there," she told him. "But you needn't walk that far with me. I mainly wanted to leave with you so I could thank you."

He began to stroll toward the parking area and Anna walked along at his side.

"No need to thank me," he said. "I've not done anything."

"Yes, you have. You've been extra nice. Especially about helping Hunter."

Malachi grunted. "That's what he pays me for."

"I know, but I also got the impression you took on his share tonight, and that you did it for my sake."

He smiled vaguely at her. "That's true. But I'm doing

it for Hunter, too. Not because he pays me or because it's my job. When I said he needed a break, I was serious. To see him spending time with you—it's good. But he'll only take that time if he knows I'm looking after the livestock. He wouldn't trust anyone else."

She thought for a moment, then asked, "Does he not take time for himself very often?"

"Rarely. And as for women—well, since I was hired on with the Flying H, I've not seen him with any. I know he gets lonely. I can see it on his face sometimes. So I'm really glad he's taken notice of you."

Her cheeks warmed as she thought of how much notice she and Hunter had taken of each other. Had Malachi already guessed they'd become closer than mere friends?

"You really care about him, don't you?" she asked.

"More than you could guess. When I met Hunter, I was living on the rez, scrounging around for odd jobs and barely managing to keep my head above water. He gave me a chance and turned my life around. I'll always be grateful to him. And I want him to be happy. That's how it is when you care about somebody—you want them to be happy."

Malachi's heartfelt comment touched her in a way she'd not expected. It also reminded her that these past four years, she'd not allowed herself to care that much for anyone. Yes, she'd made friends, but she couldn't say she was especially close to any of them. The fact was not only sad, it made her wonder about herself. Was there something missing in her? Was the amnesia preventing her from caring deeply about others? Or had she always been emotionally distant? Strange that she'd never considered such a thing about herself before now.

But Hunter and his friends seemed to be opening her eyes to many things.

She glanced at him. "Did Hunter mention to you that I'm suffering from amnesia?"

"He did. Said you had an automobile accident. That was bad luck. But look at you now. You're all good. And even without your memory, you've learned that you can keep on living. That's the most important part."

Yes, she could keep on living without her memory. And, foolish or not, meeting Hunter had her thinking more of the future, rather than bemoaning her lack of a past.

"You're so right, Malachi. And who knows, someday I might wake up and remember. But if I don't, it's like you just said, I can still keep on living." She looked up to see they'd reached a chain-link gate that led out to the parking area. "My car isn't that much farther from here. You don't have to keep escorting me."

He flashed her a grin. "No problem. The parking lot is a little dark. I want to make sure you get to your car safely."

She laughed softly. "We just passed a security guard less than two minutes ago."

His laughter joined hers. "Well, it's not often I get to walk with a girl like you. I want to make the most of it."

Amused, she asked, "A girl like me? What does that mean?"

"A girl with real class."

His response took her by surprise. Mainly because she'd never thought of herself as classy. When she thought of the word, she pictured someone glamorous and sophisticated—and that wasn't her. But she did try to dress nicely and behave like a lady. To Anna, those were commonsense rules to follow, but now that Malachi had set her thinking, she realized that class—or lack of it, really—came from a person's personality rather than their outward appearance. Where that part of her had come from, she might never know. Had her mother taught her manners and how to dress? Had her father warned her about being crass or rude? The simple questions made her realize she might never know anything about her parents or how they'd raised her.

"Thank you for the compliment, Malachi, but I'm just a regular girl." She pulled the key fob from her purse and punched the button to unlock the door.

He said, "Hunter doesn't think so."

What could she say to that? Hunter would be in Red Bluff for four more days. After that, she figured it would be the end of their time together.

She opened the car door and slid into the driver's seat. "You're a nice guy, Malachi. Thanks for escorting me to my car."

"My pleasure. See you tomorrow night."

He shut the door and waved her off. As Anna drove away from the rodeo grounds, her thoughts remained on Hunter and how meeting him had opened up her life in ways she could've never foreseen. Most likely she wasn't the woman named Willow he'd been acquainted with. And in all probability, he couldn't link her to her true identity. But those things no longer seemed to determine her future. Now *he* had become the important thing in her life. And the reality that her happiness hinged on Hunter Hollister was enough to shoot holes of fear right through her heart.

Chapter Eight

"Grace, I understand you're busy, but—"

His sister cut off the remainder of his sentence. "Busy! That's an understatement, Hunter. It's only eight thirty in the morning and at this very moment my waiting room is already full. Plus, patients are waiting in three different examining rooms. A stomach virus has been going around town. It's been chaos here at the clinic. I don't have time to draw breath, much less take time to track down a neurologist I've not talked to in months!"

He blew out a frustrated breath as he stood in his hotel room and waited for the mini coffee maker to finish filling the cup.

"All right. I understand," he said to her. "But saying I'm stressed would be an understatement, Grace. This thing with Willow is getting out of hand."

He could hear Grace draw in a sharp breath and he felt bad about adding to her stress. But his sister was the only person he could think of who might be able to help him. Sure, he could talk to a doctor in Red Bluff about the situation, but ultimately he or she would want to talk with Willow face-to-face, and that would raise too many red flags.

Grace turned his comment into a question. "Out of

hand? You haven't done anything rash and told her that she's your ex, have you?"

"Not exactly," he muttered as he picked up the cup of steaming coffee.

"What does that mean? *Not exactly*?" Grace asked warily. "I don't like the indecisiveness in your voice, Hunter. It worries me."

He snorted. "If you're worried that I'm getting involved with Willow again, don't bother. But ever since she left Stone Creek, things between us have been unresolved. Yeah, there's a set of divorce papers in a drawer back at the house, but what did they ever mean? I've spent the past four years wondering about her—about us. I guess all that time I've been lost, because she was lost. And now that I've found her, I'm living a lie. It's tearing me up, Grace. I need help and you're the only person who can help me."

Hunter could hear his sister's heavy sigh and the sound only made him feel worse. He didn't want to burden her with his romantic problems—especially when he'd once caused problems in her love life when he'd tried to talk Grace out of marrying her old flame, Mack. Not that Hunter had ever had anything against his brother-in-law. He'd simply been afraid his sister might be hurt all over again. Thank God she'd had enough courage and trust in herself and in their relationship to marry Mack anyway. He was the love of Grace's life and she couldn't have found a better husband if she'd looked all over the world.

"I'm so sorry, Hunter. I really am. And I want to help, but I'm not trained to deal with Willow's problem. If I told you to suddenly spring the truth on her and she went into some sort of breakdown, you'd hate me for the rest of my life. I'd hate myself. Just try to hold on for a few more days. Dr. Bickford should be back from his vacation soon. I'm sure he'll know what kind of advice to give you. In the meantime, what have you told Willow? Or have you seen her since that night you ran into her?"

Even though Grace couldn't see him, hot color washed up Hunter's neck and onto his face. If he admitted to his sister that he'd not only seen Willow, but that he'd held her close and kissed her as deeply as when they'd been husband and wife, she'd probably think her brother had turned into a creep. And maybe he was a jerk for kissing Willow and holding her under slightly false pretenses. But how could he not reach for her, when the love he had for her ached inside him?

He walked over to the large plate glass window overlooking the east side of the building where a grassy courtyard was surrounded by a low brick wall that matched the hotel's facade. The area was dotted with huge shade trees, wrought iron benches and contoured flower beds that held a few late blooming roses. It was a pretty spot and he wondered if Willow ever ate lunch there whenever the weather was nice. With her boss, perhaps? No. He didn't want to let his thoughts go there.

After taking another sip of coffee, he said, "Yes. I've seen her several times. I'll see her tonight, in fact. She's coming back to the rodeo."

"Willow at a rodeo?" Grace asked with disbelief. "You obviously have the wrong woman, Hunter. Your Willow didn't like rodeos, remember? Even worse, she had the idea you'd be better off without them. Face it, brother, she wasn't good for you when you were married.

She didn't try to understand your dreams or needs and I seriously doubt she'd be any different now."

He couldn't argue with any of that, Hunter thought grimly. But he hadn't necessarily tried to make Willow's dreams or needs come true, either. "That's what you're not going to believe, Grace. Willow is different. In all the ways she needed to be different. She isn't hiding herself away anymore. She's outgoing—at least, compared to what she used to be. Not only with her looks, but her personality, too. She jokes and laughs. She has self-confidence—something she needed in the worst way."

"Hmm. This definitely doesn't sound like Willow. On the other hand, if she does actually have amnesia, the medical condition could be affecting her personality. Mind you, I'm not suggesting this as a doctor. Like I've said, I'm not a neurologist. I'm only voicing an idea."

He sipped the hot coffee while hoping the brew would chase away the grogginess in his brain. After Willow had left the rodeo grounds last night, he'd considered forgetting his hotel room and bedding down in his trailer. But he'd decided he didn't want the cost of the room to go to waste so he'd driven back into town. Once he'd entered the hotel lobby, he'd walked straight to the bar and ordered a double shot of bourbon. He'd thought the drink would soothe his raw nerves. Instead, he'd sat at the same little table they'd shared that night he'd accidently bumped into her and tried to imagine how it would be if she suddenly recognized him. The alcohol and the memories had ruined his sleep and left him feeling like hell.

He said, "There's no doubt about Anna being Willow. And she clearly has amnesia." He paused and wiped a weary hand over his face. "I tell you, Grace, sometimes when I look at her, I think maybe it's better that she doesn't remember her childhood or her life as an Anderson."

"I can understand your thinking, Hunter. Her grandparents did their best, but they struggled financially. Even after Willow was grown, there were some people around Beaver County who never let her forget her modest upbringing, or how her parents had been two worthless individuals. She did some suffering before you took notice of her. And I've often wondered if deep down that's why she never felt comfortable on Stone Creek Ranch. Not that we're super rich or snobby. But I think she never felt she measured up to you—or any of us."

"Yes. She did feel that way. That's why it was a struggle to talk her into marrying me." With a heavy sigh, he said, "I can't change any of the past, Grace. But I want to make her life better now. I just don't know how to do it—without running the risk of harming her."

"I left a message with Dr. Bickford's receptionist to have him call me as soon as he returns to his office. When that happens, I'll hopefully get some answers for you. Until then, don't beat yourself up, Hunter. You're trying to do the right thing for Willow. If that includes holding back the truth for a little while longer, then just think of holding back the truth for now as giving her doses of medicine to help her get well."

He groaned. "Thanks, sis. I'll do the best I can. In the meantime, I'd appreciate it if you didn't tell Jack and Cord about our conversation."

"Why keep those two brothers in the dark?" Grace asked. "What about Flint and Quint?"

"Flint and Quint are more respectful of my feelings toward my ex-wife. Jack and Cord—well, they outright curse at the thought of me getting involved with Willow again. That's why."

"Can you blame them? They love you. They've seen you go through hell over her."

He was still going through hell over Willow, Hunter thought dismally. That's why this time he had to do everything right. He had to be patient and hope and pray that she would eventually remember he was the man who'd always loved her.

Grace went on, "Anyway, I won't mention this to anyone else in the family. I realize they all know you've run into Willow again, but I don't think they've guessed how deeply you've become involved with her again. So I won't say anything to them. At least, not before you leave Red Bluff. You are coming home for Christmas, aren't you?"

"I'll be there," he told her. "Unless some unforeseen catastrophe happens. I imagine Mom and Bonnie have everything decorated and ready for the parties."

"Of course. Cord helped Mom put up the tree a few days ago. Everything looks beautiful. It'll all look better though, Hunter, when you get here."

Hunter was about to thank his sister and tell her good-bye, when he heard a female voice calling to her from a distance.

"Uh—I can hear you're needed, Grace. I'll let you go," he said quickly.

She said, "Call me if there are any changes."

He had to smile at her very doctor-like response. "Yes, Doc. I love you."

"I love you more," she said and ended the call.

He was about to slip the phone into his shirt pocket when a ding notified him of an incoming text message.

Seeing it was from Malachi, he promptly opened it.

Ground crew needs your input. Rain and a bit of snow here last night.

Hunter quickly tapped out a reply.

Be there in a few minutes.

From what Hunter could see out the window, it hadn't rained or snowed here in town. Which meant an isolated shower had decided to let loose over the rodeo grounds.

Just what he needed to start the day, he thought, as he grabbed his jacket and hat on the way to the door. Mud puddles in front of the bucking chutes and the barrel racers worried about their horses slipping on slick ground.

Yet even the concerns of getting the arena dried out for tonight's performance wasn't enough to block Willow from his mind. Especially when he stepped off the elevator and passed through the lobby. Fortunately, he didn't know where her office was located inside the hotel, or he'd be tempted to find her and try to persuade her to leave her desk and spend the day with him.

As if she'd take a chance of jeopardizing her job to be with me, he thought miserably, as he walked outside and headed toward his truck. She had to support herself financially and every other way. She had no one else to help her. But then, she'd had no one to help her four years ago when she'd decided to take a powder. The financial security of being a Hollister had meant nothing to her. And clearly, neither had he.

"You know, we should have gone to the pancake breakfast some of the rodeo sponsors were putting on this morning. It was free to the public and only a couple of blocks from here," Celia said to Anna as the two women drank coffee on their afternoon break. "There might've been some of those cute cowboys hanging around there."

Anna glanced across the small utility table at the impish expression on her friend's face. "And what do you think you'd get if one of them took notice of you? They'll be leaving town when the rodeo is over."

Celia's brows lifted. Chuckling, she leaned toward Anna and said in a lowered voice, "I wouldn't be expecting an engagement ring. I might be silly at times, but not that silly. No, all I'd expect was a good time and fond memories to relive whenever I'm sitting home alone."

Frowning, Anna lifted the coffee cup to her lips and took a long sip. "You're not asking for much."

Celia snorted. "Anna, you know what's wrong with you? You expect too much out of a man. If not, you would've already snatched up Ian and moved to his minimansion in the ritzy part of Red Bluff. And now, with Christmas coming, it would be the perfect time to let him know you're interested. Think about it. He'd lavish you with all kinds of gifts."

Anna groaned, then glanced around to make sure none of the other hotel staffers in the break room could overhear her. "Celia, I don't want or need a bunch of lavish gifts. Furthermore, the mere thought of sharing a bed with Ian is—repulsive to me."

Celia's mouth formed a shocked O. "Wow! That's saying it pretty plainly. And why, may I ask, do you find the idea repulsive? Ian is clean-cut and kinda cute. And he's nice."

"True. But he's more like a brother to me."

"How would you know what it's like to have a brother? You don't know if you had any siblings at all," Celia retorted, then shook her head. "Sorry, Anna. That was a mean thing for me to say."

Anna shrugged. "Why? You were only speaking the truth. I have no idea as to whether I ever had brothers or sisters. But I do know that if I did, they didn't make much of an effort to find me," she added bitterly. "I'd rather believe I didn't have any siblings than to have some who disowned me."

Celia sighed. "Oh, Anna, you're always thinking too seriously about everything. I was hoping your date with Mr. Hollister last night would've loosened you up a little."

Anna stared into her coffee. If Celia only knew how loose she'd gotten with Hunter, her friend would be shocked and worried. And now, in the light of day, Anna was a bit stunned herself. There couldn't be any future with the rodeo man. So what was she doing letting herself get closer and closer to him? Was she following Celia's plan to simply make pleasant memories?

"I had a good time," she said.

Celia snorted again. "Boy, you're really telling me a lot."

"What more can I say? The rodeo was exciting. We had dinner with some of Hunter's trick riding friends and then he showed me some of his livestock. It was all enjoyable. In fact, I'm going again tonight."

Celia's eyes widened and then the surprise on her face was replaced with a look of concern. "You are? Oh my, Anna, I'm—getting worried. This isn't like you. Not at all."

Frowning, Anna placed her coffee cup on the table, then used her fingers to massage the pounding in her forehead. Once she'd returned to her apartment last night, she'd set the alarm and gone straight to bed, but instead of sleeping, she'd stared at the shadowy walls of the bedroom and thought about Hunter. Her mind and her heart were becoming consumed with him.

"I have to admit that you're right, Celia. This isn't like me at all. And yet in spite of my common sense telling me I'm headed toward a heartache, I seem to be—" she looked hopelessly up at her friend "—becoming infatuated with the man. And it has nothing to do with the fact that he might possibly be able to connect me to my past. It has everything to do with how right it feels to be with him. How perfect it all seems when I'm with him."

Celia bit down on her bottom lip—a reaction that very nearly made Anna laugh. Celia had always been keen for Anna to date and find herself a man. Now that she'd done that very thing, her friend was acting like Anna was about to walk off the edge of a high cliff.

"Oh dear, it sounds like you're falling in love with Mr. Hollister. Are you?"

Was she? Last night, before she'd finally fallen asleep, she'd asked herself that very question, but her mind had refused to come up with an answer. Probably because the answer was too scary to contemplate.

"I can't be," Anna told her. "I've only known him for a few days."

"Haven't you ever heard of love at first sight?"

"I don't believe in such things," she said with a grimace, then rose from the folding chair and disposed of her trash. "Our break is nearly up. We'd better start walking back."

Celia dealt with her cup and a half eaten bag of potato chips before the two women left the break room. As they started to the nearest elevator to take them up to the business offices, Celia said, "You know, the more that I think about it, the more I think that love at first sight doesn't describe you and Mr. Hollister. I'm beginning to wonder if the two of you might have known each other before your accident. Has that notion crossed your mind?"

Anna paused and stared at her. "Well, yes, it has. Remember, he thought I was a woman he used to be acquainted with. And I do wonder if I could be her."

"No. I don't mean being old acquaintances. Maybe you two dated. Or were even lovers at one time and he's just not telling you."

A chill rushed over Anna that had nothing to do with the hotel ventilation. She couldn't comprehend such a thing. If true, that would make Hunter an outright fraud. "You're wrong, Celia. Hunter wouldn't be so cruel. If he knew for certain who I was, he wouldn't keep it from me. Why would he? What would he gain from such a deception?"

"I don't know. I only know that you two have gotten very chummy, very quickly."

Irritated now, Anna began walking on toward the elevator doors. "Is there anything wrong with that? You just admitted you wished you could've picked up a cowboy at the pancake breakfast."

Celia chuckled guiltily. "Okay. You've made your point. And I guess I am sticking my nose where it doesn't belong. As usual. But, Anna, you've become such a dear friend to me that I care about you. That's all."

When you care about a person, you want them to be happy.

Malachi's words suddenly drifted to her and the idea that Celia did actually care about her had Anna slanting the young woman a warm, grateful smile.

"You've become a dear friend to me, too, Celia." Then with a soft chuckle, she added, "Even if you can be a real pest at times."

When Hunter met Willow on the steps of the stadium later that night after the rodeo, he announced he had a surprise for her. He took her arm and wasted no time leading her straight to his truck.

"What kind of surprise?" she asked. "Are we going somewhere?"

"We're going out to a real sit-down dinner." He helped her up into the cab of the truck, then went to the back to grab the small surprise he'd stashed there for her—a small ceramic planter filled with white-and-purple violets. While they'd been married, she'd always loved the flowers, so from time to time he'd surprised her with little pots of them. Whether she would enjoy them now was just a hope and a guess on his part.

He climbed into the driver's seat and handed her the flowers. "I hope you like violets."

Her brown eyes were suddenly glistening as she

gazed down at the tiny blooms. "Oh, I love violets, and these are so beautiful. Thank you, Hunter."

His heart swelling with warm emotions, he smiled at her. "You might've liked a regular bouquet better, but I wanted you to have flowers you could keep and grow. My sisters would say that's practical and not romantic. But that's kind of the way I am."

To his surprise, she leaned across the console and placed a soft kiss on his cheek. "You couldn't have pleased me more. I have a perfect spot for these in a north window of my living room. When you're gone back to Utah, I'll look at them and think of you."

"I'm hoping—"

He managed to stop himself from blurting out the rest of his thoughts. How he was hoping something would trigger her memory and the two of them would leave Red Bluff together.

"What?" she prompted.

He started the engine and backed the truck out of the parking spot.

"Uh—I was just going to say I'm hoping we get to spend more time together before I leave town. The days already feel like they're spinning by." And he wasn't getting any closer to a solution of helping Willow discover she was really Willow Anderson Hollister, he thought grimly. It had been an understatement when he'd told Grace on the phone this morning that he was going a bit crazy. Truth was, he was somewhere between a panic and a breakdown and he was afraid to guess which was going to come first.

"I'd like that, Hunter." She looked awkwardly down at the flowers she was holding on her lap. "I guess—well,

I guess I've made it fairly obvious that I like you—a lot. And to be honest, I hate to think of you leaving."

She glanced over at him and he turned his head just enough to see a wry smile twist her features.

"You're the first man I've met since my accident that I've wanted to be with. But I understand you have to leave. That's the nature of your job."

The nature of his job. She might understand now why he and his convoy of livestock traveled from town to town, but she hadn't four years ago.

A hard lump suddenly filled his throat. It made his voice husky when he replied. "Yeah. Rolling on. That's my life."

"Well, we can enjoy the next few days together," she said, then shot him a bright smile. "Now, where are we going to eat? Actually, I wouldn't have minded another hot dog. This time we might have gotten them down without interruptions."

Relieved that she'd moved on from the subject of him leaving town, he chuckled. "Maybe. But I wanted to treat you—and myself. I've made reservations at the River Road Restaurant north of town. Have you been there?"

"No. But I've heard about it. And—" She glanced doubtfully down at her black jeans and white blouse. "I'm not sure I'm dressed for the place. From what I hear, the restaurant is where people go for a special dinner."

"You look lovely, Anna. You won't appear anymore out of place than I will in my jeans and boots. As long as they don't turn us away, we'll be fine."

"Well, I did happen to bring my best coat with the faux fur collar and I'll be sure and put my lipstick on before we go in. That might help."

Lipstick would help all right, Hunter thought wryly. Help remind him of how much he wanted to kiss her. Not once, but over and over. Until she forgot that she couldn't remember and he forgot how this time with his ex-wife was nearly over.

The restaurant was a two-story log structure situated on the side of a mountain, overlooking the river. To Hunter and Willow's relief, there didn't seem to be a restrictive dress code. They were greeted warmly by a hostess, who led them to a small square table with a partial view of the valley.

Once they'd removed their jackets and were seated comfortably, Hunter surveyed the red linen tablecloth and twin candles flickering gently in the center. In one corner of the large room, a massive blue spruce decorated with silver-and-gold ornaments gave off the crisp scent of evergreen, while glittery stars and garlands hung from the wooden beams supporting the ceiling.

"This is a step-up from a rodeo hot dog in a travel trailer," he said with amusement. "I hope you approve."

She looked at him, then turned her attention to the view beyond the window. "I definitely approve. I only wish it was daylight and we could see more of the landscape. But look, Hunter, there's just enough moonlight to make the river look like the silver garland on the Christmas tree. It's beautiful."

And so was she, he thought, as he allowed his gaze to travel over the dark, wavy hair grazing her shoulders and her features softened even more by the candlelight. Strange, he thought, how her appearance hadn't changed at all since the days they were married even while her personality had completely transformed. Willow would have shied away from having dinner in this upscale restaurant, but Willow was clearly appreciating her surroundings.

Resisting the urge to clear his throat, he said, "Yes. It is beautiful. Perhaps we can come back in daylight hours so we can see the entire view of the valley. Before I— have to leave town, that is."

She looked at him and nodded. "That would be nice, Hunter. But you're very busy during the day and I have my job."

"There might be time after the Sunday matinee performance. We'll see."

"Yes. We'll see," she repeated softly.

He was trying to think of a gentle way to steer their conversation away from his leaving, when a waiter suddenly arrived with glasses of ice water and menus. Hunter ordered a bottle of the restaurant's best wine and a plate of their most popular appetizers.

Once the young man had left the table, she said, "I hope you're hungry. If I eat more than two pieces of the appetizers, I'll be too full to eat the main meal."

He grinned. "Don't worry. I'll eat them for you."

Hunter added, "I'm surprised you've not visited this restaurant before tonight. I would've thought some—" At the last minute, he decided not to finish what he'd been about to say, but she promptly ended the sentence for him.

"Some guy would have brought me here for dinner and dancing?"

He arched a brow at her, then glanced around the quiet dining area. "When we first came in, I thought I heard music overhead. Is there a dance floor upstairs? Because there's obviously not one down here."

She nodded. "I think the music starts at ten and goes until one in the morning. And I only know that because my best friend at work was here on one occasion with some of her family. As for me being here on a date, that hasn't happened. Until now." She shot him a sheepish smile. "Unless what we're doing doesn't count as a date."

His pulse took a foolish leap as he spotted a provocative glint in her brown eyes. "I wouldn't know what else to call it," he murmured. "Except—wonderful."

The corners of her lips tilted upward and with an all-out grin, he reached across the tabletop and pressed her hand between both of his. "I know that sounded terribly cheesy. You can laugh at me if you'd like. But I—I'm feeling a little reckless tonight."

The glint in her eyes changed to a smoky shadow. "I'm not going to laugh at you tonight. I'm going to enjoy you. And I'm going to confess—I'm feeling a little reckless, too."

Hunter breathed deeply as mixed thoughts tore through his head. Did being with Willow like this and not revealing the truth to her make him a creep and a fraud? On the other hand, wouldn't turning his back and waiting for her to learn the truth on her own make him look equally bad? And that didn't even account for the damage he might do if he just told her about her past. Oh Lord, he couldn't let himself worry about any of that now. What really mattered was that he was doing this for her and for the two of them.

"Anna? Is that you?" a male voice sounded somewhere behind them.

Hunter looked around to see a tall man with a thin frame and short, dark blond hair striding toward their table. The look of astonishment on his face closely matched the awkward surprise etched on Willow's features.

"Hello, Mr. Brennan. Are you having a special dinner tonight?"

Hunter instantly recognized the name as that of her boss. The man who made her feel uncomfortable with his interest in dating her.

The man gestured over his shoulder to a smartly dressed older gentleman standing near the exit door. From all appearances, it looked as though the two men had already eaten and were on their way out of the restaurant.

"Mr. Sanders is from our sister hotel in Redding. He's in town to sample some of our local cuisine since the owners have plans to expand the menus in our restaurants." His curious gaze encompassed Hunter and Willow. "I never expected to see you here, Anna."

Any other time Hunter would've let loose the sarcastic retort burning the tip of his tongue, telling this man to find himself a new secretary and leave his wife alone! But Willow wasn't his wife, he thought hopelessly. And he had no right interfering in her private life.

"Tonight is the first time I've ever visited this place," she told him, then gestured to Hunter. "Ian, this is Hunter Hollister. He owns and operates the Flying H Rodeo Company. He and his crew are putting on the big River Bend Christmas Stampede this week. And, Hunter, this is Ian Brennan. He manages the hotel where you're staying."

Ian stepped closer to the table and extended his hand to Hunter. The friendly gesture surprised Hunter and he quickly rose from his chair to shake the man's hand. No matter the situation with Willow, he wasn't one to rebuff a man's handshake.

"Nice to meet you, Mr. Hollister. I hope you're enjoying your stay at our hotel. It's not the biggest in town, but we like to think it's the best."

"Good to meet you, Mr. Brennan. And the hotel couldn't be better. Have you taken in the rodeo yet?"

"No. I'm afraid I haven't had the chance. Unfortunately, my evenings for this whole week are tied up with work obligations."

"In that case, maybe you can make it out for the Sunday matinee performance. It's the last show, but it's usually the best. The champions are decided that day."

Ian glanced at Willow. Judging by the expression on her face, Hunter got the feeling she wanted to jump up and run or crawl under the table.

"If things work out, I might try to make the rodeo Sunday. Now, I'd better be going before my dinner guest gets impatient. Glad to meet you, Mr. Hollister," he said to Hunter, then looked at Anna. "I'll see you tomorrow, Anna."

She nodded and he quickly walked away. Meanwhile, Hunter sank back into his chair.

"So that's your boss," he said, stating the obvious. "He seems like an okay guy."

Groaning, she said, "He is. But—"

"You don't like the way he looks at you?" he asked pointedly.

"No. I don't like it."

He shot her a wry smile. "I didn't like it either. But I can hardly blame the guy for thinking you're beautiful."

The strained look on her face relaxed and she suddenly chuckled. "You know, now that I think about it, I'm glad he happened to be here tonight. Seeing us together will hopefully make it clear to him that I'm not interested."

And was she interested in him? Not just as a possible link to her past, but simply as a man? He wanted to ask her the critical question. And maybe he would, later. But for now he wanted their dinner to be easy and relaxed.

"It might've given him a strong message," he replied.

She started to say something, but paused as the waiter walked up carrying a tray with their wine and appetizers. She took a short sip of her red wine and leaned back in her chair.

"You know, I would love to hear about your family back in Utah," she said. "In fact, you mentioned you were going to explain about your sister Bonnie taking on another job of some sort."

He reached for one of the appetizers and as he popped the tiny roll stuffed with hot pepper cheese into his mouth, he thought about how talking about his family to Willow might be a good thing. With any luck, it could possibly trigger something deep in her memory bank. On the other hand, he needed to be careful not to blurt out something that would cause her to suspect he was hiding information from her. At this point, it would be catastrophic to try to explain the truth to her.

"That's right, I did say I'd tell you about Bonnie's third job. But I warn you, it's probably going to sound convoluted and strange."

"Now you really have me curious," she said.

He swallowed the appetizer and followed it with a

sip of wine before he replied. "Well, it all started about three years or so ago when our father, Hadley, received a letter from a stranger—a woman down in Arizona by the name of Claire Hollister. Claire and her husband, Gil, own and operate Three Rivers Ranch, which happens to be one of the largest ranches in the state, plus another ranch by the name of Red Bluff." He grinned. "In case you're wondering, the name has no connection to this town. The area down in Arizona where it's located has red bluffs."

"Two ranches," she repeated thoughtfully. "These people must be exceptionally wealthy."

"Exceptional is one way of putting it. But I can truthfully say that in spite of their money, they're very down-to-earth, hardworking folks."

"I see. So with their name also being Hollister, are they your relations?"

He reached for another appetizer. "Yes, we're related. But at the time Claire sent the letter none of us knew that. She'd been working on a family tree and some of her genealogy research kept bringing up Dad's name, so she had a suspicion that our families might be connected in some way. Eventually, Dad sent my brother Jack down to Arizona and he, along with one of Claire's sons, submitted to a DNA test. The results showed our families were related, but to this day we still don't know how. We think it has something to do with our grandfather, Lionel. Because research on him comes up blank. See, he died a few years ago and his birth certificate can't be found. Nor is his birth registered in the state of Utah, so far as we can tell."

Willow's features were a picture of puzzlement. "And

Hadley doesn't know the exact date of his father's birthday?"

Hunter shook his head. "Well, Dad thought he knew. At least, he knew the date Grandfather celebrated his birthday, but it doesn't match anything on the genealogy searches."

"How odd. Well, surely your father has some old federal tax records showing your grandfather's birthday."

"We've already thought of that idea, but none can be found. See, when my dad turned twenty-one, Grandfather transferred the ownership of Stone Creek Ranch to him. After that, all the tax filings were done in Dad's name. That's how it's been for the past forty-five years. So you see, any papers concerning Grandfather Lionel were probably destroyed decades ago," he told her.

"Oh my, that does pose a problem. Do you think Lionel was purposely hiding his birth date? Or maybe his parents told him the wrong date back when he was a child?"

"That's anybody's guess. Nothing about this whole mystery makes sense. A person has to have a birth certificate for identification purposes and things of that sort. Dad thinks the document might've burned in a fire that destroyed a couple of rooms of the ranch house. He's not sure about that, though. Still, even if it had burned, the state should have the birth documented."

"Has your sister tried searching Arizona birth records?" she asked. "Perhaps Lionel was born in that state."

"Hmm. I'm not sure if Bonnie or any of them have looked into that possibility."

Her brows arched with curiosity. "What about Lionel's wife? Or does your father have siblings who might have answers?"

Shaking his head, he said, "Well, that's another hurdle the family is trying to jump over. Lionel and his wife, Scarlett—my grandmother—divorced when Dad and his two brothers were only small boys. Once she left, she never contacted the family in any form again."

"Oh, that's unfortunate. And Hadley's brothers? Are they still living?" she asked.

"Yes. They're both a few years younger than Dad. But none of them are what you'd call close. Neither one of them was interested in ranching and both left Utah years ago. As for Scarlett, neither of my uncles knows anything about her. And frankly, I don't believe they care to know."

"Sounds like a dead end there," she replied. "So have you stumbled onto any other leads that might be helpful?"

He said, "A few months ago, Bonnie did happen to track down Scarlett's whereabouts. She resides in an assisted-living home up in Idaho. Beatrice and her husband, Kipp, actually visited the woman last year, but unfortunately, she couldn't tell them anything. She's suffering from advanced dementia."

She groaned with dismay. "Oh, how awful. Do you know if Scarlett remarried? Or had any other children? Maybe they might know something about their mother's first husband. I know it's a long shot, but there might be a chance."

He shrugged. "Beatrice found out she has a couple of daughters, but we can't locate them. At least, not yet. Anyway, my sister-in-law Vanessa first began working on this family mystery while she was still living in Arizona, before she and Jack married. But recently, Vanessa gave birth to her and Jack's son, plus she teaches school in Beaver County, so she doesn't have time for genealogy. That's why Bonnie has taken on the task. Which means, she's trying to work on all this family history while doing bookkeeping for Stone Creek Ranch, plus doing the books for the Flying H. It's beginning to be too much for my sister."

"I can see why," she said with a nod. "But I have a feeling finding someone else to do your books won't be easy. Especially someone you can trust as much as you trust your sister."

"Right," he said. "But hopefully someone suitable will come along. Actually, I haven't talked to Bonnie about this yet. She'll argue that she isn't overloaded with work. You see, she's never been much of a social flower, so she thrives on her jobs."

"Hmm. With her twin getting married recently, I'd think she'd be wanting to follow in her footsteps. I've often heard that's the way it is with twins."

He grunted. "No. Bonnie and Beatrice have totally different personalities. Bonnie doesn't date much. She's very particular about the guys she goes out with."

She thoughtfully sipped her wine. "Are your sisters identical?"

Nodding, he said, "Pretty much. Family and close friends don't have trouble telling them apart. But most folks can't distinguish one from the other."

A thought suddenly struck him and he pulled out his phone. When Jack had mentioned showing her pictures of her grandparents or snapshots of Willow and himself while they were married, he'd quickly nixed the idea. That would've been the same as outright telling her the truth of her identity. But showing her photos of his family couldn't hurt, he thought. "I have a few pics of my siblings," he said. "Would you like to see them?"

"Yes, I would," she said eagerly.

He moved over to the chair kitty-cornered to her left elbow and held the phone so that she could view the screen along with him.

"I took this of the twins at Beatrice's wedding. Bonnie was her maid of honor."

Anna smiled as she gazed at the image of the two young women with long blond hair and blue eyes. "Oh, they are identical!" she exclaimed. "And so very beautiful."

"Thanks. As you might guess, since they are the last-born, Dad has been guilty of hovering over them. Especially when they were younger. However, Mom is more inclined to make sure each of her children get equal attention."

Willow chuckled. "Your mother must be the diplomatic sort."

"Yeah. If feathers get ruffled between us siblings, she's always the first to try and smooth them over."

She looked curiously at him. "Does that happen often? Getting feathers ruffled?"

"No. Not at all." But there would be plenty of hackles raised if Jack and Cordell could see him now, he thought with regret. As far as Jack and Cordell were concerned, Hunter had never used good sense when it came to Willow. And perhaps his older brothers were right. He'd not been able to keep his wife happy for the two years they'd been married. There was no reason to think he could make her happy now.

Shaking away the dismal thought, he scrolled through the photos and paused when he ran across a photo of Jack, Quint and Cordell all grouped together on horseback. The three men were dressed in batwing chaps and heavy ranch coats with woolen mufflers wrapped around their necks. The ground around them was dusted with snow.

"They must have been working in very cold weather," she mused aloud.

"Yes. The weather gets bitterly cold in the dead of winter. I think on this particular day they were headed off to the mountains to make sure there weren't any calves left behind in brush. When the weather is at its worst, Dad has us bring the cattle in closer to the ranch where they can find shelter in the barns and the thick stands of juniper."

She slanted another curious glance at him. "You used the word *us*. Does that mean you always help on the ranch whenever you're home? Or just on certain occasions?"

"When I'm home I'm always helping work the cattle or sheep. Actually, I love doing ranch work. And I love working with my brothers. But—"

With an understanding smile, she finished for him. "But you love producing rodeos even more."

Strange that she seemed to understand his feelings now. Whereas four years ago, her mind had been totally shut to the idea that the Flying H should be so important to him. Nodding, he said, "Yes. It's been a dream of mine since I was a kid."

"It's nice that you succeeded in making your dream come true and even nicer that your family supports you," she replied.

He shrugged. "There are times I catch a bit of flak for not coming home often enough, but for the most part, my family is proud of me." He rolled the picture of the men from view and continued to scroll through the photo album until Grace's image filled the screen. "This is Grace, my sister who's an MD. Her private clinic in Beaver County is always running over with patients. You'd think she was the only doctor in town."

"She isn't?"

"No. But the townsfolk like her and trust her. She needs help, but I can't picture her sharing her clinic with another doctor. She's too particular about the care of her patients."

"Like you're particular about your livestock and their care," she stated.

This was getting eerie, Hunter thought. Now that her memory had been wiped free of the conflicts of their marriage, she seemed to understand him completely.

"Yes," he said. "I guess in that way, Grace and I are alike." He scrolled to another photo. "This is another brother, Flint. He's a little older than Quint and the twins, but younger than Grace."

She peered at Flint's image, then, with a thoughtful frown, leaned in for a closer look. "Flint," she repeated. "He looks familiar to me. I suppose I must've seen some-one who looks like him. Was your brother ever around Red Bluff?"

His heart skipped a couple of beats, then thumped

hard and fast. Was it possible that seeing his family was chipping away the barrier of her blocked memory?

"Uh—no. As far as I know he's never been in this part of California. He works as a deputy sheriff for Beaver County. He and Bonnie and Quint and Clementine are the only ones who still live in the big house with our parents."

She continued to stare at the photo of Flint. "You probably told me this when we first met, but I've forgotten. Is he married?"

"No. He dates but doesn't have a steady girlfriend. Mainly because he's always working. Either for the sheriff's department or on the ranch. You might say he's the quietest one of us Hollister brothers."

"Quiet. Yes, his face projects that image to me." She smiled wanly up at him. "Strange, isn't it? That I should think he looks familiar."

Actually, even knowing everything there was to know about Willow's past life, it *did* seem odd that Flint was the one who sparked something in her mind. Yet, the more he thought about it, the more he realized he shouldn't be that surprised. Willow had always been drawn to Flint and Bonnie more than to his other siblings. He supposed that was because the two of them were quiet and introverted. Like she used to be.

"Yes. A little strange. But if—" He paused, unsure that he should finish what he'd been about to say.

She frowned. "If what?"

Shrugging, he glanced away from her and took a long sip of wine before he finally said, "I was only going to say that if—well, if you are the Willow who used to live in Beaver County, then you might have seen Flint around town. He's been working as a deputy for probably ten years now."

Her brown eyes widened slightly and he could see she was thinking hard, as though she could will her mind to make the connection.

"Do you really think that might be a possibility?" she asked. "I've been getting the impression that you've been thinking the idea of me being Willow is a real long shot."

He slipped the phone back into his jacket, then reached for his wineglass. With any luck, the alcohol would dull the anguish tearing through him. "I've not crossed off the idea. It's just that I—haven't had time to contact the people who might've known you. I'm sorry about that, Anna."

She reached over and gently placed her hand on his forearm. "Don't apologize. It's not your job to search for my background. But I have been wondering something these past few minutes."

His breath momentarily caught in his throat in a way that made his voice sound strained when he did finally speak. "Wondering about what?"

"Well, you've been talking about your family, and I was wondering if you thought there might be some old county records about the Andersons. Something that might reveal whether I was a relative. Or maybe an obituary listed in an archived newspaper? I realize it's a long shot, but it might be worth a try."

He shook his head. "Those records would list Willow as a granddaughter, but that's something we already know. It wouldn't tell us whether that granddaughter was actually you."

She looked a bit disappointed, but not totally deflated.

"True. I'm not thinking, Hunter. I guess my brain is overreaching for answers. But there is something else I wanted to ask you about the Andersons. You've not mentioned Willow's parents. Was she orphaned or something?"

Or something, he thought sickly. "No. I don't believe she was an orphan. From what I heard, the parents—uh—were incapable of raising a child. So the grandparents stepped in and took over."

"Oh. That's—sad." She reached for her wine, but instead of taking a sip, she wrapped both hands around the goblet and held it tightly. "It makes me think—I wouldn't want to be Willow Anderson."

Maybe Grace was onto something, Hunter thought. Maybe this was the reason why Willow's mind refused to remember her true identity. She didn't want to be Willow Anderson, or Hunter's ex-wife. She'd rather be Anna Jones without all that sad baggage. The idea was troubling, but he refused to let it ruin their evening.

"I tell you what I think, Anna. For tonight, I think we should forget all the family mysteries and just enjoy our dinner together."

Smiling, she put down the wineglass and reached for the menu. "The only mystery I have on my mind at the moment is whether this place serves chili dogs. I'm starving."

Chuckling, he reached over and squeezed her soft fingers. In that moment, he decided that he had to believe he and Willow had found each other for a reason. And that reason was for them to be together again. His heart refused to believe anything less.

Chapter Nine

After Hunter had eaten a thick rib eye with sautéed mushrooms and Anna had consumed most of her grilled fish and a medley of stir-fried vegetables, he suggested they go upstairs and check out the dance floor.

"Hunter, I should warn you that you're risking injury to your feet," she told him. "If I danced in the past, I don't remember it."

With his hand wrapped securely around hers, he led her up a wooden staircase to the second floor.

"You're telling me you've not danced since your accident?"

"No. Dancing hasn't exactly been on my survival list," she said in a joking way.

He glanced at her. "Well, it's about time you put it on your necessity list. And I'm guessing you probably have danced at some point in your life. It will all come back to you. If it doesn't, just follow me and fake it."

She laughed. "I'll do my best."

When they entered the small ballroom, the band was playing a torch song from the 1940s. As Hunter pulled her into his arms and began to guide her across the floor, she hummed along to the sultry melody.

"How are you familiar with this song? I'm not much

of a music buff, but I'm fairly sure this tune goes way back to long before my parents were born," he said.

"You're right," she said. "One of those great bandleaders of the swing era made it a huge hit. I guess it does seem a bit strange that I remember songs and singers."

He leaned his head back far enough to look at her and Anna could see a look of disbelief flicker across his face.

"That doesn't make any sense to me. I'd like to hear a neurological doctor explain that one."

With a shake of her head, she said, "I've been to several doctors. None can pinpoint the reason my memory is blocked or why I remember random things like old songs but nothing specific about myself or my past. To be honest, I've totally given up on finding medical help."

A wry smile tilted the corners of his lips and she wondered if he realized how much she wanted to kiss him again. Could he guess how very right and wonderful it felt to be in his arms like this, with one strong hand pressed against her back and the other wrapped tightly around hers?

"Well, I can give you the answer to one question," he told her. "You haven't forgotten how to dance. My toes are still intact and I'm not even wearing my steel-toed boots tonight."

She laughed softly. "You should probably wait until the song is over before you brag on me."

His head lowered and she sighed as he pressed his cheek against the top of her hair.

"I don't need to wait for the song to end to know how good you feel in my arms," he murmured close to her ear.

Instinctively she snuggled closer to the hard warmth of his body. "You feel just as good to me."

He didn't reply to her confession. Instead, he pressed her head against his shoulder. As her cheek rested against the crisp cotton fabric of his shirt, she felt his nose nuzzle the side of her hair.

All day long she'd fantasized about being in Hunter's embrace. Now that her dream had become a reality, she felt sure her feet were floating across the floor. The thought that she never wanted the song to end was drifting through her mind when the music finally stopped. But Hunter didn't make a move to ease her out of his arms, nor did he suggest they leave the dance floor. Instead, they remained in the same spot until, seconds later, the band began playing again. This time, the tune was a traditional holiday song with an even slower tempo. As they circled the floor in each other arms, Anna could feel something electric thrumming between them, flowing back and forth with a current hot enough to weld two pieces of steel together.

He must have been equally aware of the sexual energy sparking between them because this time when the music ended, he took her by the hand and led her off the dance floor.

Once they were a few steps away from the crowd, he said, "I think—it's time we—uh, left this place. Or would you rather dance some more?"

The sultry look in his dark blue eyes matched the desire that was simmering deep inside her and she didn't hesitate to wrap her hand over his forearm. "If you're ready to leave, I am, too."

Downstairs, Hunter took care of the bill and, after they'd donned their coats, they walked out in the cold night. Except for the sound of the wind rushing through a nearby stand of evergreens and the crunch of gravel beneath their feet, the parking lot was quiet. Even so, Anna could hear a dim *thump, thump* in her ears that sounded strangely like her heartbeat. After a moment, she realized the mere thought of Hunter making love to her had sent her heart into a rapid frenzy.

Make love? You might be thinking in those terms, Anna, but Hunter is probably thinking something altogether different. Like physical pleasure. Like plain ole sex. Can you live with that reality?

Could she? Anna refused to answer the self-imposed question. Anyway, if sex was the most she'd ever have with Hunter, she could live with that. At least, she'd have something to remember him by.

They both remained quiet and thoughtful as he drove them toward Red Bluff, but before they reached the outskirts of the city, he looked over at her.

"Where do you want to go?"

She drew in a deep breath and reached for his free hand. "Why don't we go to your hotel room?"

In the faint light glowing from the instrument panel, she could see one eyebrow arch toward the brim of his hat.

"Are you sure, Anna?" he asked gently. "Sure about what you're saying?"

She tightened the hold she had on his fingers. "I'm very sure. I'm saying I want to be with you. If that's not what you want, please tell me. I'll understand."

He groaned. "What I want? If I pulled over to the side of the highway right now and showed you what I want, I'm afraid we'd never make it to the hotel!"

A provocative smile tilted the corners of her lips. "Then you'd better not pull over."

* * *

Hunter came close to breaking the speed limit as he drove the last few miles to the hotel. Throughout the drive, his mind whirled with the right or wrong of what he was about to do.

Right or wrong? Hell, Hunter, why would you think it wrong to make love to your wife? She once carried your name, slept in your bed, and eagerly gave her body to you. How could it be wrong to be intimate with her again? Just because there's a paper stuffed away that says you're no longer man and wife?

Hell, no, Hunter barked at the taunting voice going off in his head. The divorce papers were the last thing on his mind. The only thing eating at him now was Willow's missing memories of the past. She wouldn't know she was making love to her ex-husband. And if she did suddenly remember him, would she hate him for the deception?

As he parked the truck and went around to help her to the ground, he purposely shook away the questions tearing through his thoughts. She wanted him and he wanted her. For now, he had to believe that was enough to justify taking her to his bed.

With her arm looped around his, they entered the hotel and walked straight to the elevator doors. The exact spot where she'd caught up to him on that rainy night just a few days ago. So much had changed since then. She no longer saw him as a stranger. On the other hand, she still didn't see him as the man who'd once been her husband.

"I hope none of your coworkers are anywhere around," he said, as he slipped a security card into the slot to allow the elevator doors to open.

"At this hour of the night, no one I work with directly would be in this part of the hotel," she told him. "Why do you hope they aren't?"

He glanced down at her. "I wouldn't want to ruin your reputation."

The doors swished open and as they stepped into the empty cubicle, she chuckled softly. "I think it would take more than seeing us together to ruin my reputation. Besides, my coworkers see me as a wallflower. Except for Celia. I've told her that I've been seeing you."

He looked curiously at her. "And what does she think about you *seeing me*?"

She chuckled again and it thrilled him to see she was happy to be with him. Thrilled him that their evolving relationship wasn't worrying her. At least, not for the moment.

"Truthfully, I think she believes I've slipped a cog or two. Up until now, she's thought of me as a practical woman and I've given her no reason to think otherwise. Until you came along. She's worried I'm going to get my heart broken because you're a rambling man. She's been advising me to marry Ian. In her mind, he can give me everything I want." She grimaced. "The only thing he could possibly give me would be a headache."

Smiling, he reached over and placed his palm against her forehead. "How's your head right now?"

Laughing, she turned and slipped her arms around his waist, then tilted her head back in order to look up at him. "Not one tiny ache."

Desire and joy washed through him all at once and he couldn't stop himself from bending his head and placing a long, lingering kiss on her lips.

When he eventually broke the contact, she looked questioningly up at him. "Uh—Hunter, I don't think we're moving," she said "Did you press the button for our floor?"

A slow grin crossed his face. "Umm, no. I forgot. Because you were pressing all the right buttons."

He reached over and punched a number on the panel to send the elevator into motion. They reached the right floor quickly, and after a short walk down the empty corridor, they entered his room.

This morning when he'd left the hotel, he'd not bothered to close the drapes on the window. Now the distant streetlamps shed a dim light across the bed and a nearby armchair. Clothes that he'd worn the day before were strewn on the bed, while two pair of boots and a duffel bag were piled on the floor near the closet door.

"Sorry. I left the room messy this morning," he told her. "Malachi was texting me with a message I was needed before I could swig down a cup of coffee. And I left a sign on the door for the cleaning staff to skip my room. I—uh—wasn't expecting company."

Which was quite an understatement, he thought, as he tossed the rumpled pieces of clothing onto the armchair, then quickly added his coat and hat to the pile. He'd been hoping this night would be a turning point for the two of them. He'd even sensed her growing closer to him, but he'd not expected her to suggest they go to bed together. Was there something deep within her wounded memory bank pushing her toward him? Were memories of the two of them making love slowly digging their way to the surface of her mind? He could only hope.

He turned to see she'd also removed her coat and was

placing the garment and her handbag on the top of a long dresser running along one wall.

"I'm glad you're not seeing my apartment," she said. "It looks like a tornado has come through it. Since you and the rodeo came to town, I've not exactly had much time for house cleaning."

He paused by the floor lamp situated next to the arm of the chair. "Do you want me to turn on the light?"

"I don't need it."

He glanced at the window. "Would you like for me to close the drapes?"

Shaking her head, she walked over to him. "We're up too high for anyone to see in. And it gives the room just enough light for me to see your face." Reaching up, she touched her fingertips to his cheek then marked a trail down to his chin. "And it's such a strong, dear face."

"I wouldn't know about that," he said, his voice little more than a husky whisper. "But I'm sure glad you've used your time on me instead of tidying your apartment."

"I'm glad, too," she said softly.

Sliding his arms around her waist, he drew her closer. "Are you really?"

Stepping into his embrace, she tilted her head back and studied him through lazy eyes. "Hunter, it scares me to think we might have never met. If you'd entered the hotel earlier that night. Or if I'd decided to continue working a few minutes longer, we wouldn't be together like this." Lifting her head, she pressed her cheek against his. "And I wouldn't be aching for you to make love to me."

For four long years—and most every day of those years—he'd thought how it might feel to hold her once more, to feel her lips against his skin, the warmth of her fingers pressing into his flesh. But despite all those fantasies, he'd believed he'd never experience those pleasures again in his life. And yet here she was telling him words he wanted to hear, touching him in ways he'd needed for so long. Except this was Anna Jones saying the words. Anna who was touching him in a way that robbed his breath and fired his desire. Not Willow Hollister.

But this was really Willow, his mind screamed in protest. She just didn't know it.

With a thumb beneath her chin, he tilted her face up to his. And as he lowered his lips to hers, he closed his eyes and shoved away the sorrowful thoughts. Tonight their names didn't matter. They were simply a man and a woman who wanted to be together.

"Let's not forget the rain," he whispered against her lips. "Otherwise we wouldn't have collided. But we did collide; and I'm so very thankful we did."

"Yes. Thankful," she repeated just before his lips closed over hers.

He kissed her over and over, until his lungs were burning for oxygen and his legs felt like he'd ridden a horse for twenty miles. When he finally forced his mouth away from hers, he recognized the way her fingers were clinging tightly to his shoulders and the purring sound in his ears that was coming from somewhere deep in her throat.

"Oh, Hunter, I think—maybe we've stood long enough. My legs are about to buckle."

With a needy groan, he bent and scooped her into his arms. "Hopefully mine won't buckle before I get us to the bed," he said as he quickly carried her over to the king-size mattress.

Once they were both sitting on the side of the mattress, he kissed her again, then with trembling hands began to remove her blouse, boots and jeans. When she was finally stripped down to nothing but her panties, he turned his attention to his own clothing and in a matter of seconds his jeans and boots and shirt had joined hers on the floor.

She reached for him at the same time he reached for her and as they listed sideways onto the bed, he felt her shiver in his arms.

"You're shaking. Are you cold?"

He reached for the rumpled comforter and pulled it over them, then cradled her in the circle of his arms.

Resting her head against his shoulder, she placed a hand on the middle of his chest. "No. I'm—my head is spinning, Hunter. This all feels like déjà vu."

He went still for a moment and then he gently smoothed the back of his hand across her cheek. "Oh, Anna, you've surely made love to a man before. Your mind is reliving the experience, that's all."

She leaned her head back far enough to look into his eyes. "No. That isn't the reason for this eerie feeling. It's like—oh, Hunter, please don't laugh at me— but these thoughts running through my mind are—it's like you and I have been together before—like this." Tears formed in her eyes and slipped down her cheeks. "I know it doesn't make sense. And it—I don't understand. And—it scares me."

His heart was aching and for one split second the truth nearly burst out of him. But he could plainly see she was confused and shaken. Springing the reality of the situation on her now might truly send her into some sort of confused panic.

Wrapping his arms around her, he drew her tightly to his chest. "My little darling, don't be afraid," he whispered against the top of her head. "Everything is going to be good. No, it's going to be more than good. It's going to be wonderful. Don't think about what was or what might have been. Just concentrate on you and me at this moment and how much we want each other."

Groaning, she turned her head just enough to press her face against the curve of his neck. "Oh, Hunter, nothing else matters as long as I'm lying next to you."

Willing his mind to go blank, he shifted position in order to align his face with hers. To his relief, when their lips met, he could taste desire in her kiss and feel the tremors in her body quieten. She trusted him. The idea was bittersweet and he promised himself that someday, when her memory was healed, he'd make up for all this subterfuge.

Yes. Someday she would remember he was the man she'd once loved. Someday...

His kisses seemed to go on forever. Or maybe it felt that way because with each deep search he made of her lips, the desire he was fueling in her continued to grow to an unbearable ache. And just when she thought she couldn't possibly want him more, his mouth left hers and slowly migrated on a downward path to her breasts. By the time his tongue circled one taut nipple, she expected to combust right there in his arms.

Desperate for relief, she wrapped her legs around his

and pressed the juncture of her thighs to his swollen erection. The contact caused him to groan and throw his head back. The emotion she saw on his face was so raw and real that it caused a hot lump to collect in her throat.

No matter what tomorrow might bring, for tonight she had to believe that he cared about her. She had to think she was more than just a warm female body in his arms and that her well-being and happiness mattered to him.

"I—uh, think we need to get out of our underclothes, don't you?"

The low chuckle in her throat put a smile on his face. "Things might work better if we did."

Once her panties and his boxers were tossed aside, they reached for each other at the same time and together sank back to the mattress. She sighed as his mouth found hers once again, while at the same time, she wrapped an arm around his neck and drew herself closer.

His skin was as hot as a furnace and the heat invited her hands to roam over his arms and shoulders, across his back and around to his chest. Up until tonight, whenever she'd touched him, the barrier of his clothing had prevented her from getting a full impression of his body. Now that her hands were free to explore the heated flesh, she was amazed at the rock-solid strength of his muscles and the pleasure that touching him gave her.

It wasn't until he began pressing a trail of kisses down the side of her neck that a thought suddenly struck her. She placed a hand against his shoulder to prevent him from going any further.

"Hunter—I wasn't thinking earlier. I should tell you I'm not on any sort of birth control."

Lifting his head, he gave her with a wry grin. "No

problem. I think I have some condoms packed some-where. I don't exactly have much use for them. But just in case—"

The sound she made was meant to be a laugh, but it came out more like a choked sob. "I haven't had *any* use for birth control. Not since my accident."

Astonishment flashed in his eyes. "I remember you saying you haven't been dating, but I didn't realize—four years is a long time to be celibate."

Her hands slid over his back. "Not when you're wait-ing for the right man to come along. And he finally has."

Closing his eyes, he lowered his head and whispered against her cheek. "Oh, sweetheart. You can't guess what you're doing to me—how special you are. I've never wanted anyone the way I want you. I hope you believe me. I hope when I touch you that you can feel how much I need you."

"I do feel your need, Hunter. And it matches mine."

She felt a lungful of air rush out of him before he eased away from her and climbed off the bed. "I'll get the condom," he said.

He plucked the duffel bag off the floor and after a quick search, found what he was looking for. Watching his movements, she knew he was fitting himself with the condom. For one flash of a nanosecond, she could picture her own hands rolling the protective barrier onto his shaft. The image was like a Technicolor dream, yet so real it stunned her.

Why would she be seeing herself touching Hunter in such an intimate way when she knew it had never happened? It was crazy, even scary. Was the amnesia making her brain go haywire and form false memories?

As she watched Hunter return to the bed, her first instinct was to tell him about the strange image. But he'd probably think she was remembering some other man in her past and that would be worse than throwing cold water over him.

He climbed onto the bed. Determined to shut the disturbing thought from her mind, she closed her eyes and reached for him.

By the time Hunter rolled her onto her back and positioned himself over her, he was amazed that he'd managed to stay in control, but he wasn't at all sure how much longer the tenuous grip would hold. Especially when she parted her thighs and pulled him down until he was touching the wet folds of her womanhood.

And then he was slipping inside her. As their bodies melded into one, he was rapidly overwhelmed by a slew of powerful sensations. Some of the feelings were sweet and familiar, others raw and new, but all so overwhelming he wanted to cry out the name he'd carried for so long in his heart. Yet he stifled it back in his throat even as he repeated it over and over in silence. *Willow. Willow.*

His head was whirling at such a speed, he hardly knew when she started to move against him or when he began to match the urgent arches of her hips. The room had turned into a kaleidoscope of light and gray shadows spinning around the bed. The only thing he could see was her closed eyes and swollen lips, her silky dark hair lying against her pale porcelain skin.

To love her like this was like a fantastic dream from which he never wanted to wake. But this wasn't a dream.

It was incredibly real and he wanted to hold on to every second for as long as he could.

But all too soon, he could feel the both of them reaching their ultimate height. She was writhing desperately beneath him and he was plunging into her faster and faster until his lungs were struggling to keep up and his heart felt as if it was on the verge of bursting in his chest.

"Hunter, I—can't keep going!" The words came out on a frantic gasp at the same time her hands clamped over the ridges of his shoulders. "I—oooh. Oh, my darling! My sweet—sweet—darling!"

From somewhere far away he heard her groan and mutter his name, while her fingers dug deeper into his flesh. He slipped his arms around her and pulled her so tight against him that there was scarcely enough room for either one of them to draw breath. But breathing no longer mattered as he felt his last thread of control snap and all of a sudden he was soaring off to a place filled with a million brilliant stars. The brightness blinded him, but he didn't care. It was a glorious sort of blindness that wrapped him in velvety warmth and made him forget everything but her and the love she was giving him.

For long, long moments he didn't hear anything except his heartbeat roaring in his ears and his own harsh breaths as he tried to regain control over himself. Then finally he heard her voice next to his ear. She was whispering his name like a mantra, as though she was in a shocked stupor, and the sound sent a shaft of fear racing through him.

Quickly, he rolled onto his side and tilted her face up to his. "Anna, are you okay?"

Closing her eyes, she released a long sigh. "I'm sorry.

You must think I'm going a bit crazy. But it felt so good to say your name when you were close to me like this that I didn't want to stop." She cradled her palm against the side of his face. "If I say your name again will you kiss my lips and seal it there?"

"Oh, sweetie, I'll kiss you for any reason."

A wan smile tilted the corners of her lips. "Hunter Hollister. You're everything I want."

To keep his promise he kissed her deeply, then rubbed his cheek against hers. "Does it feel sealed now?"

"Mmm. Very sealed."

"Good." He reached for the edge of the comforter and pulled it up over their shoulders. "Warm and comfy?"

She tilted her head just enough to press her lips against his shoulder. "I could stay here forever. Unfortunately, I'll have to leave early enough in the morning to go to my apartment and get ready for work."

He frowned as he forced his mind to think that far ahead. "Since your car is at the rodeo grounds, I'll have to drive you."

Her forefinger marked lazy loops upon his chest and he couldn't help but think back to the many times they'd lain together like this when they'd been married, her fingers making those same delicate tracks across his skin. The bittersweet memory caused emotions to swell in his throat until he was forced to swallow.

She said in a lazy voice, "I forgot about my car. But there's no need for you to bother driving me. I'll call a taxi."

"We'll argue about that in the morning," he said as he combed his fingers through her long hair. "Right now there's something I want to talk to you about. Something more important."

She must have sensed the serious note in his voice, because she eased her head back and studied his face. "Hunter, please, don't ruin what time we have left of this night. There's no need for it. I'm not expecting flowery promises from you." A wry smile twisted her lips. "Actually, I'm fairly sure I'll never see you again after the rodeo leaves. Unless you happen to get contracted to do the River Bend Christmas Stampede next year. But I don't want to think about that now. Not after the— not after what we just shared. It was incredible for me, Hunter. And that's what I want to remember. Not sad goodbyes."

He groaned, filled with misgivings. All along she'd been thinking he was only seeing her for a little company while he was in town. Oh, if she only knew the truth of the matter. If she only knew how he'd ached for her these past four years, how losing her had left a giant void in his life.

Cupping his hand around her chin, he locked his gaze with hers. "Sweetheart—you have everything wrong. And that's probably my fault for not making my intentions clearer."

Surprise flickered in her eyes. "Your intentions?" she repeated blankly. "What are you talking about?"

His heartbeat quickened as he searched for some sort of explanation that would make sense for two people who had known each other for only a few days. "I'm talking about you and me. I'm not sure how you feel about me, Anna. I mean, I realize I've only been in town a few days, but I think there's something special growing between us. And to be honest, I don't want our time together to end. I think we need more time. We need to figure out if what we shared tonight is something that— will go beyond this week and continue on."

She stared at him in wonder before she lifted her head and propped it with one hand. "Hunter, are you being serious?"

"Yes. I wouldn't be here with you like this if I wasn't serious."

A look of disbelief twisted her features. "Do you really think I'm *that* naive? Yes, I've been purposely living a sheltered life since my accident, but that doesn't mean I'm a fool. You want me to believe you're celibate? That you haven't been with another woman like this before?" She paused and made a cynical snort. "I'm sure you used the word *serious* on those occasions, too."

Oh hell, how could he explain? He couldn't. Not tonight. Maybe never if she refused to go along with his plan.

With a heavy sigh, he said, "Okay, Anna. I guess I didn't say that exactly right. I'm not going to pretend I've never had casual sex. But that's not what tonight was for me. And I'm not just spouting words. I meant everything I said."

She studied his face for several long seconds before her eyes closed and she swallowed hard. "All right, you're being honest with me. But I can't see how we can think about any sort of relationship after you leave."

He slid a hand down her arm, then back up to the wave of dark hair cascading over her shoulder. "Are you trying to tell me you're not interested? I thought—a few minutes ago it felt like you cared about me."

Her eyes opened and his heart winced as he recognized a sheen of tears gathering over the brown orbs.

"I must be as transparent as plastic wrap to you," she said glumly. "Even if I tried to pretend I didn't care, you'd see through me."

Frowning, he said, "You make it sound like you've done something foolish or rash in caring for me."

"No. Not rash. Just hopeless."

He scooted up to a sitting position and gathered her into his arms. "I'm going to ask you something, Anna, and you're probably going to think I'm expecting too much from you. But I just can't let these next few days slip by without being—frank."

Resting her hands against his chest, she tilted her head just enough to meet his gaze. "Then ask me," she murmured.

He drew in a deep breath. "Will you come home with me to Stone Creek Ranch? I want you to spend the holidays there with me and my family."

Her soft gasp told him he'd shocked her, while at the same time he could see an array of emotions swirling in her eyes.

"To Utah? To celebrate Christmas?"

He tried to smile, but his lips felt like they were twisted into a stiff line. She couldn't know the risk he was taking. Not only with her mental well-being, but with any kind of future he hoped to have with her.

"I live there, too. Whenever I'm not on the road," he reminded her. "But I always spend Christmas at home. I want you to be there with me. And to meet my family."

"Yes, but—I—" Pausing, she shook her head. "This is all happening so fast, Hunter. And I'm not sure why—"

She broke off awkwardly and he finished for her.

"Why I want you to go home with me?"

She nodded. "I'm wondering if you've really thought this through."

He stroked strands of tumbled hair away from her face. "I've thought long and hard, Anna. I know what I want. But I understand I'm asking a lot from you. Do you think you could take off from your job for a while? I'll understand if you can't. I don't imagine Brennan will be too pleased if you tell him you want the time to spend with me, and I don't want to make things difficult for you."

He could see her mind was spinning, but it couldn't be whirling any faster than his. Ever since the idea of taking her home to Stone Creek Ranch had entered Hunter's mind, he'd been assailed with doubts and fears. Yet, he realized if he was ever to get his Willow back in his life, he had to risk the dangers of losing her once and for all.

"I do have vacation time coming. He can't deny me that time off," she said thoughtfully. Then she asked, "When were you expecting to travel back there? I thought next week you had to take the Flying H to another town south of here."

Nodding, he said, "There's another rodeo a few days after New Year's Day. If we could leave for Utah this Sunday after the last performance here, that would give us a week at home. As for moving the Flying H to Barstow, it's a big job, but Malachi will handle things."

"So you've already talked to him about this?"

"I've already talked to him about going home for Christmas, but he doesn't know I was going to ask you to make the trip with me. Not yet. I wanted to make

sure you would agree to go first," he said with a sheepish grin. "I'd look pretty red-faced if I had to tell him
you turned me down."

Her expression solemn, she cupped her palm against
the side of his face. "Did you honestly think I could
turn you down?"

He turned his head just enough to plant a kiss in the
middle of her palm. "I've been praying you wouldn't."

"Oh, Hunter!" With a little cry, she buried her face in
the middle of his chest. "I have to go with you. Because,
like you, I want to know if this thing between us is real
and lasting. And I'm not ready to tell you goodbye. Not
a forever goodbye."

Once he'd suggested her joining him in Utah, he'd expected her to bring up the connection between Beaver
County and Willow Anderson. He'd thought she might
express excitement over the idea of someone back there
recognizing her. But so far she hadn't, and the major
part of him was happy that *he* seemed to be the main
thing on her mind, rather than finding a link to her past.

Stroking fingers down the middle of her back, he said,
"You've made me a happy man, Anna."

She nuzzled her cheek against his chest—and once
again desire flickered deep in his loins. Making love to
her had left him astounded. It had him wondering how
he'd managed to survive the past years without being
able to touch her soft body, bury himself in her warmth
and love.

"This is like a dream, Hunter. Am I really awake?"

He playfully pinched one cheek of her buttocks. "Yes.
You're awake. And maybe I shouldn't mention this now,

but it might give you another reason to go traipsing off to Utah—besides me."

Smiling pensively, she cut her gaze up to his face. "What could be more important than you?"

She might not remember her true name, but she remembered how to feed a man's ego, he thought.

"Someone around Beaver County might recognize you as Willow Anderson."

"Or they might recognize me as a woman who looks like her," she said. "Truthfully, that notion hadn't entered my mind, Hunter. Not for anything would I want you to think I agreed to this trip for that reason. It's such a long shot, anyway."

Many things about their future together were long shots, but he wasn't going to think about that tonight. Later on, when they got to Stone Creek Ranch, he'd worry about everything that might go wrong.

He cautiously chose his next words. "I wouldn't call it a long shot. Who knows, something about the place or the people might trigger your memory."

A thoughtful look crossed her face. "You mean, if I truly am Willow Anderson? You still think that might be a possibility?"

Unable to hold her gaze, he looked across the room to where the distant lights of the city obscured the starlit sky. "I'm not ruling out the chance."

She sighed. "Oh my, that would be too good to be true. Especially now that you've entered my life. To find out whether I had a family in the past would make a future with you more possible."

He scooted downward until his back was resting flat against the mattress before he draped her upper body over his. With his hands roaming her shoulders, he savored the sensation of her smooth skin beneath his fingers, the warm, eager look in her eyes.

"We'll cross that bridge later, Anna," he murmured. "For now, let's just enjoy us being together."

She wriggled upward until her lips were hovering over his. "Together. I can't think of a sweeter word."

Only one more word would make it sweeter and that was *forever*.

Forever together.

The thought filled his mind as he closed the tiny space between their lips, but as she deepened the kiss, all he could think about was making love to her again. And again.

Chapter Ten

The next morning, Anna had been asleep less than two hours when Hunter woke her with a kiss and presented her with a cup of coffee from the mini coffee maker in the hotel room. After quickly downing the reviving drink and pulling on her clothes, Hunter drove them to her apartment in order for her to shower and dress for work.

In spite of the lack of sleep and every muscle in her body screaming with soreness, she was brimming over with joy. Even when she entered Ian Brennan's office, she could hardly contain her happiness. But the moment she'd informed him that she wanted to start her vacation Monday in order to travel to Utah with Hunter, her boss had deliberately put her on the defensive. And soured her mood from joyful to resentful. From the time she'd first started working at the hotel, she'd been a devoted employee. She'd rarely taken time off. In fact, she probably worked more overtime than anyone in the business department.

"You want your vacation time to go to Utah with Hunter Hollister?" he asked in an astonished voice. "Look, Anna, I realize your personal life is not my business, no matter how much I'd like for it to be. But I feel—

well, I can't remain quiet about this. You've only just met the man! You don't really know anything about him!"

And you think you do? She wanted to fling the question at his smug face. She also wanted to tell her boss that if she lived to be eighty years old, she still wouldn't find him attractive.

Clearing her throat, she said, "Hunter and the Flying H are known all over the western states. He's a reputable man. You can ask most any city official in town and anyone on the Red Bluff rodeo committee. They've dealt with him over the past few years."

Grimacing, he whacked a pen against his palm. "I'm sure he's a good businessman. That's not what I'm talking about, Anna. You couldn't know much about his personal life. He might be a serial womanizer."

Anna wanted to point out that unlike him, Hunter didn't have the leisure time to be a serial womanizer, but she was already pushing the boundaries of appropriateness for their boss-secretary relationship. She didn't want to turn this into a personal issue, even though he appeared to be doing just that.

"If he is, I'll soon learn about it," she said crisply. "I'm only planning to see his home and meet his family. That's hardly the same as signing a marriage license."

He must've realized he was offending her, because he sighed and shook his head. "I'm sorry, Anna. I'm out of line. It's just that—okay, I'm disappointed. All this time you've been working as my secretary, I've been hoping—"

Thankfully, he stopped when she held up her hand. "Please, Mr. Brennan. I like you as a boss and a friend, but that's all. Don't make this more awkward for me than it already is."

"All right, then. Back to business," he said flatly. "You plan to finish out the week. Which is today and tomorrow. You have two weeks of vacation time. Are you planning on being gone the whole two weeks?"

At this point, Anna didn't know anything concrete about their plans, except that she was leaving Red Bluff Sunday with Hunter. He'd told her to pack plenty of things, because they'd be staying at Stone Creek Ranch for a week. But to be honest, Anna wouldn't care if Hunter asked her to remain with him longer than her vacation warranted. If she ended up losing her job, then so be it. At least, for once in her life, she'd have the chance to experience real passion with a man who was beginning to set up residence in her heart.

"I haven't decided on that yet. I'll let you know when to expect me back," she told him. "In the meantime, I'll make sure everything you've noted as important has been taken care of before I leave. That way it will be easier for a temp to take over."

"I'm not calling in a temp," he informed her. "Michelle will be filling in for you and a temp will take over her desk."

Michelle was a vivacious redhead who worked in the hotel's advertising-and-marketing department. She was certainly savvy enough about the hotel's inner workings to fill Anna's job. Actually, she was probably overqualified for the job and Anna couldn't help but think Michelle would fit perfectly into Ian's home in the ritzy part of town.

"I see. Well, with her at my desk, I'm sure everything will run smoothly."

He leveled a pointed look at her. "Michelle isn't you, Anna."

Yes, just like he wasn't Hunter. So much for not making things awkward, Anna thought ruefully.

She glanced at her watch. "If that's all, Mr. Brennan, it's past time for my lunch break."

He rose from the executive chair and walked over to a double window that framed a picture-perfect view of a white church steeple and a distant mountain peak. Ian had one of the most luxurious offices in the whole building and, like Celia often reminded Anna, he owned a massive home, fancy cars, clothes and whatever else money could buy. But in her eyes, he couldn't compare to Hunter. He never would.

"That's all, Anna. Have a nice lunch."

"Thank you."

She hurried out of his office and was fetching her handbag from the bottom drawer on her desk when Celia stuck her head around the outer door to Anna's office.

"Anna, it's getting so late we're going to have to forget Loretta's and hurry over to the Happy Hen! I looked in here twice and you were nowhere to be seen. What's going on? Is Ian piling on the work?"

Anna snatched her jacket from the back of the chair and carried it and her handbag over to the door where Celia was waiting.

"I was in his office," she confirmed in a lowered voice, just in case he might pick up their conversation through the connecting wall. "Let's get out of here. I'll explain as we walk over to the diner."

Five minutes later, the two women were seated in a booth, sipping coffee and waiting on their orders to be filled. On their way over to the Happy Hen, Anna had explained to her friend that she was going to Utah to spend the holidays with Hunter. Since then, Celia had gone unusually quiet. Which was so out of character, Anna couldn't help but prod her to talk.

"Okay, Celia, what's wrong? Are you angry with me because I'm going to be gone for the next few days and won't be here for Christmas? You have your grandmother and you've said your parents are coming down from Redding to see you. Don't you think I have the right to spend my holiday with someone who's special to me?"

Celia groaned and rolled her eyes toward the ceiling. "Yes, but this is more than just celebrating the holidays. You're going off with a man, and not just any man. From the description you've given me of the man, Hunter Hollister is a hunky cowboy who would make any normal woman lose all common sense. What are you expecting out of this, Anna? You're not the brief-affair type!"

Anna felt her cheeks turning red. "No. I'm not a brief-affair kind of woman. But I—when Hunter asked me to travel with him to Stone Creek Ranch, I didn't have to mull over the invitation. When I'm with Hunter—I can't understand or explain it, but I feel like I've known him forever. I feel like—I don't know—like we're perfect together."

Celia regarded her with a suspicious look. "You know what you sound like?"

"A fool?"

"That depends on how you define *fool*." With a wry shake of her head, she leaned toward Anna and lowered her voice. "If you ask me, you sound more like a woman in love."

Just hearing Celia say it caused a jolt to her system. Had she already fallen in love with Hunter? True, from the moment they'd met, she'd thrown caution to the wind. And the more time she'd spent with him, the more infatuated she'd become. But last night had been a revelation for her. The feelings Hunter had invoked in her had been much more than physical passion. Wrapped in his arms, she'd felt her heart pouring out to him.

"I'll be frank, Celia. I get a little scared when I ask myself how I feel about him. I think—well, he's rapidly become very important to me. And when he asked me to accompany him to Utah, I was thrilled. Does that mean I'm in love with him? I'm not ready to say yes, just yet. Ask me again when I get back from the trip."

Just as Celia opened her mouth to make a retort, the waitress arrived with their lunch orders. After she'd placed the grilled chicken salads in front of them and refilled their coffees, she moved on to the next table, but Celia ignored her food. Instead, she shook her head at Anna and said, "I don't expect you'll be back, Anna."

Frowning, Anna picked up the pepper shaker and sprinkled some on her salad. "That's ridiculous, Celia. Sometimes your thoughts go way off in some sort of fantasy land."

Celia stabbed her fork into a piece of chicken. "Okay, go ahead and make fun of me. I can take it. But I have a feeling that once you go to Utah with Hunter your life is going to change. And don't ask me how. I can't tell you that."

Anna groaned. "Celia, you need to get out more. I

think you've been spending too much time with your grandmother. I know she's the mystic type. Obviously she's rubbing off on you."

Celia laughed, but Anna noticed it sounded strained and a little sad.

"Maybe you're right. I haven't been on a decent date in ages." She ate a couple of bites of salad, then asked, "So how did Ian react when you told him you wanted time off? Bet he wasn't too pleased."

"He could hardly forbid me from taking my vacation time."

"No. But you didn't give him much warning."

"You're right. And I feel a little bad about that, but it can't be helped." She wasn't about to tell Celia everything Ian said to her. Even though she didn't always mean to, Celia often chattered to all her coworkers in the bookkeeping department about things that should've been labeled private. "Anyway, Michelle is going to be filling in for me."

This news caused Celia's eyes to pop wide open. "Michelle? Seriously? He's bringing her over from marketing? I always knew she was a gold digger. I wonder how she swung this?"

Anna shrugged. "I wouldn't jump to conclusions about Michelle. She couldn't have known I was planning on taking my vacation. I only told Mr. Brennan about it this morning. Obviously, *he'll* be contacting *her*. Not the other way around."

Celia sighed. "Oh well, he would've never chosen me, anyway."

Anna frowned at her friend. "Look, Celia, Mr. Brennan would be the last man on earth to make you happy.

For one thing, he's too old for you. And another, he's too much of a stuffed shirt. You need a guy like you—full of life."

With a woeful smile, Celia reached across the table and gave Anna's hand an affectionate squeeze. "I'm going to miss you so much, Anna."

Anna gave her an indulgent smile. "Celia, you make it sound like you're never going to see me again. I'll be back in Red Bluff before you know it."

"Sure, Anna. Whatever you say."

Thankfully, throughout the rest of the lunch break, her friend dropped the subject. Even so, Celia's comments continued to swirl around in Anna's head. She couldn't imagine anything that might happen at Stone Creek Ranch that would prevent her from returning to Red Bluff. It wasn't like Hunter was suddenly going to propose marriage to her or even ask her to stay with him on a permanent basis. He'd not mentioned anything of the sort. Nor did she expect it.

Yes, going with Hunter to Utah was impulsive and out of character for her, maybe even reckless. But no matter what the future might bring, this time she had to follow her heart.

"Look guys, you go find some shovels right now and get busy!" Hunter pointed to one end of the bull pen where water was puddled ankle-deep around the animals. "I want this pen trenched and drained! Who the hell left the water running in the trough, anyway?"

The two young men glanced anxiously at each other before one of them ventured to explain. "It has an automatic float, Mr. Hollister. It must have gotten stuck or something. We only found it a few minutes ago."

Heaving out a heavy breath, Hunter pushed back the brim of his Stetson and pinched the bridge of his nose. It wasn't like him to scold his employees. He'd always tried to be an understanding boss, not a taskmaster. But he wasn't himself today. And not because he'd gotten very little sleep after making love to Willow until the wee hours of the morning. No, if he was honest with himself, his short temper was because he was worried.

"Sorry, Jay. Sorry, Daniel. I shouldn't have barked at you that way," he said after a moment. "I realize you have lots to do around here and you can't keep an eye on everything all the time. Just do what you can with the pen. In the meantime, let's move the bulls over to the next lot."

Jay, a tall slender guy in his early twenties, said, "We can move the bulls over, Mr. Hollister, but there's no water trough in that pen."

Hunter muttered a curse under his breath. "Well, don't worry about it. Just hang up a few buckets and make sure they stay filled."

The two men assured him they'd get the job done. Hunter was turning to move on to the horse pens when Malachi's voice sounded behind him.

"What's the matter with you? Did you eat gravel with your biscuits this morning?"

Hunter walked over and stood next to his grinning assistant. "I didn't eat breakfast this morning."

"Didn't have time?" Malachi asked coyly.

The first thing Hunter had done this morning when he'd arrived at the rodeo grounds was to take Malachi aside and inform him that Willow would be spending the next week with home on Stone Creek. He'd expected his trusty assistant to assure him he'd take care of moving the livestock down to Barstow, but he'd not planned on Malachi being so happy about the news. And from the looks of him, he was still pleased about the sudden turn of events.

"No. Actually, Willow's vehicle is still parked here at my trailer. So I hung around to take her to work."

The smile on Malachi's face disappeared. "Hunter, when we talked earlier about you and Willow going to Stone Creek Ranch, you didn't mention anything about her amnesia. You've spent quite a bit of time with her here lately. Has she remembered anything? Has anything you've said or done triggered a memory?"

Hunter glanced over his shoulder to see Jay and Daniel were already moving the bulls into the adjoining pen. Satisfied the men were handling the task, he nudged Malachi's shoulder in the direction of his travel trailer.

"Let's take a little coffee break," he said.

"I'm all for that."

A few short minutes later, after Hunter had made a pot of coffee in a quick-drip machine, he poured two cups and gestured for Malachi to join him at the table.

While his assistant stirred two spoonsful of sugar into his cup, he eyed Hunter. "Since Willow has agreed to go with you to Utah, I'm assuming you two had a special date last night."

"We did. Very special." His hands locked around the warm cup, Hunter stared into the brown liquid as memories of making love to Willow flashed through his mind. Being with her again had shaken him even more than he'd first realized. Even now, he could detect a slight tremor to his hands. He didn't want Malachi to see him in such a vulnerable state. "It was almost like we were man and wife again. Almost. In her mind, I'm just a man she met a few days ago. So to answer your earlier question, no. She still doesn't remember me or anything about our past."

"That's a hell of a thing, Hunter. She's such a nice, pretty lady. And I know you love her. You both deserve better."

Hunter raised the cup to his lips and took a long sip. "Yeah. I think so, too. That's why I wanted to take this next week off and spend it with her."

"I thought you were thrilled she agreed to go. Why are you looking so glum? Changing your mind about the whole thing?"

He looked over at his friend and coworker. "No. But I am worried, Malachi. Really worried. Last night when I invited her, I wasn't thinking. I guess I wasn't even thinking clearly this morning when I first talked to you about the trip. But as the morning has ticked on, all sorts of scenarios have come to my mind." He set the cup down on the tabletop and wiped a shaky hand over his face. "Loving a woman shouldn't be this hard on a man."

"What are you worried about, Hunter? Even if you go home and she doesn't remember anything, you'll still be together. Maybe not the way you want the two of you to be together, but it's better than not having her at all, isn't it?"

"Honestly, her not remembering and everything going along like it has been for the past few days might be the best-case scenario. I'm going to tell my family ahead of time to treat Willow as though they're meeting her for the first time. Of course, they'll say she looks like Willow— she's going to expect them all to bring it up, so it wouldn't seem normal if they don't make mention of her—but no one in my family is going to tell her about Willow's past."

"And what are they going to say? Oh, you look just like Willow Anderson?"

"Yes. But since they've not seen her in years, she could just be someone who looks like her. So I think I can get by with that problem. But I'm pretty sure Willow is going to want to drive into Beaver County and look the town over. And this is where the worries begin. We're bound to run into people who knew us as a married couple. The first thing they're going to ask is when did we get back together? I'd look like all kinds of fool if I tried to pass her off as a look-alike. No, it would be worse than me looking like a fool. Willow isn't dumb. She'd instantly put two and two together and—well, I don't know what would happen."

"Oh. I see. Willow still doesn't know that you were married to Willow Anderson."

"No. I couldn't reveal that to her. I'd obviously know my own wife, and it seemed too risky to make that big of a revelation to her. I couldn't be sure she'd take it well. It might actually hurt her, physically. So I had to pretend that Willow was just a past acquaintance who lived in Beaver County."

His expression grim, Malachi nodded. "Yeah. I see your point. And to tell you the truth, that thought hadn't crossed my mind either. I don't know, Hunter, but it sounds like you've gotten yourself in a hell of a fix."

He wiped another hand over his face. "Last night when I asked her to make the trip I wasn't thinking about the risks. I was only thinking that I wanted us to have more time together—plus, I was hoping that seeing our home on Stone Creek Ranch would jar her memory bank. Malachi, if someone blurts out to her that she's Willow Hollister, I'm afraid it might send her over the edge."

"You mean like put her into a shocked stupor, or something?"

"Yes. That's been one of Grace's worries, too. So you see, where Willow is concerned, I've tangled myself into a web of pretense."

Malachi tapped his fingers thoughtfully against the tabletop. "Well, I suppose you could always back out on your invitation. Use me as an excuse and tell her I can't manage to move the Flying H without your help. Explain that you can't go to Utah until later. And then later won't have to come."

Hunter shot him a disgusted look. "Hell, Malachi, do you honestly think I could do such a thing and then live with it?"

His shrug implied he didn't think the suggestion was all that out of line. "Maybe you could. If you thought it would spare Willow lots of heartache."

Spare her heartache? One thing he knew for sure, he didn't want to cause her any more pain. Not for any reason. But how could either of them find happiness if he allowed fear to rule his thinking?

"Don't you see, Malachi? All this week, I've been pretending, dancing around the truth just to save her from pain and confusion. I can't stop now." Misery swung Hunter's head from side to side. "I can't stop until—her amnesia clears. And God only knows when that might be."

"Well, since you appear to be dead set on taking her to Stone Creek Ranch, all I can say is that you'd better make sure she stays there on the ranch instead of going into town. The way I remember it, Beaver County is a small place where most everyone is an acquaintance or a relative. If she goes there, she'd be bound to run into someone who will let the cat out of the bag."

Hunter wished he could douse his coffee with a heavy amount of brandy. Not only would the spirits warm his insides, they would slow the whirling in his mind. But he and Malachi had plenty of work to do before tonight's performance. He needed a clear head. Besides, dulling his raw nerves wouldn't solve his problems.

"I can only make so many excuses to avoid going into town. After a while, she's going to get suspicious."

"Well, my friend, you can always hope for a miracle."

Hunter had already experienced one miracle when he'd stumbled into Willow on his first night in Red Bluff. If he was lucky, perhaps a second miracle would occur. Otherwise, he feared he could lose Willow once and for all.

"A Christmas miracle might just be my last chance, Malachi."

He drained his cup. As he carried it over to the sink, he felt his cell phone buzz with an incoming text message. Probably the fifth since he and Malachi had sat down with their coffees.

Resting his back against the cabinet counter, he pulled out the phone to see the notification. The text was from a member of the rodeo committee from Barstow.

Groaning, he quickly scanned the short message, then looked over at Malachi. "The rodeo committee in Barstow expects me to meet with them on January 2. I'm going to tell him you'll be standing in for me until I get there."

Malachi stared at him wide-eyed before he let out a sly

chuckle. "Imagine me, a scrawny kid from the rez, attending a committee meeting. That's a good one, Hunter!"

"You're not only going to attend the meeting; you're going to be the top dog there. So don't try to weasel out of it—you're up to the task. You know what the Flying H can and cannot do. I trust you to be sensible and diplomatic. All you have to do is assure them you'll have everything ready to go when it's time for the Barstow Roundup to begin."

Rolling his eyes toward the ceiling, Malachi laughed again. "Okay, Hunter. I'll do my best. But do you have some extra cash on you?"

Frowning slightly, Hunter reached to the back pocket of his jeans for his wallet. Malachi never asked for money. Not for a loan or an advance on his salary. So he couldn't imagine why he was asking now. "I do. How much do you need?"

"Oh, at least enough to buy a suit. I can't go to a committee meeting looking like this," he joked, while gesturing down to his mud-splotched jeans and plaid western shirt.

Recognizing his assistant was joking, Hunter chuckled and jerked his thumb toward the door. "Drink up. We have work waiting on us."

Malachi jumped up from the table. After placing his cup in the sink with Hunter's, he said, "Don't worry, Hunter. If I can make it through a rodeo committee meeting, you can definitely make it through a week with Willow on Stone Creek Ranch."

Forcing a grin on his face, he gave the younger man's shoulder a grateful slap. "Put like that, Malachi, I don't have a worry in the world."

* * *

Later that afternoon, after a short luncheon meeting with the two men who were announcing the rodeo, Hunter returned to the rodeo grounds and climbed up to the announcers' stand to get a good view of the arena floor. He took a seat in one of the folding chairs supplied for the timers and bookkeepers and called his father to explain the situation with Willow.

He'd expected Hadley to be a bit irked about his son's plans to throw such a tense situation on the family, especially at Christmas when everyone would be gathered together and celebrating, but he'd been wrong. His father assured him everyone would be on their toes when Willow was around. He'd even told Hunter how very much he wanted things to work out for him and his ex-wife.

"You don't know how much I appreciate that, Dad. I wasn't sure—" He was forced to pause and swallow at the thickness that had suddenly clogged his throat. "Well, I haven't really talked to you about Willow in a few years. Not since the divorce. I know you weren't happy about the situation then."

"Hell no, I wasn't happy. You were hurt. She hurt you. It's as simple as that. But I like to think I'm a fair man, son, and there are always two sides to everything. Especially a relationship between a man and a woman. I figured Willow had problems she couldn't deal with, and she took the easy way out by running. And now— well, if you think you can trust her, we'll just have to see, won't we? I hope the two of you can be together and happy again."

Hunter drew in a deep breath and let it out. "I think

that's going to depend on her amnesia and—a lot of things."

"Like the Flying H?" Hadley asked sagely.

Hadley had always been a wise man who Hunter loved and respected. He understood that Hadley had watched his own father die a bitter man over the woman he'd divorced and that he didn't want that same sort of wasted life for his son.

"That's one of them. But I believe in second chances. Don't you, Dad?"

"Of course I do, son. So my advice to you is to make the most of this one."

"Thanks, Dad. I'll see you in a few days."

"You mother and I will be looking forward to seeing you and Willow again."

Hunter wanted to thank his father again for being so gracious, but this time Hunter couldn't swallow away the hot lump in his throat.

"Bye, Dad," he said in a choked voice, then quickly ended the call.

Hunter climbed down from the announcers' stand to go in search of the two men who oversaw the ground crew. He found them at the far end of the arena, hooking up a giant harrow to a tractor. After he discussed the issue of spreading more sand in front of the roping chute, he left them to make his way over to the Dalharts' trailer. Halfway there, his phone rang. Seeing it was Bonnie, he stopped and rested a shoulder against a nearby pipe fence.

"Dad just told me about you and Willow coming home to the ranch for Christmas," she said in an incredulous voice. "Have you lost your mind, Hunter? How can this possibly work?"

Of his twin sisters, Bonnie was the reserved, practical one. She wasn't one to take chances or venture off into the unknown, so it was hardly a surprise to hear her expressing doubts about his plans. Still, her heart was as soft as a marshmallow and he knew she was expressing her fears because she loved him.

Before Hunter could attempt to answer her question, she continued in a remorseful voice, "I'm sorry, brother. That was an awful thing for me to say to you."

"Bonnie, listen, it's okay to tell me you wish I'd keep Willow away from the ranch—and that I'd stay away from her, too," Hunter told her. "It's not like I've forgotten how everyone felt when she left and sent divorce papers in the mail. I think you all hated her. And probably still do."

"Oh, Hunter, we don't hate Willow. At least, I don't," Bonnie told him. "I'm just concerned about you."

"You shouldn't be," Hunter told his younger sister. "I'm a big boy. Whatever happens—I can take it. I mean, it can't get much worse than the hell I went through these past four years, can it?"

"If you're such a big boy, then you should know, Hunter, that things can always get worse. But let's not think in those terms," she said, deliberately injecting a cheerier note in her voice. "I'll be praying that everything gets better."

"Thanks, sis. Is that the only reason you called? To talk to me about Willow?"

"Actually, there is another reason. I wanted to let you know I've received your contract for the rodeo in Ely. From the looks of it, the first performances will start a week after Barstow winds up. Do you still want to sign it?"

He didn't hesitate to answer. "Certainly. Why wouldn't I? It's a whale of a sum of money. I'm thrilled the Ely rodeo committee is trusting the Flying H to put on the show."

"Yes, I can see it's a very lucrative contract. But after I heard about Willow—I didn't know if you'd be taking time off to be with her or—whatever."

Hunter sighed and ran a hand over the tense muscles at the back of his neck. "Look, Bonnie, producing rodeos is my job. It's what I'll always do."

"And if Willow still can't live with that?" Bonnie asked pointedly.

Yeah, what then, Hunter asked himself. Could he stick his heels in the dirt one more time and watch her walk away? Oh God, he could only pray it didn't come to that.

"Willow is a different person now. And I like to think I'm a little different, too."

There was a long pause and then Bonnie said, "Okay, Hunter. I'll sign and put this contract in the mail tomorrow."

"Thanks, Bonnie. Has anyone told you lately that you're the best sister ever?"

She laughed softly. "I think Bea told me that yesterday. Bye, Hunter."

The next three days passed like a whirlwind to Anna as she packed bags, made sure her bills were scheduled to be paid and her mail was put on hold. She also used one of her lunch hours to shop for Christmas gifts for Hunter and his family. As for her job, she'd expected Ian to pile extra work on her just out of spite, but he'd been surprisingly nice. She was grateful he'd made her last two days at work a breeze to get through.

Now, as Hunter loaded the last of their bags into his truck and gave last minute instructions to Malachi regarding the Flying H, Anna stood to one side and waited for the Dalhart sisters to say their goodbyes.

"I don't suppose you'll be joining us down in Barstow, will you?" Cheyenne asked. "It would be such fun if you could. Being in the Mojave Desert, it should be quite a bit warmer. And the crowds are usually great."

Instinctively, Anna glanced over to the tailgate of the truck, where Hunter and Malachi continued to talk. She'd spent the last three nights with Hunter and she was certain the time together had drawn the two of them even closer. Yet, she hadn't missed the fact that when Hunter spoke of the future, it was only in the short term. She didn't know if that was because he was reluctant to commit himself to anything permanent or if he simply couldn't plan that far ahead.

Anna wanted to believe that somehow they could make a long-distance relationship last, but she had her doubts. Relationships took time and nurturing to strengthen into something meaningful. With her in Red Bluff and Hunter traveling all over the west, she couldn't see that happening. But she'd been telling herself that she wasn't going to dwell on that problem for the next few days. Once her time on Stone Creek Ranch with Hunter was over, then she could start worrying about the future.

"I can't make any promises, but it sounds like fun. And I've not been to that part of the state. At least, not in the four years that I can remember."

"Gosh, I still have to stop and remind myself that prior to your accident you don't know where you've been," Cheyenne said. "I can't imagine how weird that must feel."

"It is weird. But I've learned to live with it," she told the middle Dalhart sister, then gave them all a smile. "I'm truly going to miss visiting with all of you. And miss seeing your trick riding acts."

"Now, Anna, don't make it sound like this is a forever goodbye," Carlotta said. "We'll be coming back to Red Bluff next year. Hunter will make certain of that."

A year. Would it be that long before she saw the sisters and Malachi again? More importantly, how much time would pass before she and Hunter would be together again?

Shaking away the pesky question, she said, "You're right, Lotta. I'll see you three again when the Stampede comes back around—if not before."

The three of them had just finished giving Anna a hug, when Hunter walked up and announced they had to be leaving.

"You three make a safe trip down to Barstow. Have a merry Christmas and I'll see you there before the first performance," he said to the sisters.

"That's only a week and a half away," Carlotta said. "You need more of a vacation with Anna than that."

"Just be glad he's taking time for the holidays," Chastity told her sister, then slanted an impish glance at Anna. "From what I hear, he's never taken this much time off for Christmas. You must have said the right thing to him, Anna."

"And you're not ever going to know what that right thing was," Hunter joked, making all three sisters laugh.

He wrapped an arm around Anna's shoulders and urged her over to the passenger's door of the truck. Once he'd helped her into the cab, he took his place in the driver's seat. As he started the engine, the women began waving goodbye.

Anna waved back at them, but as Hunter put the truck into motion and headed away from the rodeo grounds, it dawned on her that Malachi hadn't hung around to see them off.

"What's wrong with Malachi? I thought, at least, he'd tell me goodbye. I might not see him again for a long, long time."

A wan smile on his face, he glanced over at her. "You sound like you've grown fond of my assistant."

Nodding, Anna said, "I have. I like him a lot."

"Well, I have news for you. Malachi likes you a lot, too. And he's not good at goodbyes. He told me to tell you he'd see you later on down the trail."

It surprised Anna to hear the tall, strong Shoshone had such a sensitive side to him. On the occasions she'd been around him, he'd always seemed laid-back, without a single worry.

"Hmm. Is there a specific reason he doesn't like goodbyes?"

"He's gone through some tough losses. I think he tries not to let himself develop close relationships with anyone, because he figures he'll ultimately get hurt."

She slanted him a wry glance. "Malachi obviously has a close relationship with you."

"That's because he trusts me." He arched a brow in her direction. "Do you?"

Smiling, she reached for his hand. "I wouldn't be

going to Utah with you if I believed you were anything less than trustworthy."

He squeezed her hand. "Then I'm going to do my best not to disappoint you."

"How could you disappoint me, Hunter? You've opened up my life to things I never thought I'd experience. You've made me see that my life shouldn't be limited just because I have no memory of my past. I'll always be grateful to you for that and for—making me very, very happy."

"Once you see our—uh, my home on Stone Creek Ranch, I hope you'll still be saying that, Anna."

She'd not missed the slip of the tongue. But why had he started to say "our" home? Had he unconsciously included her in his remark and then changed it when he'd realized how he'd sounded?

You're making a big deal out of nothing, Anna. Hunter's home isn't your home. It never will be. So don't go ruining this coming week by wishing for the impossible.

Shoving away the taunting voice in her head, she looked at him. "Why wouldn't I? I expect I'll love everything about your home."

"We'll see. Tomorrow we'll be home on Stone Creek Ranch."

Tomorrow we'll be home. She couldn't think of anything sweeter he could've said to her. Except maybe, *I love you.* And it was too early for that, she thought. Maybe in a few days, when they left Utah and headed back to California, they'd both know whether they loved each other.

Chapter Eleven

After an overnight stopover in Reno, they rolled into Beaver County the next afternoon. Not wanting to take any chances, Hunter avoided driving into town. Instead, he cut off on a county road that led straight to Stone Creek Ranch.

As they drove through the sweeping mountain ranges with valley floors that ran for miles, Anna gazed out the window, her attention captivated by the landscape.

"This is so incredibly beautiful, Hunter!" With a breathless little laugh, she looked over at him. "I guess you can tell I'm in awe."

The joy she was expressing over the ranch's rangeland gave him hope. Even if these next few days didn't trigger anything in her memory, at least in her new state of mind, she didn't find the remoteness of the ranch unpleasant.

"I'm glad you think it's beautiful. I've always thought of this land as a little slice of paradise."

She tilted her head to one side as she studied him. "And yet you leave this place behind more than you stay. I realize you love your job, but after seeing this land— well, it's a bit confusing to me, Hunter."

The fact had always confused her. She'd never understood how, in spite of his love for the ranch—and for the home he shared with her—rodeo life was in his blood. In the same way wild geese had to leave their home and fly south to stay warm, he had to hit the road with his livestock to feel complete.

"Sometimes a man's dreams take him in unexpected directions. I like knowing I have a nest to come back to, but I also have a need to fly out of it from time to time."

She nodded slowly. "If I hadn't met Malachi or the Dalton sisters, I doubt I would understand what you mean. But after a few nights of being with you and them, I can see you're all like a family—a traveling family— and you need each other. Just like you need your family here. Am I getting any part of that right?"

He smiled at her and silently sent up a prayer of thanks. He'd told Bonnie and Grace that Anna was a different woman now—more rounded and open-minded. He could only hope that if she did remember she was Willow, that she would remain as understanding as this woman sitting next to him.

"You're getting a whole lot of parts right, Anna."

She shot him a pleased grin, then she scooted to the edge of the seat and peered out at the northern ridge of mountains lying directly in front of them. "Are we almost to the ranch headquarters yet? I'm getting excited to meet your family. But Hunter, I hope you told them that I don't want to be an intrusion this week. You know, the two best times of having a guest is when they arrive and when they leave. I don't want to be a pest in between."

He chuckled. "I won't let you be a pest, Anna. As to

your question, we should be there in ten more minutes. I'll warn you in time enough to put on your lipstick."

Smiling, she looked over at him. "You're such a sweet cowboy."

No, he thought ruefully. He was her forgotten cowboy. But he had to hope that seeing his family would flip on a light in her dark memory—and that if it did, she wouldn't hate him when their shared past came to light.

Minutes later, Hunter parked the truck beneath a huge tree at the edge of the lawn. The massive limbs had lost their leaves and turned the ground below into a red-and-rusty-brown carpet. As soon as Hunter helped her out of the truck, she was struck by the scents of juniper and pine blowing down from the mountains, while somewhere in the far distance she could hear cows bawling and dogs barking.

Mesmerized by her surroundings, she stood gawking at the house. Somehow the place looked just as Anna imagined it would—majestic, yet homey. A giant wreath of evergreens and holly hung from the front door, while enormous red bows were attached to the post supporting the roof over the porch.

"This is the original ranch house," Hunter said as he wrapped a supportive hand beneath her elbow. "Grandfather Lionel started building it back in the early 1960s. As you can see, Mom and Bonnie have decorated for Christmas."

As the two of them walked across the brown lawn, Anna continued to gaze up at the large, two-story structure. The outside walls were a combination of large round rock and lap siding. The steep, shingled roof matched the soft gray color of the siding, while white board shutters bracketed several windows on the front. On the north side of the house, an enormous stone chimney rose high above the roof. Presently, a trail of woodsmoke spiraled up into the blue sky and Anna thought how lovely it must be to have a real fireplace to enjoy in the cold months.

"This is incredible, Hunter. I'm in awe." She glanced at him. "So this is the house you grew up in?"

"That's right. Me and my seven siblings. When we were all still living at home the house was bulging at the seams. Now, not so much."

"Who still lives with your parents?" she asked.

"Bonnie, Flint, and Quint and Clementine. Which makes the house seem almost empty. Mom and Dad wouldn't be able to stand it if there weren't some kids around."

"Hmm. How wonderful that your parents had eight children." She laughed lightly. "Although, I imagine it was chaotic at times when you were all growing up."

Smiling fondly, he nodded. "Mom and Dad always wanted a big family and I think they expected the commotion that went with it."

"I'd be thrilled if I could have half that many children."

She could feel his gaze on the side of her face and she wondered what he was thinking. Did he believe that she was throwing out subtle hints? She hoped not. As much as she wanted Hunter in her life, she never wanted to make him feel cornered or pressured.

"Would you?" he asked.

Nodding, she said, "Oh yes, I want to have babies. One of the first things I asked the nurses and doctors when I woke up with amnesia was whether I had children. I told them that if I did, I wanted to see them. Later—well, I've accepted the fact that I probably don't have any little kiddos yet. But I've not given up hope for the future."

He gently squeezed her elbow. "You shouldn't give up on your dreams, Anna."

Dreams. She wanted the wishes in her heart to be more than dreams. That was one of the reasons she'd traveled with Hunter nearly eight hundred miles. She was searching for a way to make her dreams come true.

They climbed two short steps to a porch made of planks that stretched across the entire front of the structure. Covered with the same shingled roof as the house, the long space was filled with chairs and love seats made of bent willow branches and topped with brightly colored cushions.

As they climbed the steps to the porch, Hunter said, "In the summer months, Mom has loads of potted plants out here, but it's obviously too cold those now. And unfortunately, the rose garden has already been covered for the winter."

She looked at him with interest. "Oh. Your mother has a rose garden?"

"It's in the backyard. The roses were Grandfather Lionel's babies. He planted them when he built the house and trust me, he made sure they got as much tender loving care as the livestock. Mom helped him care for the roses, especially after Grandfather grew feeble. And after he passed they became her babies."

"Sounds like the roses were very important to your grandfather," she remarked.

"They were. Dad asked him one time why he worked so hard to keep the flowers perfect and all he said was that he liked them. You have to understand that Grandfather was a man of few words. Until he got angry. Then you could hear him all over the house."

He couldn't know how hearing about his family made her long for one of her own. Ever since her accident, she'd been alone and because no one had come searching for her, she'd continued to wonder if she'd grown up without a family, perhaps in a series of foster homes. Or even worse, her relatives might have shunned or abandoned her. But none of that had to matter now. Hunter had brought her here to his home and he was opening up a whole new world to her.

"I'll bet you never angered your grandfather," she teased.

He chuckled. "Of course not. I was always a good boy."

He punched the doorbell, then not waiting for anyone to answer, he opened the door and ushered her into a foyer.

"Mom is probably in the kitchen," he said as he snaked an arm around her waist. "And Dad might be at the cattle barn or in his office. Let's go see if we can find someone."

They left the foyer and were walking through a long, formal living room furnished with rich wood-and-leather furniture when Anna heard approaching footsteps. A second later, a couple somewhere in their sixties appeared in the open doorway. Anna instantly knew the pair had to be the matriarch and patriarch of the Hollister family. The man, dressed in typical ranch clothes, was tall and burly with dark hair, while the woman at his side was petite with streaks of silver threaded through her blond hair. She was wearing a multicolored maxi skirt with a matching deep blue sweater and cowboy boots. The pair made a striking couple, but she wouldn't have expected anything less from ranching royalty.

"Hunter! Why didn't you warn us that you were about to arrive!" the woman exclaimed. "We would've met you on the porch!"

"I wanted to surprise you," he told her as he urged Anna toward his parents. "Mom, Dad, I'd like for you to meet Anna Jones. And, Anna, this is my parents, Claire and Hadley. And, Anna, before they have a chance to start telling tales on their oldest child, don't believe any of them."

Laughing softly, Anna extended her hand to Claire first. "I've been looking forward to meeting you, Ms. Hollister. You're lovelier than even Hunter described."

Smiling warmly, Claire gave Anna's hand a firm shake. "Thank you, Anna. And you're, uh—just exactly how Hunter described you. Hadley and I are very happy to have you here on Stone Creek Ranch, Anna. Especially for Christmas."

"Thank you," she said, then offered her hand to Hadley. "It's a pleasure to meet you, Mr. Hollister. I'm going to assume that Hunter inherited all his charm from you."

Chuckling, Hadley patted the top of Anna's hand. "I can already see we're going to get along great, Anna. But before we go any further, I don't want to hear any more of this Ms. and Mr. stuff. We're Claire and Hadley, right, honey?" He directed the question to his wife.

Anna looked over to Claire to see the woman was

studying her with a strange sort of expression. It suddenly dawned on her that she and Hadley were probably thinking how much she resembled Willow Anderson.

"Yes, that's exactly right," the woman said. "You must call us Claire and Hadley."

"Excuse me, Claire, but I noticed you were looking at me as though you'd seen me before," Anna said.

Claire cleared her throat as she darted an awkward glance at Hunter. "I'm sorry, Anna. I didn't mean to stare. You must think I'm rude."

Hunter's hand gently squeezed the side of Anna's waist. "Mom is staring because you're so beautiful," he said.

"And because I look like Willow Anderson, right?" she said, then encompassed the couple with a reassuring smile. "Don't worry. Hunter has already explained there was a woman who looked like me who used to live in Beaver County. I would've found it strange if you hadn't noticed a resemblance."

Hadley's brows lifted with faint speculation. "Well, you do look an awful lot like her. But I think Hunter is on the right track—we're staring because you're so lovely. Our son was a lucky man when he stumbled on you."

"Thank you," Anna told him. "Thank you both. You're so gracious to have me."

Grinning now, Hadley stepped forward and, wrapping a hand around Anna's arm, pulled her away from Hunter's grasp. "Come along, Anna. I'll show you to the den where you can get comfortable in front of the fire. Hunter, you go with your mother and help her make us all some coffee."

Hunter laughed. "Do I have a choice, Dad?"

As Hadley led Anna away, he glanced back at his wife and son. "No. You don't have a choice," he told Hunter, then added, "Claire, honey, dig out a bottle of brandy. We need to give Anna a warm welcome."

As soon as Hadley and Willow disappeared down the hallway toward the den, Claire hustled Hunter into the kitchen and carefully shut the door behind them.

"Oh Lord, Hunter, you were telling the truth! That's Willow in there!" Claire exclaimed with a gasp. "I—didn't know—before when you said you were bringing her here—I thought—well, to be honest, I thought you were bringing a woman to visit, who merely resembled Willow."

Bewildered, Hunter stared at her. "Mom, why would I make up something like that?"

"Because—well, you were so in love with Willow that I thought you were probably just settling for someone who reminded you of her."

"That's ridiculous, Mom. Think about what you're saying. If you lost Dad, would you settle for a man who only looked like him?"

She shook her head. "No. But—oh, son, she doesn't know us! She truly doesn't know!"

All of a sudden Claire was crying and Hunter could only gather his mother in his arms and give her a reassuring hug. "I'm sorry I'm putting such an emotional load on you and Dad and everyone else, especially here at Christmastime, but I'm hoping and praying that seeing all of you and the ranch will help her."

Claire sniffed and eased out of his arms. "Don't worry about me. That's not why I'm so emotional. It just hurts me to see you and Willow in such a—twisted situation. As for your dad, you needn't worry about him. He'll be good for her."

He gave her a wry grin. "Yeah, Dad has a way about him."

Sighing, Claire hurried over to the cabinet and began putting the coffee makings together. "I can't help but wonder, son, what might happen if Willow does remember. She left us once. She might do it again. And I'd hate for you to be hurt like that a second time."

His mother was only saying what Hunter had been thinking from the first night he'd bumped into Willow in the rain. Who was to say she wouldn't hurt him again? But he had to try to build something with her. Otherwise, he'd always view himself as a coward, choosing fear over love.

Joining his mother at the cabinet counter, he gently patted her shoulder. "Mom, life is all about taking chances. This is one of those times when I have to take one."

She paused in dumping the scoop of ground coffee into the paper filter and leveled a shaky smile at him. "You always were a big dreamer, Hunter. I only hope this one comes true for you."

"Me and you both," he said. "Now, where do I find the brandy? I'll get it and some cups ready."

The den was located on the bottom floor at the back of the huge ranch house. A long room furnished with three couches, four stuffed armchairs and a couple of cushioned rockers, it was warm and especially cheery with Christmas decorations adorning tables, windows and the mantel over the fireplace.

To one side of the room, safely away from the blaz-
ing logs in the fireplace, an enormous fir rose up to the
high beamed ceiling. The branches were trimmed with
red-and-silver garlands, countless twinkling lights and
so many colorful ornaments Anna wondered what kept
the branches from sagging from the weight.

Drawn to the beautiful tree, Anna walked over to give
it a closer look. All sizes of brightly wrapped gifts were
piled beneath the branches, but it was the tip-top that
caught her attention, where a blonde angel with a white
dress and gossamer wings held a wand tipped with a
golden star.

The sight of the angel struck a chord in Anna, and for
several long moments she gazed up at her.

"You like the angel?" Hadley asked as he came to
stand next to her.

Smiling faintly, she looked at him. "Everything about
the tree is gorgeous. But she's my favorite ornament. I
love the fact that she's holding a star."

"Claire has had that angel for years. And she's not
satisfied unless Cordell sets the angel up there."

"Why him?"

Hadley chuckled. "Probably because he was always
the rowdy one of our kids and Claire thought he needed
contact with an angel more than the rest. But to be fair,
Cord has always made it a point to help his mother with
the tree. Even though he's usually overworked at this
time of year. Sometimes he and Quint are in the saddle
from sunup to sundown and beyond."

"I suppose the winter weather keeps everyone on the
ranch extra busy with the increased haying and feeding,"
she said. "Hunter mentioned that most of his siblings

and their spouses would be here for dinner tonight. I'm eager to meet everyone."

An odd look flashed in his eyes, but then he quickly smiled and Anna decided she must have imagined his strange reaction. After all, she couldn't imagine how her comments would've been seen as out of line.

"Everyone will be here except for Beatrice and Kipp," Hadley replied. "He couldn't get away from their ranch in Idaho until later this evening. So they won't get here until early in the morning. But Jack and Van and their baby son, Jackson, will be here. Little Jack, as we call him, won't celebrate his first birthday until March. And Cordell and Maggie will be here with their little girl, Bridget. Most of them aren't here at the moment because several inches of snow are supposed to hit tomorrow, so Quint and Clementine have been herding the sheep up to the barns and Cord and the ranch hands are making sure all the cattle are in sheltered areas. They're all working overtime, but they'll be here for dinner. And Flint, of course. Unless there's an emergency involving the sheriff's office. Otherwise, he has a coworker who is kind enough to cover his shift sometimes, like tonight, so he can be here with everyone. And we're hoping Grace and her husband, Mack, don't run into any emergencies at their clinics. Hunter has probably already told you that Grace is a medical doctor and Mack is a veterinarian. They both have their own private clinics in town."

"He has mentioned Grace and her husband," Anna told him. "But I don't think he said whether they have children. Do they?"

"Two. A daughter, Kitty. She's six now. And an eight-year-old son, Ross."

The fact that Hunter had nieces and nephews made Anna wonder if he'd ever wanted children of his own. That first night they'd met and shared a drink in the bar, he'd told her he wasn't married. And she'd assumed he'd never been a husband or father. But had he ever wanted to be? There'd been several times this past week that she'd wanted to ask him those questions, but she'd been afraid they might put him off to the point where he wouldn't want to see her anymore. But now that they were surrounded by his family, she was beginning to need answers.

"Sounds like everyone is trying to juggle time for the holidays. I hope the snow doesn't hinder travel for your daughter and son-in-law driving down from Idaho."

Hadley chuckled. "Trust me, Bea and Kipp are accustomed to traveling in bad weather. A snowstorm is actually one of the reasons they ended up married. But that's another long story. You'll have to get Bea to tell you about it while she's here." He gestured over to the furniture situated in front of the fireplace. "I'm sure you must be tired, Anna. Have a seat and relax. Hunter and Claire should be showing up with the coffee soon."

She walked over to a cushioned rocker that was near enough to the fire to feel the warmth but was angled just enough toward a wide picture window to give her a view of the backyard and beyond. Her gaze immediately went to a low rock wall that fenced off two sides of the lawn. Next to the wall, a sea of gray tarps stretched over what she assumed were the rose bushes Hunter had told her about.

"Hunter mentioned that Claire's rose garden would be covered," Anna said. "But in the springtime I can imagine how beautiful the plants must look beside the rock wall. The whole thing reminds me of an English garden."

"I'm sorry you're not seeing her roses at their best, but for now, Claire had a couple of the ranch hands string Christmas lights along the patio and on the juniper trees to make up for the ugliness of the tarps. When it gets dark, the backyard looks fairly festive. As for reminding you of an English garden…most everyone who sees the yard says that very same thing." He eased into a stuffed armchair a few steps away from where she sat. "We used to tell Dad that he must have been an Englishman at heart. He had a penchant for sheep, too. And Quint obviously took his love for the animals after his grandfather."

He squared around in the chair and pointed out the window toward a distant mountain range covered with snow. "See that tallest peak?" he asked.

"Yes. It makes for a majestic view from here."

"Well, we call it Snow Mountain because the only time it loses its white cap is in the dead of summer. Anyway, at the foot of that mountain is where Quint and Clementine are gathering a few hundred head of Merino sheep on horseback today. With the help of four dogs," he added.

"Is that area where the sheep usually stay?" she asked.

"Yes. The western range of Stone Creek Ranch is mostly used for sheep grazing. The cattle are kept on the eastern range. And since we recently purchased another ranch running adjacent to the northern boundary of Stone Creek, we've put more cattle on that land."

"Sounds as though you're expanding," she said.

He smiled and shrugged. "When I first brought up the notion of buying more land, I think most of my children thought I was growing senile or reckless. Especially Jack. He comanages the ranch with me. But after a while, Jack and the rest of the family were pleased. Especially now that the risks of investing are paying off."

She nodded. "Building something always requires risks," she said. "As far as that goes, just plain ole living requires risks."

"So does building relationships. Claire and I have been lucky in that regard. We've been together for forty-two years and counting, but it hasn't always been easy. Sometimes we have to work at being happy together."

Anna wondered if Hadley was saying all of this for her benefit. Surely he wasn't thinking that Hunter had marriage on his mind. He'd only invited her here to the ranch for a short visit and to give them a chance to get to know each other better. But she wasn't going to point that out to Hadley now. The man was being extremely cordial to her and the more she talked with him, the more comfortable she felt. Like he was the father figure she'd always hoped for.

She'd always hoped for? How did she know she'd *always* hoped for a father figure? It was impossible for her to know whether she'd had a father in the past or a mother, or any kind of family!

Perplexed by her odd thoughts, she looked at Hunter's father. "Hadley, did you know Willow Anderson's parents?"

Frowning slightly, he shrugged one big shoulder. "What I know of them is mostly hearsay. From what I've heard other folks say, they were a worthless pair. However, I was acquainted with her grandparents, Angus and Marcella. Those two were good, hardworking people.

They sure didn't deserve that pitiful excuse of a son." He arched a brow at her. "Have you talked with Hunter about the Andersons?"

"A little. When he explained how much I looked like Willow, I was naturally interested. I'd hoped there might be some connection that would lead me to my real identity. But now—well, after meeting you and Claire I can see that was a hopeless idea."

He opened his mouth as though he was going to speak, then just as quickly closed it, leaving Anna to wonder what he'd been about to say.

Finally he asked, "Why do you think it's a hopeless idea?"

His eyes narrowed shrewdly and Anna got the strange feeling that he was hiding something. But what? What could he possibly have to tell her that would make any difference about her amnesia?

"Well, you and Claire obviously know that I'm not Willow. Otherwise, you would have told me the instant we met."

"Hmm. I see." He swiped a hand over his face, then turned and stared out the window. "You know, Anna, I've learned through my sixty-five years of living that most anything is possible. Did you ever think that you could've been related to the Andersons somehow? Maybe you were a cousin or a niece who never lived around here."

"Were you aware of the Andersons having other relatives?"

"Don't recall any mentioned," he replied. "But that doesn't mean much."

Anna said, "Well, the idea that I might be a relative of

Willow's never entered my mind. But it's said that every person has a twin somewhere in the world. Willow and I could have simply been look-alikes and nothing more."

Glancing over his shoulder at her, he said, "Maybe you'll know someday. Until then, I want you to enjoy your time here. Especially with us celebrating the holidays."

She smiled wanly. "I've spent the last three Christmases alone. So you'd better believe I'm going to enjoy every moment I'm here with you Hollisters."

"Ho, ho, ho," Hunter called out as he entered the den carrying a loaded tray. "Coffee and brandy are here. Finally."

"Sorry it took so long," Claire announced as she walked at her son's side. "I should've asked Santa for a new coffee maker. This one is getting slower and slower."

"Dad, the way I see it, Mom is the one getting slower," Hunter teased. "She just isn't willing to admit it."

"That's what you think," Claire said with a laugh. "I'm still running this household with an iron fist."

"Better watch out, Dad." Hunter continued to joke. "Mom is sounding tough."

Hadley's expression was full of love as he curled an arm around his wife's waist and hugged her to his side. "She's as tough as a marshmallow."

Anna enjoyed seeing the obvious affection Hunter's parents had for each other, yet it was also a bittersweet experience. She wanted, even needed, that same sort of affection. She longed to think that years from now a man would be looking at her the way Hadley gazed at Claire. Would it be foolish of her to hope that man would be Hunter?

Anna rose from the rocker and walked over to where he was placing the tray with the coffee and brandy on a low table in front of the couch.

"I'm glad the coffee maker was going slow," Anna said. "It's been extra nice visiting with Hadley."

Straightening to his full height, Hunter glanced at her. "I imagine Dad has been telling you all about the ranch."

"Among other things. I'm learning that Stone Creek Ranch is a very busy place."

"Because of all the extra feeding and haying and making sure the animals are where they can find safe shelter, the workdays here in the winter months are very long and hard," Hunter said. "And sometimes when calving starts in the latter part of winter, the nights are even longer than the days."

"You got that right, son," Hadley spoke up. "But let's hope tonight isn't interrupted with barn emergencies."

Claire filled all the cups with coffee and splashed a measurable amount of brandy into each one before she handed the first one to Anna, then passed the others to her husband and son.

"Hunter tried to get me to drag out the eggnog, but I'm saving that for tonight. For now, this should warm things up," Claire said. "Here's to a happy Christmas Eve."

Hunter stepped over to Anna's side and wrapped an arm around her shoulders. In that moment, she could see herself standing next to Hunter in front of this very fireplace. His arm was around her in the same way it was now and she could hear female laughter somewhere in the background. But the image was from the past. How could that be? She'd never been to this ranch before today! Something was wrong with her. Seriously wrong!

"And to Anna," Hunter added.

"Hear! Hear!" Hadley seconded his son's toast.

As the four of them lifted their cups, Anna tried not to panic. With any luck, the brandy-laced coffee would help to clear the tangled confusion in her brain.

She was leaning slightly against Hunter's side, sipping the hot drink and trying to focus on the present, when a female voice suddenly sounded from the open doorway.

"Wait a minute! Are you guys having something good to drink without me?"

Anna looked around to see a young, slender woman with long blond hair hurrying into the den. A white silky blouse showed off her tiny waist, while a red plaid maxi skirt swished around the ankles of her boots. A broad smile was on her face and the closer she came to the group, the more Anna was drawn to the woman she recognized from the photo Hunter had shown her.

"Sorry, Bonnie, we should've rung your desk and told you that Hunter and Anna had arrived," Hadley said to his daughter. "We're just now having a toast of coffee and brandy. Want to join us?"

"Sure. I'll fetch another cup from the bar," she told him. "But first, I want to give Hunter a hug and say hello to Anna."

After giving Hunter an affectionate embrace, she walked over and offered her hand to Anna. "Hi, Anna. I'm Bonnie. One half of Mom and Dad's twins. We're the lastborn of the bunch."

She was a lovely woman somewhere in her later twenties. Her eyes were azure blue and her complexion resembled cream-colored satin. Yet none of those things about Bonnie had snagged Anna's attention. It was something about the shy smile on her lips and the incredible kindness she spotted in her eyes that had Anna staring at Hunter's younger sister.

This was Bonnie, who'd wanted to stay hidden. This was Bonnie, her kindred spirit.

Dizziness rapidly engulfed Anna as the whispered words dashed through her mind, but somehow she managed to place her hand in Bonnie's.

"It's so nice to—"

The rest of her sentence trailed away as the room turned blindingly white. She swayed on her feet and barely noticed when someone caught her cup before it dropped to the floor.

"Anna!"

Hunter's frantic voice calling her name was the last thing she heard before her legs crumpled and she pitched face forward.

Chapter Twelve

"I think she's coming around, son," Hadley stated. "Her eyelids fluttered. Maybe if you prop up her head."

The moment Willow had crumpled in Hunter's arms, he'd rushed her over to the nearest couch and laid her flat on the cushions.

"Oh Lord, she's as pale as a ghost!" Hunter exclaimed as he reached for a throw pillow to tuck beneath her head.

"No! Don't do that," Bonnie ordered. "Leave her head lying flat so she'll get more blood flow to her brain. I'll go get a wet cloth for her face."

While Bonnie rushed out of the room, Claire and Hadley continued to hover near Hunter's shoulder as all three of them peered anxiously at Willow.

"Hunter, I'm thinking we should drive her to the ER!" Claire exclaimed.

Neither one of his parents were the panicking type. Living on a ranch with eight children, Claire and Hadley had dealt with all sorts of accidents and medical events. But Hunter could clearly see from the worried expressions on their faces that they were highly concerned about Willow.

"If she doesn't come around in the next minute or

two, I'll drive her straight to the hospital," he assured his mother.

"Has she done this before?" Hadley asked.

"Not around me. And she's not mentioned anything about having fainting spells," Hunter answered. "But she's eaten very little today, plus the long hours of traveling— it's probably taken a toll on her," Hunter explained.

He was sending up a silent prayer for Willow's eyes to open when Bonnie reappeared with a damp washcloth. Hunter quickly placed the cool compress on her fore- head and the instant it touched her skin, she began to groan. Seconds later, her eyes opened and she squinted up at the anxious faces hovering over her.

"Hunter?" she asked groggily. "What happened?"

Not waiting for him to answer, she attempted to sit up, but Hunter placed a deterring hand on her shoulder.

"You fainted," he explained. "Don't try to sit up yet. Just lie there for a minute and give yourself time to re- cuperate."

He continued to gently press the cloth to her fore- head and her fingers reached up to investigate. "Did I fall and hit my head?"

"No. I caught you before you fell," Hunter told her. "Is your head hurting?"

"No. My ears are ringing, but that's all." She glanced at the other worried faces peering over Hunter's shoul- ders. "Oh, this is embarrassing! I apologize for causing such a commotion! I'm okay now. Really."

"There's no commotion, Anna," Hadley assured her. "We just want you to be well."

Claire cast a worried look at her husband, then turned back to where Anna was lying on the couch. "I think we should take you into town, Anna, and have Grace examine you. I'd feel better if she said you were all right."

"You're so kind to be concerned, Claire, but I'm fine," Willow told her, then reached for Hunter's hand. "Would you help me sit up so I can get my bearings?"

Hunter helped her to a sitting position before easing himself down beside her, still holding on to her hand. Thankfully, he could see a rosy color seeping back into her cheeks and her eyes looked clear. In all honesty, he agreed with his mother. He wanted to take Willow straight to a doctor. But to do so would be taking a huge risk of running into someone who'd immediately recognize her. In her fragile state, the shock might flatten her completely.

"Are you sure you're feeling better?" he asked.

"Please don't worry," she told him, then glanced at Bonnie and his parents. "This happens to me every once in a while. My doctor believes it has something to do with my amnesia. In any case, he told me not to be overly concerned about fainting. It's the fall that could harm me. Or the danger of it happening while I'm driving. But I usually have a warning that something feels off before it happens."

Claire let out a breath of relief. "It's good that you have an explanation—and that you've talked to a doctor about this already."

"Yes. Really good," Bonnie spoke up. "Maybe if you drank your coffee now, Anna, it would help revive you. Do you feel like sipping Maybe eating a cracker or cookie?"

"Thank you, Bonnie. Yes, I think it might help."

Bonnie fetched a cookie from a plate on a nearby table and handed it, along with the coffee cup to Willow. Hunter noticed that as Willow accepted the food and drink, she was eyeing Bonnie gratefully. He'd also noticed earlier, before she'd fainted, that she'd been looking at Bonnie with a strange sort of fascination. Had the sight of his sister awoke something in her memory bank? Moreover, had it triggered the fainting spell? If so, what might happen when the rest of his family arrived tonight?

These past few days, he'd been worried about Willow meeting up with old acquaintances in town, but it might be that seeing his family could be even more shocking to her system. Oh God, what had he done by bringing her home? Was this Christmas Eve going to be memorable for all the wrong reasons?

"I think it's time we all joined Anna in drinking our coffee before it gets cold," Hadley suggested.

"I agree. Maybe some Christmas music might cheer things up," Bonnie said before crossing the room to turn on a satellite radio station. After she rejoined the group and everyone was seated and sipping their drinks, Hunter looked over at Willow and squeezed her hand.

"Feeling better?" he asked softly.

"No worries, Hunter. I'm feeling perfectly okay." Smiling, she gazed up at the angel at the top of the tree. "How else could I feel with an angel and your wonderful family looking out for me?"

Hunter's heart felt full to the brim and as he looked at Willow's lovely profile, he realized if Malachi could see the glaze of moisture that had gathered in his eyes, he'd be surprised to learn his friend could be so sentimental.

"We're going to always look out for you, Anna. And

tonight is going to be a special Christmas Eve. The angel told me that," he added with a gentle grin.

She squeezed the hand he had wrapped around hers. "It's already a special Christmas Eve, Hunter."

Hunter placed a kiss on her forehead, then glanced over to see both his parents were watching the interaction. And even though it didn't show on their faces, Hunter knew they were both worried.

Nearly two hours later, after Anna had napped for a while in one of the guest bedrooms, she showered and changed her clothes for the dinner party tonight. Now, as she stood in front of the dresser mirror and fidgeted with the bangs she'd attempted to drape near one eye, she was grateful the ringing in her ears had stopped, along with the odd swimmy feeling that had struck her right before she'd fainted.

More than a year had passed since she'd fainted and that incident had occurred at work in the middle of a very stressful day. But what had caused her to black out in the den hadn't been stress. *More like fear*, she thought ruefully. For a few seconds, as the strange images had paraded through her mind, she'd been terrified she was suddenly losing her sanity. And then when Bonnie had walked in, she'd taken one look at her and felt like she'd been tossed into another dimension. Why else would a woman she had never met seem so shockingly *familiar*? But thankfully, the weird feelings were now gone and she was super excited for the evening ahead.

A knock at the door pulled Anna out of her thoughts and she called out, "Come in."

Bonnie stepped into the bedroom and as soon as she

spotted Anna standing near the dresser, she clapped her hands with approval.

"Anna, you look beautiful! Like a Christmas angel," Bonnie said.

Anna glanced down at the tiered white skirt she'd paired with a fuzzy white sweater. She'd not wanted to look overly dressed for the evening, but she'd wanted to wear something nicer than a pair of jeans. "I wasn't sure if any of you would be wearing dresses," she told Bonnie. "But for Hunter's sake, I wanted to look decent when I met all his family."

Bonnie walked over and took the brush from Anna's hand, then smoothed the hair hanging down the middle of her back. "You care about him a lot, don't you?"

Other than a paid hairdresser, Anna couldn't remember anyone brushing her hair for her. Bonnie's act of kindness filled her with warm pleasure.

"A whole lot." Her tongue burned with the words *I love him*, but she bit them back. She wouldn't say those words to anyone before she said them to him. When and how that might come about, she wasn't sure. But it was becoming clear to her that she'd fallen in love with him. Completely and irrevocably in love.

"Well, it's pretty obvious he cares a lot about you." She gave Anna's hair one last swipe with the brush then stepped back and studied her with an appreciative smile. "I can't wait for Bea to see your skirt. It has just enough western flair to make her happy. Did you know she designs clothing?"

"No," Anna answered. "Hunter hasn't mentioned that. I took it for granted that she probably helped her husband on their ranch in Idaho."

"Actually, when Bea and I were younger we loved to do ranch work. And, not to brag, but we're both good with horses, in and out of the saddle. But as we got older we developed other interests. In college, Bea directed her studies toward design and I aimed for a ranch management degree, like Jack and Hunter. These days, Bea works at a boutique in the town near their ranch and designs in her free time. But once a ranch girl, always a ranch girl. We still ride when we have the chance."

Anna leveled a knowing smile at her. "That couldn't be very often. Hunter tells me you're overworked doing the books for Stone Creek Ranch and the Flying H. Honestly, Bonnie, I don't know how you keep up."

The compliment put a sheepish smile on Bonnie's face. "I love what I do. I wouldn't want to be idle."

"Well, you can be assured that Hunter appreciates all you do for him," she said.

Another knock sounded. Expecting it to be Hunter, Anna was surprised when Bonnie opened the door and a tall woman carrying a medical bag walked into the bedroom. She was dressed in a glittery red blouse and skirt, while a playful headband adorned with reindeer antlers held back her long blond hair.

"Doctor calling," she chimed cheerfully.

"Oh Grace, it's such a relief to see you!" Bonnie greeted her sister with a kiss on the cheek. "Please give Anna a thorough examination. We don't want her fainting again!"

Grace gave Bonnie a reassuring pat on the shoulder. "Don't worry, sis, I'll do my job." She walked over to Anna and held out her hand. "Hello, Anna. There's probably no need to tell you I'm Grace—the doctor of the family. Human doctor, that is. My husband, Mack, is the animal doctor."

Anna was instantly drawn to Grace's gentle smile. "It's a pleasure to meet you, Grace. And I apologize for interrupting your evening. If it means anything, I'm feeling fine now. There's no need for you to examine me."

"Just looking on the outside, you look more than fine, Anna, you look beautiful. But if I didn't give you a thorough going-over, Hunter and Mom and Dad would disown me. Now come sit down and let me see if I can spot anything wrong."

With a hand on her arm, she ushered Anna over to a wooden chest with a padded top that was situated at the foot of the bed.

"Bonnie, you can play nurse for me, if you don't mind," Grace said as she picked up Anna's wrist and felt for her pulse. "Open my bag and dig out my stethoscope and the blood pressure cuff. Oh, and my penlight."

Bonnie let out a good-natured groan. "Poor Cleo and Poppy. Is this the way you order your nurses around?"

Grace chuckled. "I don't have to order my nurses around. They're always Johnny-on-the-spot."

Twenty minutes later, after Grace had given Anna a thorough exam, she packed her instruments away and gave her a happy thumbs-up sign. "Anna, from what I can see, you're a healthy woman. Of course, if the fainting spells continue, you'll need to undergo further tests. But I don't foresee that happening. Hunter explained you've had a long day without much to eat."

"He's right. I haven't eaten much. I guess all the excitement of getting here to the ranch kind of made me forget."

"Well, my doctor's advice to you is to enjoy a big Christmas Eve dinner," Grace told her.

"Which won't be hard to do, Anna. Mom and Van and Maggie are in the kitchen putting a feast together. It's going to be a smorgasbord tonight. Smoked brisket, roasted duck and grilled fish. We even have fresh authentic tamales," Bonnie told her.

Surprised at the last food item, Grace looked at her sister. "Authentic tamales? Where did those come from?"

"Arizona. Maureen and Gil had them shipped up to us on overnight express. Reeva, her cook on Three Rivers Ranch, makes them with her granddaughter, Sophia. From what Jack says, eating at their dinner table is like eating food at a five-star restaurant."

Grace leveled a pointed look at her sister. "Well, the food on Stone Creek Ranch isn't exactly chuckwagon grub."

Bonnie frowned. "There's nothing wrong with chuckwagon grub. Ours is delicious."

Laughing, Grace looked at Anna. "She might not look it, but Bonnie is a ranch girl through and through."

Anna rose to her feet. "Well, I think you're both being far too kind to be giving me this much attention."

"Nonsense," Grace said, while giving Anna's shoulders a brief hug. "You've been one of the best patients I've had in days. Now, I think it's time we joined the rest of the crowd."

Bonnie said, "Maybe we'll get lucky and Dad will have made a pitcher of margaritas."

Grace let out a good-natured groan as they left the bedroom. "If Dad made margaritas, half the family will end up flat on the floor."

"Oh, then I'd better skip the cocktails then," Anna said impishly. "I've already been flat on the couch. I don't want to hit the floor."

As the three of them walked side by side across the upstairs landing, Grace glanced questioningly over at her. "You're joking, right?"

A little perplexed by her question, Anna chuckled. "Well, yes. I mean, I might as well joke about fainting." She glanced at both women. "Why? Did I say something silly or wrong?"

Grace quickly shook her head while Bonnie said, "Oh no. We're just glad you can joke about it. Right, Grace?"

"Right. We're glad you can joke with us, period." She cleared her throat, then gave Anna a wide smile. "I know it's sometimes hard when you go somewhere and meet people for the first time. It's not always easy to be relaxed. We're happy that you feel comfortable with us."

Anna reached for both sisters' hands and gave them an affectionate squeeze. "I know it won't make sense to either one of you. Honestly, it doesn't make sense to me. But I feel so comfortable with all of you. It's like Hunter has brought me home."

Grace paused and looked at her. "Home? You really feel that way here?" she asked.

Anna smiled sheepishly. "Sorry. I hope that doesn't offend either of you. Believe me, it's not like I'm assuming or expecting to become a Hollister, or anything. Hunter hasn't led me on, and I didn't come here with any grand expectations. But I—well, you see, with my amnesia I haven't had a real home in more than four years. So it feels nice to believe that for the next few days, at least, I have a temporary home. Especially a home for Christmas."

Bonnie's eyes filled with tears and she gave Anna a tight hug. "Oh, Anna, of course we don't mind. We're glad you're here. Truly."

"My sister is right, Anna," Grace said as she patted the back of Anna's hand. "And I'll tell you something else. You don't have to think of this home as temporary. No matter about Hunter, Mom and Dad will always open the door to you."

Smiling through her tears, she said, "Thank you. Thank you both. Now, I don't want to get maudlin, so let's go check out your mom's smorgasbord. I'm getting hungry."

"Now you're talking!" Bonnie exclaimed.

They headed down the staircase. As Hunter's sisters walked on either side of her, Anna could only think how hard it was going to be to go back to Red Bluff, to live her life alone and pretend that she was happy.

"Our plans are to add another section to the shearing barn before spring," Quint said to Hunter. "That's if the weather doesn't cause problems with the construction."

The two men sat together on a couch in the den, while their father was relaxed in an armchair with nine-month-old Jackson perched on his knee. The dark-haired baby resembled Jack and usually had the same quiet countenance as his daddy. Currently, Little Jack, as most everyone called him, was gnawing his way through a Christmas sugar cookie. Something he would've never been given if his mother, Vanessa, had been in the room.

"If you're lucky, you'll only get a few feet of snow

here on the ranch before spring arrives," Hunter replied to his brother's remark.

Quint grunted. "Yeah. And when I last checked the weather radar over Beaver County, it looked like heavy snow will arrive before the night is over. Oh well, having a white Christmas will be nice. Ross and Kitty will enjoy making a snowman. I wonder if Willow has seen much snow around Red Bluff? Or has she only been living there a short time?"

Hunter glanced over at his three other brothers. Flint and Cordell were standing on the hearth with their backs to the flames, swapping stories, while Jack was sitting half-asleep in an armchair with his feet propped on footstool. Christmas music was playing faintly in the background, joined by the pop and crackle of the burning logs. Normally, Hunter would be relaxed and enjoying the quiet time with his family. But the longer Willow and his sisters remained upstairs, the more anxious Hunter was growing.

Recognizing Quint was waiting for him to answer, he gave himself a mental shake. "Uh—yes, she's been living there since her amnesia. But Quint...when she comes downstairs, remember to call her Anna."

Quint frowned thoughtfully. "Anna. Right. Does she have any idea how she got to Red Bluff?"

Hunter nodded. "Yes, she went to Red Bluff once she was released from her hospital stay in Redding. But she has no idea why she was driving that night near Redding when she had the accident."

Quint's expression turned empathetic. "Hunter, I know we—well, where you and Willow are concerned, we brothers haven't always been supportive. I just want you to know I feel kinda awful about that."

Hunter slanted him a twisted smile. "Why feel awful now? Nothing has changed. Except that she's now back here on the ranch."

Quint shrugged. "You're wrong, Hunter. At least, you are about me. Until Clementine came into my life, I don't think I understood what love really was or could be. If she walked off now, for any reason, I'd have to go after her. No matter how much my family called me a fool. I get it now—all the heartache and loneliness you must have gone through."

He reached over and gave Quint's knee a grateful shake. "You're right. It's been a hell of a lot of heartache. And I'm not at all sure it's over with. I—"

Hunter stopped in midsentence as, from the corner of his eye, he spotted Grace entering the den. She was conspicuously alone.

Rising quickly from the couch, he said, "Sorry, Quint, Grace just walked in. I need to get her report."

Striding quickly, he met his sister before she'd reached the middle of the room. "I didn't think you were ever going to show up!" he exclaimed, then, lowering his voice, added, "Five more minutes and I was going to be knocking on that bedroom door!"

"I wasn't going to rush through my examination. And there isn't any need for you to be in panic mode."

"I'm not in panic mode!" he denied. "But don't you think I have a right to be worried?"

With a hand on his shoulder, she directed him toward the doorway leading out of the den. "Let's go out to the patio where we can be alone. Dad has the outdoor firepit going. We won't freeze."

He eyed her with misgiving. "Why can't we talk in here? You need to tell me something you don't want the rest of the family to overhear?"

Smiling patiently, she said, "No. I'd just feel better talking to you without interruption. Just think of it as going into my office at the clinic for a consultation with the doctor."

He groaned. "I've never liked consultations, but I need to hear what you have to say."

They stepped out onto the covered patio. White icicle lights hung from the edge of the roof, while a pair of juniper trees in the yard were lit with a multitude of colorful lights. Now that darkness had fallen over the ranch, the temperature had fallen drastically and a few bits of snow were beginning to fly through the air. Since neither of them were wearing a coat or jacket, they hurried straight over to the firepit and hovered over the warming flames.

"Okay, sis," he said. "Here we are, alone. Now tell me, do you think there's anything seriously wrong with Willow? I realize it's Christmas Eve and I don't want to spoil this time for her, but if you think she needs to go to the hospital, I'll persuade her somehow."

"Persuade her? Oh my, Hunter, I get the feeling she'd do anything you asked of her. But not to worry. Not about her physical health, that is. She appears to be perfectly fine. I think the fainting was just a momentary thing. Most likely a sudden drop in blood sugar from not eating, maybe mixed with a little stress from meeting the family of the guy she's seeing."

Hunter let out a long breath of relief. "Thank God," he said, then looked at her through narrowed eyes. "Did I hear a *but* in your voice? I did, didn't I? There is something worrying you. You or Bonnie didn't slip and call her Willow, did you?"

"No. Which is damned hard not to do," Grace told him. "Honestly, Hunter, I understand now the anguish you must be going through. Acting as though we've never known Willow when she was actually a part of our family is—well, it's tough."

"This deception or pretense, or whatever you want to call it, has to end, Grace." He blew out a long breath. "I can't take much more of it."

"Yes. I agree. But just blurting everything out to her—" Pausing, she shook her head. "I'm not sure, Hunter. Frankly, after talking with her, I'm dumbfounded. I've truly never seen anything like this. I mean, I did see a couple of cases of amnesia while I was in med school, but those patients were strangers to me. I had no idea who they were before they lost their memory. But Willow is—she's like herself in some ways, but so very different in others! I wasn't expecting this."

He heaved out a breath of relief. At least Grace hadn't found anything physically wrong with Willow. "Our parents weren't expecting this change in Willow, either. When we first arrived this afternoon, I could tell from their expressions that they were a little dazed by her attitude."

"Poor Bonnie. I think this whole thing has shaken her. She's so softhearted anyway. And, you know, back when you and Willow were married, I think Bonnie understood her a little more than the rest of us."

"You're right. They both wanted to stay hidden and live in their own little worlds. Thank God Bonnie has emerged from hers. And Willow—well, it's like I told you when we were still in Red Bluff. She's changed. How or why, I don't know, but the amnesia seems to have made her a more self-confident and stronger person."

"Hmm. I'm a doctor and I couldn't have said it better than that, Hunter. The old Willow would've never been so affectionate and outgoing with Bonnie and me. Before when she was here in the big house, she seemed awkward and uneasy. But now—only a few minutes ago she was telling us how much she felt at home here. And the astonishing thing about it, Hunter, is that she truly means what she's saying. This isn't an act she's putting on. I could see the real emotion in her eyes and her face."

Closing his eyes, Hunter swiped a hand over his face. "Sis, tell me, am I a fool for hoping that someday she's going to remember me? Remember that I was once her husband?"

Grace laid a gentle hand on his forearm. "You want that more than anything, don't you?"

He opened his eyes to see the glow of the fire illuminating the lines of concern on Grace's face. "More than anything," he agreed. "And Grace, I'm sorry for trying to steer you away from Mack. When you reunited with him, I didn't understand how you truly felt. But I do now."

She gave him a lopsided grin. "Everything you've ever said to me was said out of love. Don't be sorry for that. Anyway, I think you've learned things about yourself since you found Willow."

He returned her grin with a wry one of his own. "You

mean, I've learned things about life that I should've learned a long time ago?"

"Something like that. Anyway, my concern for Willow now is what might happen if she does remember everything," Grace said. "Even as a doctor, I don't have a clue if she'd revert back to being the old Willow or keep on being this new-outgoing version."

Hunter grimaced as he thought how Grace had pretty much summed up his worries for the past week. "You're leaving out the big question, Grace. Will she still want me to be in her life?"

"I guess that is the big question." Smiling, she gave his forearm a reassuring squeeze. "But, Hunter, it's Christmas Eve. We can pray for a miracle."

Quint and Clementine, Cordell and Maggie, Jack and Vanessa. Not to mention the kids. It was a lot to keep up with, but before dinner was served, Anna finally met Hunter's married brothers, their wives and children. Then she'd met Flint, the brother who was still single and working as a county deputy sheriff. She'd recognized all of them from the photos Hunter had shown her on his phone, but like that time, Flint was the one who gave her an odd déjà vu feeling. All through dinner, she'd tried to ignore the strange idea that she'd met him before. But in spite of her effort, she kept racking her brain, trying to think of where she might have run across someone who looked like him. Because it seemed certain that she'd never met him in real life before tonight.

After dinner, everyone had dessert and coffee in the den and then Grace's kids, Ross and Kitty, passed out Dirty Santa gifts. Most of the inexpensive gifts drew loud groans and laughter. Especially when Anna ended up with a sack of horse treats.

Sitting next to Hunter on a comfortable love seat, she handed the sack of treats to him. "I'll give them to you, Hunter. You have plenty of horses to treat with peppermint candies."

"Okay, then you can have these red furry earmuffs. They'll look cute on you." To prove his point, he settled the earmuffs onto her head and adjusted them over her ears. "See, they look perfect."

Laughing, she lifted the muffs off her head. "Thanks, but I can't hear with these on."

"If you go outside you might want them," Vanessa said, as she stood holding little Jack in front of the picture window. "Looks like the snow is already beginning to cover the ground."

Little Jack began to point toward the window and whine in what Anna took as an effort to tell his mother he wanted to go outside and get a closeup view of the snow. While Vanessa tried to explain to the baby that they needed to stay inside, Bonnie expressed her concerns about Beatrice and Kipp.

"I thought they might be here by now." She looked at Hadley. "Do you think they might have to stop over for the night and finish the trip tomorrow?"

"Oh, for them to have to travel on Christmas Day would be just awful," Claire spoke up.

Across from the love seat where Anna and Hunter were sitting, Maggie was perched on the arm of Cordell's chair. The pretty redhead cast her mother-in-law an insightful look.

"Not nearly as awful as them being injured in a crash on the highway," Maggie told her.

Anna glanced at Hunter and the pained expression on his face told her he was thinking about her own car accident and the toll it had taken on her life. She touched her hand to his to let him know the reminder hadn't troubled her. Actually, in a strange way, she was grateful for the tragic incident. Otherwise, she wouldn't be sitting here with Hunter, soaking up the joy of being with him and his family.

Cordell smiled up at his wife. "Spoken like a true ER nurse, honey."

"And a mother," Maggie said as she gazed lovingly down at their daughter. After plenty of romping and playing with her older cousins, the fiery-haired toddler had finally fallen asleep in her father's arms. "Now that we're parents to Bridget, I think about safety issues even more."

Hadley held up a hand to ward off any more worries concerning the pair of travelers. "This is Christmas Eve. We're supposed to be laughing and singing, not worrying. Less than ten minutes ago I got a text from Bea saying they were making good time and the roads were still fairly clear. She figures they'll be here by midnight."

"Hadley! Why didn't you tell us this earlier?" Claire exclaimed. "You ought to know how Bonnie worries about her twin!"

"Oh, Mom, don't scold Dad," Flint spoke up. "Tonight is a time for fun. Anyway, my coworker who's out patrolling the county roads says presently the highways are okay."

Flint's remarks put an end to the travel worries and

after a few minutes, the conversation around the room turned to tomorrow and the family's plans for opening gifts and preparing for the big dinner.

Eventually, Anna felt herself growing drowsy from all the food and drink and the warmth of the fireplace. When she rested her cheek against Hunter's shoulder, he glanced down at her.

"I think it's time we called it a night, don't you?" he asked.

She nodded. "As much as I'm enjoying being with your family, I am getting a little tired."

Hunter helped Anna to her feet and quickly announced they were leaving for his place. The whole room howled out a protest and, surprisingly, Bonnie was the loudest.

"But don't you want to stick around to welcome Bea and Kipp?" she asked.

"Under the circumstances, I think Bea will understand that Anna has had a very long day and needs to rest," Hunter answered.

"Oh, sorry, Anna, I guess I'm so excited about Christmas I wasn't thinking." Bonnie walked over and hooked an arm through Anna's. "I'll walk with you and Hunter to the door."

"Good night, everyone," Anna said to the whole group.

Hunter added, "You'll see us in the morning bright and early. So have the coffee going, Mom."

After everyone called their good-nights to them, Bonnie walked with them as far as the front porch, then waved them off as they hurried through the falling snow to the truck.

The short drive to Hunter's house took them over a

tall rise, then past a working ranch yard equipped with several large barns and a network of corrals. Yard lamps illuminated the area and cast spooky shadows over the empty lots.

As she gazed out the windshield, she said, "I don't see any cattle or sheep."

"Most of them are snuggled up under the loafing sheds or inside the barns. You'll see them tomorrow morning. The men will be spreading hay."

"On Christmas Day? But I suppose a rancher's work never takes a holiday," she said thoughtfully. "I wonder how Malachi is making out with the Flying H livestock."

"I got a text from his earlier this evening. He says all is well and the weather is nice and warm."

"That's good. I've been wondering what he'll do to celebrate Christmas. He's a long distance from his home on the reservation."

"I wouldn't worry about Malachi. He and the guys will get together and celebrate. Anyway, I don't think Malachi has much of a home on the rez. Other than his dad, he doesn't have a lot of family anymore. So I figure he's happy celebrating Christmas where he is right now."

"Probably so. He has a lot to look forward to in the future. You should be proud." She glanced at him. "What about the Dalhart sisters? I didn't ask them about their holiday plans. Although I did hear Cheyenne mention their father. Were they traveling back to Wyoming to see him?"

"No. Mr. Dalhart is going to meet up with his daughters down in Barstow. He wanted to experience a warm holiday this year." He chuckled and nodded toward the scene beyond the windshield. "And we're going to have a cold white one. I hope you don't mind."

"Oh, I think it's lovely. I'm enjoying every minute with you and your family. Especially with you," she added softly.

He reached over and clasped her hand. "I don't mind telling you, Anna, you scared the hell out of me when you fainted."

Did he truly care that much? She wanted to think so, but she wasn't going to press him about his feelings now. Or even in the near future. If he was falling in love with her, she wanted the words to come from him voluntarily. Not because she'd pushed or prodded.

"There's no need for you to worry about me, Hunter. I'm fine. Truly."

He slanted a tender glance at her. "I'm going to make sure you stay that way."

They traveled less than fifty more yards on the graveled road when he turned right onto a sloping drive. As the truck climbed the incline, Anna leaned forward in her seat and peered eagerly through the windshield at the trees in the yard.

And then the house came into view. Just for a second, her heart seemed to stop. The large log structure—complete with a porch and numerous windows on the front—was incredibly beautiful. Like an image in a garden magazine, she thought. Is that why the house looked so familiar? Had she seen it in a photo somewhere?

Pushing the outlandish thoughts aside, she glanced over at Hunter. "When you said you had a house of your own, you really meant it! This is gorgeous, Hunter! I'm so impressed!"

He smiled as he brought the truck to a halt and shut off the engine. "I hope you'll like the inside just as well. I have a cleaning lady come in twice a month to keep the place dusted and tidy, whether I'm using the house or not. So it should be clean."

"I can't wait to look it over. You saw for yourself how tiny my one-bedroom apartment is. You could probably fit five of them in this house."

He unlatched his seat belt. "Come on. Let's go in. I'll get our bags in a few minutes, after you've had a chance to look around."

After helping her out of the truck, they walked arm in arm up the steps to a wide wooden door with a tall, frosted window. As he unlocked the knob and pushed the door open, Anna had the ridiculous urge to have him carry her over the threshold. She very nearly asked him if he would, but managed to catch herself just in time. Was she disoriented or something? Hunter didn't bring her to Stone Creek Ranch with the idea of making her his wife! So why did she keep imagining the two of them married? Had that fainting spell been a warning that something was going awry in her brain?

The worrisome questions were suddenly pushed aside as he flipped on a light and ushered her past a short foyer and into a spacious front room furnished with heavy wood-and-leather chairs. There was a large window looking over the front yard.

"In the daylight hours, you can see the ridge of the northern mountains from the window."

"Oh, I imagine it's beautiful." She walked over and peered out at the falling snow. With the aid of two yard lamps, she could see the white drifts already piling around the trunks of the young trees. "Hadley told me he'd purchased another ranch north of here. Does it lie beyond the mountains?"

"Partly. Most of it lies adjacent to the lower part of Stone Creek's original boundary. Before the week is up, I'll give you a look at that property and the rest of the ranch. Right now, I'll show you through the other rooms." With an arm around her shoulders, he guided her out of the living room. "Are you warm enough?"

"Feels just right," she assured him.

"There's a fireplace in the den, but the night is growing so late, I hate to build a fire and then go to bed before we can really appreciate it. We'll have one tomorrow. On Christmas Day," he added with a grin.

She smiled impishly back at him. "I'm worried that you're not going to like your gift. But I've kept the receipt in case you want to exchange it for something else."

He chuckled. "You've already given me the perfect gift, Anna. You're here with me."

She paused and rose on the tips of her toes to plant a quick kiss on his lips. "And you've already given me the perfect gift, Hunter. I'm here with you."

A wry smile twisted his lips. "Well, if you're that happy, don't you think you ought to give me more of a kiss than the one you just gave me?"

Laughing, she grabbed his hand and led him forward. "No way. If we start that, I'll never see the rest of the house!"

After that, Hunter took her on a quick tour of the den, kitchen, dining room and five bedrooms. When they finally entered the master bedroom, she smiled at the row of cowboy boots lined up on the floor and the hats hanging on the posts of the footboard.

"This is obviously your room," she said.

"It is. Do you like it?"

She walked over to him. "I love everything about the whole house. But I do have a question. You live here alone. Why is it so big? And with so many bedrooms?"

One of his big shoulders lifted and fell. "I've always wanted a big family. But—"

Her gaze connected with his and her heart thumped at the raw emotions she saw on his face. "But that hasn't happened yet," she murmured.

"Not yet. I'm still hoping."

Stepping closer, she rested her palms against the middle of his chest. "I'm still hoping, too," she whispered.

Lowering his head, he placed a kiss in the middle of her forehead. "Are you too tired to go to bed?"

She eased back her head and laughed. "Isn't going to bed the natural remedy to being tired?"

He chuckled as he circled his arms around her waist and drew her body snug against his. "Yes. But I had more in mind than just sleeping."

Purring deep in her throat, she slipped her arms around his neck. "I think I can summon up enough energy— for you."

She tilted her lips up to his and when he kissed her, she could only think she'd finally found her home right here in Hunter's arms.

Chapter Thirteen

Much, much later that night, Hunter blinked awake, not sure when he'd finally drifted off to sleep after they'd made love. The last thing he remembered was kissing the top of her head as she pillowed her head on his shoulder and then she'd murmured good-night.

He looked around, trying to figure out what had caused him to wake. He glanced over to see the spot where Willow had been lying next to him. She was gone and the sheet was cool.

Something was wrong! He could feel it!

Apprehension caused his hands to shake as he leaped out of bed and jerked on his jeans. Why had she left their bed? Had she gone to the bathroom or kitchen and fainted?

Not bothering with his boots or shirt, he rushed over to the private bathroom located in the far corner of the bedroom. The space was dark and empty.

He hurried out of the bedroom, then trotted down the hallway and into the kitchen where he'd left a night-light burning near the double sink. The fact that she was nowhere to be seen sent rivulets of fear racing down his spine.

It was happening all over again, he thought frantically. Four years ago, he'd searched every room for her and found them all cold and empty. There'd been snow on the ground that night, too, and for days afterwards he'd shivered, not from the cold, but from shock. *Oh dear God, please don't let it happen again! Not again!*

Trying not to panic, he began to methodically check every room, while calling her name. It wasn't until he returned to the living room for a second time and glanced in the foyer that he noticed the door to the front porch was unlocked.

Frantically, he snatched a pair of old boots and a jacket from the hall closet, then grabbed the small flashlight he kept near the door. Outside, the wind had picked up noticeably and the snowfall had grown even thicker.

Why would she have left their warm bed and come out in this? What could she be doing?

The questions were flying through his head when he noticed tracks leading off the porch and into the yard. He trotted after them. Each step he took brought him closer to the aspens she'd planted soon after they were married. Finally, he spotted her leaning against one of the tree trunks. Beneath her coat, he could see she was wearing the same white skirt and sweater she'd worn at dinner. The hem of the skirt was already soaked from trailing over the snow. Her face was turned away from him, but he didn't have to see it to know she was in deep distress.

Fearing the worst, he ran the last few steps to her.

"Anna! What are you doing out here?"

She looked around at him and even in the dim glow of his flashlight he could see that tears were streaming down her face.

"Oh, Hunter! Oh please, forgive me! Forgive me!"

She flung herself at him and he held her tightly for a moment as the snowy wind whipped around them.

"Darling, why are you crying? What's wrong?"

Her hands gripped his shoulders tightly. "The trees. I remember planting my aspens!"

Stunned, he lifted her into his arms and hurriedly carried her into the house and straight to the couch in the living room. But even as he sat her safely down on the cushion, she wouldn't release the tight grip she had on his shoulders.

Finally, he managed to ease her head back far enough to look at her face. "Anna, are you saying you remember something?"

Her expression full of anguish, she shook her head. "I'm not Anna Jones! I'm Willow! Willow Hollister! Oh, Hunter, I—can't believe—all this time you knew—your family knew—but you said nothing! Why?"

A ball of emotion was choking him and he had to swallow twice before he could utter a word. "We were all afraid the shock of learning the truth too abruptly might harm you mentally or emotionally. We just didn't know. Grace has been trying to get in touch with a neurologist to find out the best, safest way to sit you down and explain the situation to you. But she hasn't had a chance to speak with him yet and—oh, darling Willow, I'm sorry. We were all keeping quiet out of love. I hope you understand that."

Shaking her head again, she closed her eyes, but even that didn't prevent tears from seeping from the lids and trickling down her cheeks. "Hunter, please, I'm the one who needs forgiveness. I'm the one who was so confused and so wrong four years ago when I left here. Left *you*. At that time I thought you'd be better off with someone else. I was just a poor Anderson. I wasn't good enough to be your wife."

"Do you know how awful that sounds? How misguided you were to think that?"

She opened her eyes and his heart ached as he watched a wave of tears drench her face. "It was wrong of me—I realize it now. But back then I—I understand your family thought I didn't like them or want to spend time around them. But it wasn't like that at all. I honestly felt like a fish out of water around your mother and sisters and—you—well, you needed a woman who wasn't timid. One who wouldn't have been afraid to go with you—to help you live out your dreams."

Amazed at what he was hearing, he stared at her. "The divorce papers—do you have any idea what it was like for me when I received them in the mail? I went around in a daze wanting to hate you. But I couldn't. All I wanted was for us to be together again, but you wouldn't even come back to give me the papers yourself. You didn't give me a chance to try to fix things."

She bit back a sob and struggled to compose herself. "I had the lawyer send those papers thinking I needed to be independent. Besides, I knew I was making you miserable with all my clinging and nagging for you to remain on the ranch. Oh Lord, Hunter, I was a mess back then."

He gathered both of her hands between his. "Your accident. Do you remember what you were doing? How it happened?"

She nodded glumly. "When I received the signed divorce papers back from the lawyer and saw your signature, I realized I'd made a horrible, horrible mistake. I loved you so much, Hunter. No matter what you think or how terribly I behaved, you have to believe I always loved you. That night of the car crash—I was headed back to Utah and you. I was hoping and praying that somehow you'd forgive me and we could start over. It was raining that night—just like the night we crashed into each other at the hotel—and I was going around a mountain curve when a doe and fawn jumped out in front of me. I swerved to miss them. I suppose, because the pavement was slick, the car lost traction and went out of control. Everything went black until I woke up in the hospital at Redding. The rest you know."

He tightened his hold on her hands as he gazed deeply into her eyes. "No, Willow. The rest I don't know. Especially what happens now. Do you still want to start over, to be my wife—again? Do you think you can live with me running the Flying H?"

With a little cry of joy, she leaned forward and began smacking kisses all over his face. "Oh, Hunter, when I woke up a few minutes ago everything was strange and swimmy. I was about to panic when I looked over and saw you and then it was like a dam inside my brain burst. Memories came pouring in, and I realized I was sleeping with my husband! The man I'd divorced. I guess I went a little blank because the next thing I knew I was outside under the aspens."

His pressed his cheek to hers. "And now?"

"Now I can't wait for us to be married again. I can't wait to start traveling with you, helping you run the Flying H."

"What about your job at the hotel in Red Bluff?" Hunter asked. "I don't imagine Ian is going to take this news very well."

"He'll understand when he hears I'm back with my husband where I belong," she said. "As for the job vacancy my leaving will make, there are several women already working there who'll be eager to take my position."

Easing his head back, he looked into her eyes. "I promise you, darling, we won't live on the road forever. Once our kids grow to school age, we'll have to give up part of the nomadic life. But by then Malachi will be experienced enough to take over the reins whenever we can't be there."

She gently framed his face with her hands. "I'm not worried one bit about any of that, Hunter. We'll make it all work—together. But for now, I can't wait to hit the road with you. It's going to be fun seeing all those different places, watching the rodeos and spending time with Malachi and the Dalharts." A suggestive grin tilted the corner of her lips. "I'm a very good secretary, you know. I can take over all your bookkeeping work and give Bonnie the break she needs."

Even though he wanted to laugh with joy, he was close to crying and he swallowed hard to push away the hot lump of emotion clogging his throat.

"Willow, four years ago, I desperately wanted to hear you say these things to me. But you refused to meet me halfway. What's caused this change in you?"

"Earlier in the bedroom, when my memory came rushing back, I was shocked to realize I was Willow." Her voice was rueful as her eyes begged him to listen and try to understand. "Do you remember how reluctant I was to marry you?"

He grimaced. "How could I forget? I had to ask you— no, I had to beg you several times before you finally gave in. I was beginning to think you didn't love me.

Not enough to marry me. And then when you left and I got those damned divorce papers, I could only think I should've listened to what my brain was trying to tell me. Instead, I'd listened with my heart and ignored every warning sign."

She sighed. "My reluctance to marry you had nothing to do with love. It had everything to do with my upbringing."

He groaned with frustration. "You could hardly help the fact that your parents were no good or that they deserted you when you were less than two years old."

"I never let their desertion define me. They didn't matter. Not when my grandparents were so caring and loving. But they weren't outgoing people. Grandfather worked his little farm and Grandmother helped him—they lived a mostly isolated life and that's the way they raised me. Which wasn't a bad thing, exactly. I loved being with them. I just didn't have much experience with the outside world. The biggest town I'd ever visited was Cedar City."

"I remember. After Marcella passed away, you took a job in town doing books for the bank, but you remained on the farm to take care of Angus. That's when we first started dating."

Her lips took on a remorseful slant. "I couldn't believe you ever noticed me. And then when you proposed marriage, I couldn't believe you meant it. A Hollister wanting to marry an Anderson. You see, Hunter, even after we married, I guess I doubted myself. I doubted I could fit into your life, so I didn't try to. Not with your family or your job. I think those two years we were married I was just—waiting for you to end it. Until finally I decided to end it myself."

"Willow, Willow…" He softly repeated her name as he smoothed his fingertips over the hollows beneath her eyes. "I'm so sorry. I'm to blame, too. I should've listened more. I should've compromised. Instead of thinking you were nagging, I should've recognized you were really crying out for help and reassurance. But now—"

"I'm different, Hunter. I can't explain it. Maybe as time goes by I'll understand this shift in my psyche. But when I woke up after the accident, it became very clear that I was on my own. It only took a few days to realize no one was coming for me, no one was looking for me. I had to be strong and self-reliant—and I was determined to survive. After I landed the job at the hotel, I began to thrive. Now, with my memory back, I can see that a whole new world opened up for me in Red Bluff. At the time, I had no idea I needed to grow out of a shell, but that's exactly what happened. And you know what, darling?"

He nuzzled the soft skin beneath her ear. "I know what you're going to say. Nearly being killed when you hit the bottom of that ravine was the best thing to ever happen to you."

Her soft chuckles were full of joy and love. "Not *the* best," she murmured. "The best was when you ran into me out on the hotel portico."

"You didn't have a clue who I was," he said as he began to plant a column of kisses down the side of her neck.

Easing her head back, she gave him a coy smile. "No. But I sure did fall in love with you all over again."

"And I never stopped loving you." He placed a tender kiss on her lips. "We've been given a Christmas gift we'll never forget."

Her contented sigh brushed his cheek. "A gift of love and togetherness. What else could we ask for?"

"Mmm. Children to fill this big empty house," he said, then, rising to his feet, lifted her into his arms. "What do you say we get to work on that project right now? Are you too tired to go to bed with me again?"

Laughing, she circled her arms around his neck. "Merry Christmas, darling!"

The next day at the main Stone Creek ranch house, the Christmas Day celebration was made even sweeter when the family learned Willow's memory had returned and she and Hunter were planning to be remarried in the next few days, before they had to leave for California. She'd also called Celia in Red Bluff to wish her friend a merry Christmas and give her the news about her returning memory and plans to remarry Hunter.

Throughout the morning, as gifts were passed around and opened, the couple was bombarded with questions, along with hugs and kisses of joy. After four long years, Claire and Hadley were especially overjoyed to see genuine joy replace the lonely look on Hunter's face.

Later, when everyone was seated around the festive dinner table and dishes of turkey and dressing were making the rounds, Hadley stood and called for his family's attention.

Reaching for his wine goblet, he said, "I think a toast is in order, so everyone lift your glasses. We have so much to be thankful for this Christmas Day. We're all healthy and together. Even though Bea and Kipp had to slide their way here on snow-packed roads," he added jokingly.

Kipp batted a dismissive hand through the air. "Bea and I are old hands at traveling on snow-packed roads."

Everyone laughed. Then Hadley leveled a grateful look at Hunter and Willow, who were sitting next to each other. "I want to say how happy we are to have you back in the family where you belong, Willow. Welcome home. May you and Hunter have a long and happy life together."

Tears sprang to Willow's eyes. They would have worried Hunter if he hadn't understood her reaction was one of pure joy. His wife now realized she truly belonged in the Hollister family.

She said, "Thank you, Hadley. It's wonderful to finally be home with all of you." She glanced around the table at the smiling faces of her in-laws. "And thank all of you for being so gracious and welcoming me back."

Hunter leaned over and kissed her cheek. Everyone around the table shouted and applauded their approval.

"Hear! Hear!" Hadley boomed. "Now that's what I call a toast!"

The Hollister patriarch was about to drink from his glass when Quint suddenly interrupted.

"Wait, Dad!" Quint interrupted. "There's something else I'd like for everyone to hear."

Cordell let out a loud groan. "Quint, everyone already knows you and Clementine are getting a bigger shearing barn. And one of your ewes had twins last night. Congratulations."

Quint shot his brother a smug grin. "Thanks, Cord, but I have something a little more important to share with the family." He turned a tender look on his wife. "Clementine has just learned she's pregnant. My little sheepherder is going to have our own little lamb by the end of June!"

The announcement caused a flurry of excitement with Clementine getting showered with hugs and kisses from the women and Quint receiving hugs and handshakes from the men.

After the hoopla eventually calmed down and everyone had returned to their seats, Claire turned a question on her youngest son. "Quint, why didn't you tell us this news earlier?"

Quint glanced down the table at Hunter. "We didn't want to rob Hunter and Willow of the chance to reveal their big surprise."

Hadley let out a good-natured snort. "This family is big enough to handle more than one surprise in a day. Now, let's drink, eat and have a very merry Christmas!"

Hunter and Willow lifted their glasses and as they exchanged a loving glance, he sent up a prayer of thanks.

Later that night, everyone migrated to the den, where the adults relaxed around the fireplace and the kids played with their new toys on the braided rug.

Fascinated by the snow, which had continued to fall throughout the day, Willow walked over to the picture window and gazed out at the backyard. Kitty and Ross, with help from their parents, had built a tall snowman with a green muffler wrapped around his neck and a crumpled cowboy hat atop his head.

"He's a pretty good-looking cowboy," Hunter said as he came up behind her and slipped his arms around her waist. "Only one thing wrong with him—when it's time to go to work, he'll melt."

Willow chuckled. "Oh, I think Stone Creek Ranch has plenty of hands to help take care of this place without the snowman. I'm glad I got to see the guys again. And to meet the new men from Arizona."

Earlier that evening, the ranch's longtime employees—Chance, Brooks and Jett—all stopped by for coffee and dessert. Then later, the two brothers from Arizona, who'd come to work the Hollisters' expanded ranch property, had stopped by to give their Christmas wishes to everyone.

"Dad couldn't have better men working for him, that's for sure," he said. "And speaking of working men, I talked with Malachi while you were in the kitchen helping Mom with the cleanup."

She turned and looked slyly up at him. "Did Malachi and the Dalhart sisters know all along that I *was* actually Willow?"

Hunter gave her a sheepish grin. "I didn't say anything to the Dalharts, but I did tell Malachi. I had to. I was about to lose my mind trying to figure out what to do. By the way, he was thrilled to hear that your amnesia is gone and we're getting married—again."

He lifted her left hand and pressed a kiss just above her ring finger. Earlier today, he'd shocked her when he'd pulled out the plain gold band she'd worn when they'd been married. Even though she'd left the ring behind when she'd fled the ranch, Hunter told her he'd kept it safely locked away all this time. And when he'd slipped it on her finger, tears of disbelief and joy had spilled from her eyes.

"Since this is a day of surprises, I have another little one for you." His expression still smug, he pulled a small velvet box from a pocket of his jeans. "I purchased this back in Red Bluff with the hopes that someday I'd be able to propose to you again. I couldn't know my chance was going to come so soon."

He opened the box and Willow drew in a sharp breath as she spotted the solitaire diamond mounted on a thin gold band. "Hunter! It's stunning! Truly stunning! But I already have my wedding ring!" she exclaimed.

"A plain gold band might have been all I was able to get you to accept before, but I'm hoping that's another thing that has changed. I want this diamond to sparkle on your hand and let everyone know that you're my wife." He removed it from the box and slipped it on her finger to join the band. "I love you, Willow. Will you be my wife again?"

"Oh yes, sweetheart. Again and again."

He placed a sweet, lingering kiss on her lips then eased his head up to look at her. "You know, darling, while we were still in Red Bluff, I believed it was going to take a Christmas miracle to keep you in my life."

She reached up and placed her palm against the side of his face. "And lucky us, we were given a true Christmas miracle," she said gently.

"Hey, you two! None of us have the flu. You can come sit with us!" Jack called out to them.

With a smile of contentment, she took hold of his hand. "Come on. Let's go show everyone my ring."

They walked over first to where Claire and Hadley were sitting on a love seat. Just as they were complimenting the beautiful stone, Beatrice let out a gasp of surprise.

Everyone turned to see the younger twin standing on the fireplace hearth, staring at the face of her cell phone.

Bonnie rushed over to her. "Sissy! What's wrong?"

Beatrice's expression was incredulous as she looked around at the expectant faces of her family. "I've just received a text from the twins in Idaho. You know—Rueben and Walter Stevenson. They reside in the neighbors' place, like Scarlett."

Hadley scooted to the edge of his seat, while Kipp left his chair to go to stand at his wife's side.

"Are they wishing us a Merry Christmas or something?" Kipp asked.

Since he and Beatrice had met the two men and Scarlett, Lionel Hollister's estranged wife, Hunter was aware that his brother-in-law, Kipp, was very involved in the case.

"Yes. Yes, they sent a Happy Christmas to all of us. And then some surprising news. They've learned the names of Scarlett's daughters! They believe one lives in Idaho not far from Coeur d'Alene, and the other somewhere in Wyoming."

Beatrice looked hopefully at her father. "Dad, what do you think?"

Hadley walked over to join his twin daughters and son-in-law at the fireplace. "I think someone is going to have to go to Idaho and see if you can find this daughter."

"That's a no-brainer, Dad," Jack said. "Bea and Kipp aren't that far away from Coeur d'Alene."

Loudly clearing her throat, Beatrice looked at Jack. "Only six hundred miles or so, dear brother."

"Well, that's closer than all of the rest of you. If you need us to help, Bea and I can take on the task," Kipp offered.

Hadley glanced gratefully at his newest son-in-law. "Thanks, Kipp, but you and Bea have already done a major part in trying to unravel this family mystery. We can't keep asking you to shoulder more responsibility."

"Right, Dad," Quint spoke up. "I think Bonnie should go. She never gets to go anywhere."

"No. Bonnie will get her turn. Right now, she has too much to do." Hadley looked straight at Flint. "Son, I think it's your turn to work on this cryptic genealogy problem."

Stunned that his father had singled him out, Flint slapped a hand against his chest. "Me? Dad, I can't go! I have to work!"

"So do the rest of us," Jack pointed out.

Cordell smiled at his brother in a goading fashion. "Flint, you have enough vacation time built up to take off a few months if you need to! Surely this won't take nearly that long."

Flint rose to his feet, then walked over and stood in front of his father. "Dad, what makes you think having me go to Idaho would do any good? It'll take a miracle to find either one of Scarlett's daughters!"

Hunter and Willow looked at each other and exchanged appreciative smiles.

"Miracles do happen, Flint," Hunter said as he drew his wife close to his side. "Willow and I experienced one last night."

"Yeah, Flint," Quint spoke up. "Just look at those two and you'll know what Christmas is all about."

His heart full of love, Hunter gathered Willow into his arms. As he rested his cheek against the top of her head, his eyes lifted with gratitude to the top of tree.

Only an angel with a Christmas star could have guided them back together.

* * * * *